THE HEART OF A STRANGER

THE HEART OF A STRANGER

AN ANTHOLOGY OF EXILE LITERATURE

Edited by André Naffis-Sahely

Pushkin Press

Pushkin Press
71–75 Shelton Street
London WC2H 9JQ

Introductions and afterword © 2019 André Naffis-Sahely

The Heart of a Stranger was first published by Pushkin Press in 2019

1 3 5 7 9 8 6 4 2

ISBN 13: 978-1-78227-426-1

Designed and typeset by M Rules, London

Printed and bound by CPI Group (UK) Ltd, Croydon, CR0 4YY

www.pushkinpress.com

This anthology is dedicated to
Sarah Maguire (1957–2017)
poet, translator, friend to exiles

CONTENTS

Expulsions, Explorations and Migrations

DYNASTIES, MERCENARIES AND NATIONS

REVOLUTIONS, COUNTER-REVOLUTIONS AND PERSECUTIONS

Cosmopolitanism and Rootlessness

ORIGINS AND MYTHS

<hr>

C IVILIZATION BEGETS EXILE; in fact, being banished from one's home lies at the root of our earliest stories, whether human or divine. As the Abrahamic traditions tell us, if disobeying God was our original sin, then exile was our original punishment. In Genesis, Adam and Eve are expelled from the Garden of Eden after eating the forbidden fruit, their return forever barred by a flaming sword and a host of cherubim. Tragedy of course repeats itself when Cain murders his brother Abel and is exiled east of Eden. Genesis also tells us of the Tower of Babel, an edifice tall enough to reach heaven itself, a monument to human hubris whose destruction scattered its people across the earth and "confounded" our original language, thus making us unintelligible to one another for the first time since creation. The Tanakh, in fact, is rife with exile: Abraham sends Hagar and Ishmael into the wilderness of the Desert of Paran, while the young Moses voluntarily heads into exile after murdering an Egyptian. Genesis and Exodus tell of the captivity of the Israelites in Egypt and their subsequent escape to Sinai, while the Book of Ezra records the end of the Babylonian captivity — the inspiration behind Psalm 137's immortal lines, "by the rivers of Babylon we sat and wept / when we remembered Zion" — and the eventual return of the Jews to Israel.

Nevertheless, our religious texts tell us that exile wasn't a fate exclusive to lowly humans. In the *Ramayana*, the ancient Indian epic, Rama, the Supreme Being of Hinduism, is banished by his father, the Emperor Dasharatha, after falling victim to court intrigues and is ordered to spend fourteen years in exile in the forest of Dandaka, seeking enlightenment amidst demons and wandering holy men. Although Rama is recalled from his exile following his father's death, he decides to remain in exile for the entire fourteen years. Similarly, in Greek mythology, Hephaestus, the son of Zeus and Hera, is thrown off Mount Olympus by Hera due to his deformities, only to be brought back to Olympus on the back of a mule by the treacherous god of wine, Dionysus. While exile was often a temporary situation for many gods, it was a more permanent state of affairs for their mortal creations.

It was in Babel's Mesopotamia, towards the end of the Third Dynasty of Ur, that one of our earliest poetic epics, *The Lament for Urim*, first depicted the vicious cycle of conquest and expulsion that has largely characterized our history. In *The Lament for Urim* Ningal, the goddess of reeds, pleads before the great gods: "I have been exiled from the city, I can find no rest." Bemoaning the destruction of her beloved Ur by the invading Elamites, Ningal cries out its name:

O city, your name exists
but you have been destroyed.
O city, your wall rises high
but your Land has perished.

Employing the refrain "woe is me", Ningal chronicles the annihilation of her world: "I am one whose cows have been scattered", "My small birds and fowl have flown away", "My young men mourn in a desert they do not know". The Sumerian epic ends with a soft, sanguine prayer that Ningal's city may one day be restored, unleashing one of our first literary archetypes: the hopeful exile. In fact, if *The Lament for Urim* is any indication, the very concept of recorded history — and literature — appears to spring out of the necessity of exile, preserving in our minds what had been bloodily erased on earth.

The ancient Egyptian "Return of Sinuhe", written during the Twelfth Dynasty, however, ends on a far happier note. Sinuhe, either a prince or a courtier, depending on the adaptation, flees his native country after an unspecified plot against the throne. Although Sinuhe finds power, wealth and respect in barbaric lands, he cannot quieten the loss that turns all his foreign-won sweetness to ash: "Desire disturbed me, and longing beckoned my heart. There appeared before my eyes scenes of the Nile and the luxuriant greenery and heavenly blue sky and the mighty pyramids and the lofty obelisks, and I feared that death would overtake me while I was in a land other than Egypt." Fortunately for Sinuhe, his earnest patriotism wins the pharaoh's mercy when he returns to Egypt as an old man and he is welcomed back into the fold, able to die in his unforgettable homeland. This uncharacteristically happy conclusion to an exile's suffering shares some similarities with Luke's "Parable of the Prodigal Son", where the spendthrift younger son returns home to his father's undying love — and to the biblical tale of Joseph, who is sold into slavery by his envious brothers, but who then rises to unimaginable heights in Egypt, triggering a series of events that would lead to Moses and the Exodus to the Promised Land, the founding myth of the

Israelites. As was written in Exodus 23:9, "thou shalt not oppress a stranger: for ye know the heart of a stranger, seeing ye were strangers in the land of Egypt".

While exile has accompanied our every step, and our earliest stories and religious myths are studded with tales of woe and banishment, much has been lost precisely because of exile's oblivion-inducing force. The Greek poet Sappho (*c.*630–*c.*570 BC) is perhaps our most famous example. While we know she lived on the island of Lesbos, we do not know what caused her to be exiled to Sicily in her earlier life, and only the tiniest fragments of her reputedly voluminous works have survived. Although exile originally appears to have been the outcome of divine retribution, war or intrigue, it wasn't long before humans began to play god with the concept themselves. Greek literature shows us that exile was the most common form of retribution for murder, and exile therefore shapes the stories of many of Greece's most famous mythical heroes, like Peleus, Perseus, Bellerophon and Patroclus, all of whom were killers cast out of society until such time as they could be readmitted. As society grew more complex, however, exile came to be seen as far more useful than simply a punishment for murder. Aristotle's (384–322 BC) *Athenian Constitution* introduces us to the law of ostracism, whereby the names of powerful men suspected of abusing their political offices were submitted to a public vote. Assembling in the agora, citizens would scratch the name of the intended exile onto shards of broken pottery and the shards would be tallied up. The man with the most pot-shards was subsequently banished. The chosen exile could be sent away permanently or for a period of ten years, at which point they would be welcomed home and their rights duly restored. This practice proved popular enough to spread to the Greek colonies of southern Italy in Magna Graecia. In his *Bibliotheca historica*, Diodorus Siculus (90–30 BC) mentions the practice of petalism — from the Greek word for leaf — whereby the citizens of Syracuse wrote the names of the intended exiles on the leaves of olive trees instead of pot-shards.

Regardless of the voting method, this was the way democracy's enemies were dealt with: if a man grew rich enough to make tyranny inevitable, he was simply banished. Aside from recognizing wealth's inherent tendency to subvert the public interest, the particular wisdom of this law lay in its focus on exiling powerful individuals rather than their poorer, more numerous partisans, who were often allowed to remain in the city even when their leaders were not. Exile thus not only offered an attractive alternative to execution; it simultaneously hindered the widening of existing social rifts. Themistocles (c.524–459 BC) was perhaps the most famous of these ostracized exiles. After building the Athenian fleet into a major force and fighting the Persians at Marathon, Artemisium and Salamis, Themistocles was implicated in a plot involving the Spartan tyrant Pausanias — most accounts claim unfairly so — and he was subsequently forced to end his days serving the very Persians he had once warred against.

Almost needless to say, however, war never lagged far behind human law-making as the chief wellspring of exile. A fragment by Xenophanes of Colophon (c.570–c.475 BC) provides a clear picture of how the dispersion caused by the Greco–Persian Wars fundamentally reshaped Greek society:

When a stranger appears in wintertime,
these are the questions you must ask,
as you lie reclined on soft couches,
eating nuts, drinking wine by the fire:
"What's your name?", "Where do you come from?",
"How old were you when the Persians invaded?"

Orators, dissidents and artists could be banished just as easily as politicians in ancient Greece, and while many of them were able to secure shelter in faraway cities for some time, exile was never a solid guarantee of safety. Determined to extend his mastery over Greece following his victory in the Lamian War, the Macedonian general Antipater hired a number of "exile-hunters" to capture anyone who had once defamed or opposed his power. For these exiles, no island was distant enough, no temple imperviously sacred. One of Antipater's most infamous hunters was Archias of Thurii, an actor-turned-mercenary whose scalps included some of Greece's brightest lights, including Hypereides, Himeraeus and Demosthenes — who committed suicide by chewing on a poisonous reed after Archias finally tracked him down.

While Greek ostracism was engineered to protect a city's democracy, it was a dictator who first codified exile into Roman law. In 80 BC, Sulla's *Leges Corneliae* constitutionalized an already established practice: rather than execute convicted criminals, problematic tribunes or ambitious generals, it was deemed easier to expropriate them, thereby enriching the state's coffers, and to banish them from the city. Indeed, Polybius tells us that a Roman citizen accused of a crime could voluntarily go into exile in order to avoid being sentenced. Although banished from the capital, such a citizen could travel to certain *civitates foederatae* — allied cities of Rome — where they could enjoy safety and tranquillity, Neapolis (Naples) being a notable example. As Gordon P. Kelly points out in *A History of Exile in the Roman Republic* (CUP, 2006), refracted through the prism of Roman law, *exilium* could describe a variety of situations: "traditional voluntary exile, flight from proscription, magisterial *relegatio*, retirement from Rome for personal reasons, extended military service, and even emigration or travel". Furthermore, in order to avoid an exile's premature return, the policy of *aquae et ignis interdictio* — exclusion from the communal use of fire and water — created a buffer zone between Rome and the exile's new "home", making it illegal for anyone to offer said exile a welcome hearth or refreshment within its bounds.

Strictly speaking, however, softer shades of banishment tended to prove the most popular, given that *exilium* technically meant that a Roman could be stripped of both his wealth and citizenship, while the lesser *relegatio* ensured said citizen never lost his rights or property. Many of the more famous Roman exiles belonged to the second category. Ovid (43 BC–AD 18), banished to the Black Sea by Augustus, spent much of his time weeping, sighing and penning servile poems which he hoped would restore his good fortunes in the capital, often interrupting his lyricism in mid-flow to remind his readers that he was merely a *relegatus*. As for Cicero (106–43 BC), his letters clearly indicate he spent the majority of his eighteen-month exile hopping between luxurious villas, cursing the heavens for his undeserved misfortunes. As such, it is to the Stoic Seneca the Younger (54 BC–AD *c.*39) that we must turn for a pragmatic outlook on Roman exile: "I classify as 'indifferent' — that is, neither good nor evil — sickness, pain, poverty, exile, death. None of these things are intrinsically glorious; but nothing can be glorious apart from them. For it is not poverty that we praise, it is the man whom poverty cannot humble or bend. Nor is it exile that we praise, it is the man who withdraws into exile in the spirit in which he would have sent another into exile."

Such a sober perspective might have helped Gaius Marius (157–86 BC) make sense of his ironic fate, when, after being hounded across Italy by Sulla's wrath, he was turned away by the Roman garrison at Carthage, the very city he had once helped Rome to conquer. Marius would have undoubtedly identified with Shakespeare's Coriolanus (Act III, Scene 3):

Let them pronounce the steep Tarpeian death,
Vagabond exile, flaying, pent to linger
But with a grain a day, I would not buy
Their mercy at the price of one fair word.

Once the Republic perished, Rome's emperors began to favour the practice of *deportatio insulae*, or deportation to an island. Tiberius, Caligula and Domitian, among others, exiled quite a few of their family members and enemies — not that the two categories were mutually exclusive, especially in Roman society — to the Pontine islands in the Tyrrhenian Sea. This exilic tradition in the Tyrrhenian would last for thousands of years — until the end of Benito Mussolini's rule in 1943 — and in its final moments the Pontines housed such prisoners as the novelist Cesare Pavese (1908–50) and the politician Altiero Spinelli (1907–86), who wrote his famous pro-European *Manifesto* while confined to the island of Ventotene.

NAGUIB MAHFOUZ
The Return of Sinuhe

The incredible news spread through every part of Pharaoh's palace.
Every tongue told it, all ears listened eagerly to it, and the stunned
gossips repeated it — that a messenger from the land of Amorites
had descended upon Egypt. He bore a letter to Pharaoh from
Prince Sinuhe, who had vanished without warning all of forty
years before — and whose disappearance itself had wreaked havoc
in the people's minds. It was said that the prince pleaded with the
king to forgive what had passed, and to permit him to return to his
native land. There he would retire in quiet isolation, awaiting the
moment of his death in peace and security. No sooner had everyone recalled the hoary tale of the disappearance of Prince Sinuhe,
than they would revive the forgotten events and remember their
heroes — who were now old and senile, the ravages of age carved
harshly upon them.

In that distant time, the queen was but a young princess living
in the palace of Pharaoh Amenemhat I — a radiant rose blooming
on a towering tree. Her lively body was clothed in the gown of
youth and the shawl of beauty. Gentleness illuminated her spirit,
her wit blazed, her intelligence gleamed. The two greatest princes
of the realm were devoted to her: the then crown prince (and
present king) Senwosret I and Prince Sinuhe. The two princes
were the most perfect models of strength and youth, courage and
wealth, affection and fidelity. Their hearts were filled with love
and their souls with loyalty, until each of the two became upset
with his companion — to the point of rage and ruthless action.
When Pharaoh learnt that their emotional bond to each other and
their sense of mutual brotherhood were about to snap, he became

very anxious. He summoned the princess and — after a long discussion — he commanded her to remain in her own wing of the palace, and not to leave it.

He also sent for the two princes and said to them, with firmness and candor, "You two are but miserable, accursed victims of your own blind self-abandon in the pursuit of rashness and folly — a laughing stock among your fellow princes and a joke among the masses. The sages have said that a person does not merit the divine term 'human' until he is able to govern his lusts and his passions. Have you not behaved like dumb beasts and love-struck idiots? You should know that the princess is still confused between the two of you — and will remain confused until her heart is inspired to make a choice. But I call upon you to renounce your rivalry in an iron-bound agreement that you may not break. Furthermore, you will be satisfied with her decision, whatever it may be, and you will not bear anything towards your brother but fondness and loyalty — both inwardly and outwardly. Now, are you finished with this business?"

His tone did not leave room for hesitation. The two princes bowed their heads in silence, as Pharaoh bid them swear to their pact and shake hands. This they did — then left with the purest of intentions.

It happened during this time that unrest and rebellion broke out among the tribes of Libya. Pharaoh dispatched troops to chastise them, led by Prince Senwosret, the heir apparent, who chose Prince Sinuhe to command a brigade. The army clashed with the Libyans at several places, besetting them until they turned their backs and fled. The two princes displayed the kind of boldness and bravery befitting their characters. They were perhaps about to end their mission when the heir apparent suddenly announced the death of his father, King Amenemhat I. When this grievous news reached Prince Sinuhe, it seemed to have stirred his doubts as to what the new king might intend towards him. Suspicion swept over him and drove him to despair — so he melted away without warning, as though he had been swallowed by the sands of the desert.

Rumours abounded about Sinuhe's fate. Some said that he had fled to one of the faraway villages. Others held that he had killed himself out of desperation over life and love. The stories about him proliferated for quite a long time. But eventually, the tongues grew tired of them, consigning them to the tombs of oblivion under the rubble of time. Darkness enveloped them for forty years — until at last came that messenger from the land of the Amorites carrying Prince Sinuhe's letter — awakening the inattentive and reminding the forgetful.

King Senwosret looked at the letter over and over again with disbelieving eyes. He consulted the queen, now in her sixty-fifth year, on the affair. They agreed to send messengers bearing precious gifts to Prince Sinuhe in Amora, inviting him to come to Egypt safely, and with honour.

Pharaoh's messengers traversed the northern deserts, carrying the royal gifts straight to the land of the Amorites. Then they returned, accompanied by a venerable old man of seventy-five years. Passing the pyramids, his limbs trembled and his eyes were darkened by a cloud of distress. He was in Bedouin attire — a coarse woollen robe with sandals. A sword scabbard girded his waist; a long white beard flowed down over his chest. Almost nothing remained to show that he was an Egyptian raised in the palace of Memphis, except that when the sailors' song of the Nile reached his ears, his eyes became violently dreamy, his parched lips quivered, his breath beat violently in his breast — and he wept. The messengers knew nothing but that the old man threw himself down on the bank of the river and kissed it with ardour, as though he were kissing the cheek of a sweetheart from whom he had long been parted.

They brought him to the pharaoh's palace. He came into the presence of King Senwosret I, who was seated before him, and said, "May the Lord bless you, O exalted king, for forgiving me — and for graciously allowing me to return to the sacred soil of Egypt."

Pharaoh looked at him closely with obvious amazement, and said, his voice rising, "Is that really you? Are you my brother and the companion of my childhood and youth — Prince Sinuhe?"

"Before you, my lord, is what the desert and forty years have done to Prince Sinuhe."

Shaking his head, the king drew his brother towards him with tenderness and respect, and asked, "What did the Lord do with you during all these forty years?"

The prince pulled himself up straight in his seat and began to tell his tale.

"My lord, the story of my flight began at the hour that you were informed of our mighty father's death out in the Western Desert. There the Devil blinded me and evil whispers terrified me. So I threw myself into the wind, which blew me across deserts, villages and rivers, until I passed the borders between damnation and madness. But in the land of exile, the name of the person whose face I had fled, and who had dazzled me with his fame, conferred honour upon me. And whenever I confronted trouble, I cast my thoughts back to Pharaoh — and my cares left me. Yet I remained lost in my wanderings, until the leader of the Tonu tribes in Amora learnt of my plight, and invited me to see him.

"He was a magnificent chief who held Egypt and its subjects in all awe and affection. He spoke to me as a man of power, asking me about my homeland. I told him what I knew, while keeping the truth about myself from him. He offered me marriage to one of his daughters, and I accepted — and began to despair that I would ever again see my homeland. After a short time, I — who was raised on Pharaoh's famous chariots, and grew up in the wars of Libya and Nubia — was able to conquer all of Tonu's enemies. From them I took prisoners, their women and goods, their weapons and spoils, and their heirs, and my status rose even further. The chief appointed me the head of his armies, making me his expected successor.

"The gravest challenge that I faced was the great thief of the desert, a demonic giant — the very mention of whom frightened the bravest of men. He came to my place seeking to seize my home, my wife and my wealth. The men, women and children all rushed to the square to see this most ferocious example of combat between two opponents. I stood against him amidst the cheers and apprehension, fighting him for a long time. Dodging a mighty blow from his axe, I launched my piercing arrow and it struck him in the neck. Fatally weakened, he fell to the ground, death rattling in his throat. From that day onward, I was the undisputed lord of the badlands.

"Then I succeeded my father-in-law after his death, ruling the tribes by sword, enforcing the traditions of the desert. And the days, seasons and years passed by, one after another. My sons grew into strong men who knew nothing but the wilderness of the place for birth, life, glory and death. Do you not see, my lord, that I suffered in my estrangement from Egypt? That I was tossed back and forth by horrors and anxieties and was afflicted by calamities, although I also enjoyed love and the siring of children, reaping glory and happiness along the way. But old age and weakness finally caught up with me, and I conceded authority to my sons. Then I went home to my tent to await my passing.

13

"In my isolation, heartaches assailed me and anguish over-whelmed me, as I remembered gorgeous Egypt — the fertile playground of my childhood and youth. Desire disturbed me, and longing beckoned my heart. There appeared before my eyes scenes of the Nile and the luxuriant greenery and heavenly blue sky and the mighty pyramids and the lofty obelisks, and I feared that death would overtake me while I was in a land other than Egypt.

"So I sent a messenger to you, my lord, and my lord chose to pardon me and grant me his hospitality. I do not wish for more than a quiet corner to live out my old age, until Sinuhe's appointed hour comes round. Then he would be thrown into the embalming tank, and in his sarcophagus, the Book of the Dead — guide to the afterlife — would be laid. The professional women mourners of Egypt would wail over him with their plaintive rhyming cries..."

Pharaoh listened to Sinuhe with excitement and delight. Patting his shoulder gently, he said, "Whatever you want is yours." Then the king summoned one of his chamberlains, who led the prince into his wing of the palace.

Just before evening, a messenger came, saying that it would please the queen if she could meet with him. Immediately, Sinuhe rose to go to her, his aged heart beating hard. Following the mes-senger, nervous and distracted, he muttered to himself, "O Lord! Is it possible that I will see her once again? Will she really remember me? Will she remember Sinuhe, the young prince and lover?"

He crossed the threshold of her room like a man walking in his sleep. He reached her throne in seconds. Lifting his eyes up to her, he saw the face of his companion, whose youthful bloom the years had withered. Of her former loveliness, only faint traces remained. Bowing to her in reverence, he kissed the hem of her robe. The queen then spoke to him, without concealing her astonishment: "My God, is this truly our Prince Sinuhe?"

14

The prince smiled without uttering a word. He had not yet recovered himself when the queen said, "My lord has told me of your conversation. I was impressed by your feats, and the harshness of your struggle, though it took me aback that you had the fortitude to leave your wife and children behind."

"Mercy upon you, my queen," Sinuhe replied. "What remains of my life merely lengthens my torture, while the likes of me would find it unbearable to be buried outside of dear Egypt."

The queen lowered her gaze a moment, then, raising up to him her eyes filled with dreams, she said to him tenderly, "Prince Sinuhe, you have told us your story, but do you know ours? You fled at the time that you learnt of Pharaoh's death. You suspected that your rival, who had the upper hand, would not spare your life. You took off with the wind and traversed the deserts of Amora. Did you not know how your flight injured yourself and those that you love?"

Confusion showed on Sinuhe's face, but he did not break his silence. The queen continued, "Yet how could you know that the heir apparent visited me just before your departure at the head of the campaign in Libya. He said to me: 'Princess, my heart tells me that you have chosen the man that you want. Please answer me truthfully, and I promise you just as truthfully that I will be both content and loyal. I would never break this vow.'"

Her majesty grew quiet. Sinuhe queried her with a sigh, "Were you frank with him, my queen?"

She answered by nodding her head, then her breath grew more agitated. Sinuhe, gasping from the forty-year voyage back to his early manhood, pressed her further. "And what did you tell him?"

"Will it really interest you to know my answer? After a lapse of forty years? And after your children have grown to be chiefs of the tribes of Tonu?"

15

His exhausted eyes flashed a look of perplexity, then he said with a tremulous voice, "By the Sacred Lord, it matters to me."

She was staring at his face with pleasure and concern, and she said, smiling, "How strange this is, O Sinuhe! But you shall have what you want. I will not hold back the answer that you should have heard forty years ago. Senwosret questioned me closely, so I told him that I would grant him whatever I had of fondness and friendship. But as for my heart…"

The queen halted for a moment as Sinuhe again looked up, his beard twitching, shock and dismay bursting on his face. Then she resumed, "As for my heart — I am helpless to control it."

"My lord," he muttered.

"Yes, that is what I said to Senwosret. He bid me a moving goodbye — and swore that he would remain your brother so long as he breathed.

"But you were hasty, Sinuhe, and ran off with the wind. You strangled our high hopes, and buried our happiness alive. When the news of your vanishing came, I could hardly believe it — I nearly died of grief. Afterwards, I lived in seclusion for many long years. Then, at last, life mocked at my sorrows; the love of it freed me from the malaise of pain and despair. I was content with the king as my husband. This is my story, O Sinuhe."

She gazed into his face to see him drop his eyes in mourning; his fingers shook with emotion. She continued to regard him with compassion and joy, and asked herself: "Could it be that the agony of our long-ago love still toys with this ancient heart, so close to its demise?"

Translated from Arabic by Raymond Stock

THE TORAH
Exodus 23:9

Also thou shalt not oppress a stranger: for ye know the heart of a stranger, seeing ye were strangers in the land of Egypt.

THE BOOK OF PSALMS
Psalm 137

By the rivers of Babylon we sat and wept
  when we remembered Zion.
There on the poplars
  we hung our harps,
for there our captors asked us for songs,
  our tormentors demanded songs of joy;
  they said, "Sing us one of the songs of Zion!"
How can we sing the songs of the Lord
  while in a foreign land?
If I forget you, Jerusalem,
  may my right hand forget its skill.
May my tongue cling to the roof of my mouth
  if I do not remember you,
if I do not consider Jerusalem
  my highest joy.
Remember, Lord, what the Edomites did
  on the day Jerusalem fell.
"Tear it down," they cried,
  "tear it down to its foundations!"
Daughter Babylon, doomed to destruction,
  happy is the one who repays you
  according to what you have done to us.
Happy is the one who seizes your infants
  and dashes them against the rocks.

HOMER
from *The Odyssey*

Now at their native realms the Greeks arrived;
All who the wars of ten long years survived;
And 'scaped the perils of the gulfy main.
Ulysses, sole of all the victor train,
An exile from his dear paternal coast,
Deplored his absent queen and empire lost.
Calypso in her caves constrain'd his stay,
With sweet, reluctant, amorous delay;
In vain — for now the circling years disclose
The day predestined to reward his woes.
At length his Ithaca is given by fate,
Where yet new labours his arrival wait;
At length their rage the hostile powers restrain,
All but the ruthless monarch of the main.
But now the god, remote, a heavenly guest,
In Æthiopia graced the genial feast
(A race divided, whom with sloping rays
The rising and descending sun surveys);
There on the world's extremest verge revered
With hecatombs and prayer in pomp preferr'd,
Distant he lay: while in the bright abodes
Of high Olympus, Jove convened the gods:
The assembly thus the sire supreme address'd,
Ægysthus' fate revolving in his breast,
Whom young Orestes to the dreary coast
Of Pluto sent, a blood-polluted ghost.
"Perverse mankind! whose wills, created free,

Charge all their woes on absolute degree;
All to the dooming gods their guilt translate,
And follies are miscall'd the crimes of fate.
When to his lust Ægysthus gave the rein,
Did fate, or we, the adulterous act constrain?
Did fate, or we, when great Atrides died,
Urge the bold traitor to the regicide?
Hermes I sent, while yet his soul remain'd
Sincere from royal blood, and faith profaned;
To warn the wretch, that young Orestes, grown
To manly years, should re-assert the throne.
Yet, impotent of mind, and uncontroll'd,
He plunged into the gulf which Heaven foretold."
Here paused the god; and pensive thus replies
Minerva, graceful with her azure eyes:
"O thou! from whom the whole creation springs,
The source of power on earth derived to kings!
His death was equal to the direful deed;
So may the man of blood be doomed to bleed!
But grief and rage alternate wound my breast
For brave Ulysses, still by fate oppress'd
Amidst an isle, around whose rocky shore
The forests murmur, and the surges roar,
The blameless hero from his wish'd-for home
A goddess guards in her enchanted dome;
(Atlas her sire, to whose far-piercing eye
The wonders of the deep expanded lie;
The eternal columns which on earth he rears
End in the starry vault, and prop the spheres).
By his fair daughter is the chief confined,
Who soothes to dear delight his anxious mind;

Successless all her soft caresses prove,
To banish from his breast his country's love;
To see the smoke from his loved palace rise,
While the dear isle in distant prospect lies,
With what contentment could he close his eyes!
And will Omnipotence neglect to save
The suffering virtue of the wise and brave?
Must he, whose altars on the Phrygian shore
with frequent rites, and pure, avow'd thy power,
Be doom'd the worst of human ills to prove,
Unbless'd, abandon'd to the wrath of Jove?"

Translated from Greek by Alexander Pope

SAPPHO
Fragment 98B

but for you Kleis I have no
spangled—where would I get it?—
headbinder: yet the Mytilinean[

                ][
               ]to hold
               ]spangled

these things of the Kleanaktidai
exile
memories   terribly leaked away

Translated from Greek by Anne Carson

XENOPHANES
Fragment 22

When a stranger appears in wintertime,
these are the questions you must ask,
as you lie reclined on soft couches,
eating nuts, drinking wine by the fire:
"What's your name?", "Where do you come from?",
"How old were you when the Persians invaded?"

Translated from Greek by André Naffis-Sahely

SENECA THE YOUNGER
from *Moral Letters to Lucilius*

To enable yourself to meet death, you may expect no encourage-
ment or cheer from those who try to make you believe, by means
of their hair-splitting logic, that death is no evil. For I take pleasure,
excellent Lucilius, in poking fun at the absurdities of the Greeks,
of which, to my continual surprise, I have not yet succeeded in
ridding myself. Our master Zeno uses a syllogism like this: "No
evil is glorious; but death is glorious; therefore death is no evil."
A cure, Zeno! I have been freed from fear; henceforth I shall not
hesitate to bare my neck on the scaffold. Will you not utter sterner
words instead of rousing a dying man to laughter? Indeed, Lucilius,
I could not easily tell you whether he who thought that he was
quenching the fear of death by setting up this syllogism was the
more foolish, or he who attempted to refute it, just as if it had
anything to do with the matter! For the refuter himself proposed
a counter-syllogism, based upon the proposition that we regard
death as "indifferent", one of the things which the Greeks call
ἀδιάφορα. "Nothing", he says, "that is indifferent can be glorious;
death is glorious; therefore death is not indifferent." You comprehend the tricky fallacy which is contained in this syllogism — mere
death is, in fact, not glorious; but a brave death is glorious. And
when you say, "Nothing that is indifferent is glorious", I grant you
this much, and declare that nothing is glorious except as it deals
with indifferent things. I classify as "indifferent" — that is, neither
good nor evil — sickness, pain, poverty, exile, death. None of these
things are intrinsically glorious; but nothing can be glorious apart
from them. For it is not poverty that we praise, it is the man whom
poverty cannot humble or bend. Nor is it exile that we praise, it is

the man who withdraws into exile in the spirit in which he would have sent another into exile. It is not pain that we praise, it is the man whom pain has not coerced. One praises not death, but the man whose soul death takes away before it can confound it. All these things are in themselves neither honourable nor glorious; but any one of them that virtue has visited and touched is made honourable and glorious by virtue; they merely lie in between, and the decisive question is only whether wickedness or virtue has laid hold upon them. For instance, the death which in Cato's case is glorious, is in the case of Brutus forthwith base and disgraceful. For this Brutus, condemned to death, was trying to obtain postponement; he withdrew a moment in order to ease himself; when summoned to die and ordered to bare his throat, he exclaimed: "I will bare my throat, if only I may live!" What madness it is to run away, when it is impossible to turn back! "I will bare my throat, if only I may live!" He came very near saying also: "even under Antony!". This fellow deserved indeed to be consigned to life!

Translated from Latin by Richard Mott Gummere

PLUTARCH
from *The Life of Cleomenes*

Cleomenes, when day came, published a list of eighty citizens
who must go into exile, and removed all the ephoral chairs except
one; in this he purposed to sit himself for the transaction of public
business. Then he called a general assembly and made a defence
of his proceedings. He said that Lycurgus had blended the powers
of senate and kings, and that for a long time the state was administered in this way and had no need of other officials. But later,
when the Messenian War proved to be long, the kings, since their
campaigns abroad left them no time to administer justice themselves, chose some of their friends and left them behind to serve
the citizens in their stead. These were called ephors, or guardians,
and as a matter of fact they continued at first to be assistants of
the kings, but then gradually diverted the power into their own
hands, and so, ere men were aware, established a magistracy of
their own. As proof of this, Cleomenes cited the fact that, down
to that day, when the ephors summoned a king to appear before
them, he refused to go at the first summons, and at the second,
but at the third rose up and went with them; and he said that the
one who first added weight to this office, and extended its powers,
Asteropus, was ephor many generations later. As long, then, he
said, as the ephors kept within bounds, it had been better to bear
with them; but when with their assumed power they subverted
the ancient form of government to such an extent as to drive away
some kings, put others to death without a trial, and threaten such
as desired to behold again in Sparta her fairest and most divinely
appointed constitution, it was not to be endured. If, then, it had
been possible without bloodshed to rid Sparta of her imported

curses, namely luxury and extravagance, and debts and usury, and those elder evils than these, namely, poverty and wealth, he would have thought himself the most fortunate king in the world to have cured the disease of his country like a wise physician, without pain; but as it was, he said, in support of the necessity that had been laid upon him, he could cite Lycurgus, who, though he was neither king nor magistrate but a private person attempting to act as king, proceeded with an armed retinue into the market-place, so that Charillus the king took fright and fled for refuge to an altar. That king, however, Cleomenes said, since he was an excellent man and a lover of his country, speedily concurred in the measures of Lycurgus and accepted the change of constitution; still, as a matter of fact Lycurgus by his own acts bore witness to the difficulty of changing a constitution without violence and fear. To these, Cleomenes said, he had himself resorted with the greatest moderation, for he had but put out of the way the men who were opposed to the salvation of Sparta. For all the rest, he said, the whole land should be common property, debtors should be set free from their debts, and foreigners should be examined and rated, in order that the strongest of them might be made Spartan citizens and help to preserve the state by their arms.

Translated from Latin by Bernadotte Perrin

DARK AGES AND RENAISSANCES

W HEN ROME SLOWLY BEGAN to convert to Christianity, the ensuing ecumenical wars for the empire's soul led to high-ranking clergymen often conspiring to have their rivals exiled, pressuring emperors to intercede on their behalf and stamp out dangerous heresies, thus ensuring the empire's stability. Socrates Scholasticus (c.380– c.439) relates how, acting under the influence of Bishop Lucius of Alexandria, the Emperor Valens exiled Macarius the Elder and Macarius the Younger to an island off the coast of the Nile inhabited solely by pagans. Disconnected from their communities and fellow worshippers, it was thought the monks would be forced to abandon their faith, a wish that was irremediably dashed when the Macariuses instead converted the island's entire population to the teachings of Christ. While bishops vied with one another and the Constantinian Church acquired a lust for gold and bureaucracy, purging all forms of anti-authoritarian thought from their liturgy, monastic communities sprang up all along the Nitrian

Desert, in Lower Egypt. It is interesting to note here that while exile from the civilized world was considered a most horrible fate in Greek and Roman society, the Christian world instead taught that to remove oneself from the world's concerns was to attain a level of spiritual purity unavailable to those mired in the corrupting influences of everyday life.

The isolation of these communities afforded the Desert Fathers and Mothers, early-third-century Christian hermits who lived in the deserts of northern Egypt, the opportunity to retreat from the increasingly complex, violent and disordered world around them and to devote themselves to God, building upon foundations laid out by earlier mystics such as Saint Anthony of Egypt and Saint Pachomius. The Egyptian desert — which abounded in what Abba Andrew dubbed the three things most appropriate for a monk, "exile, poverty and endurance in silence" — would also eventually welcome the long-maligned Nestorius (c.386–450). Following Nestorius's defeat at the Council of Ephesus in 431, when his proposition that Christ's human and divine natures were separate was denounced as irredeemably heretical, Emperor Theodosius II banished him to Hibis in Egypt's Western Desert, nevertheless probably ensuring the spread of his teachings to the east, which they did, first to Persia and then on to India and China. Elsewhere, Saint Patrick converted Ireland, alongside Saint Columba, the founder of Iona Abbey, while Saint Aidan established Lindisfarne Priory off the coast of Northumberland. Islands, once home to inconvenient orators and political rivals, became safe havens for the servants of God, where exile, like in the *Ramayana*, transformed into a form of religious asceticism, a means to purify oneself. Of course, merely withdrawing from the world provided no certainty of instant holiness, as the Desert Father Abba Lucius recognized: "One day Abba Longinus questioned Abba Lucius about three thoughts, saying first, 'I want to go into exile.' The old man said to him, 'If you cannot control your tongue, you will not be an exile anywhere. Therefore control your tongue here, and you will be an exile.'"

The world the Desert Fathers and Mothers had known would be forever changed by the early Muslim conquests of the seventh century, and not long after Tariq ibn Ziyad (670–719) conquered the rock that now bears his name, the notion of exile would be again revisited by Abd al-Rahman I (731–88), an Umayyad prince from Syria, with whom the rich tradition of exilic writing in Spain arguably begins. Among the high-ranking survivors of the Abbasid slaughter of the Umayyads in 750, Abd al-Rahman spent several years roaming the cities of North Africa before amassing a small army, landing in al-Andalus and conquering Córdoba, which he made his capital, much to the chagrin of the Abbasid ruler in Baghdad, who reigned, if only nominally, as caliph over the entire Muslim world. Abd al-Rahman's most famous poem, or rather the most famous poem attributed to him, is "The Palm Tree", which takes as its subject a tree that, like the new Emir of Córdoba, has "sprung from soil" in which he is a "stranger", becoming a memento of Abd al-Rahman's lost homeland in Syria, which by then was ruled by his enemies.

Although Islam expanded its territory rapidly in the first three centuries of its existence, it would not ultimately retain many of its farthest outposts. While al-Andalus — or Muslim Spain — would last roughly from 711 to the fall of Granada in 1491, Siqilliyat, or the Emirate of Sicily, proved even more short-lived (831–1091). This might explain why, in the words of the Italian writer Giuseppe Quatriglio (1922–2017), many of the works of the Siculo-Arab poets we know are imbued with "the pain of eternal exile from Sicily". Ibn Hamdis (1056–1133) was born halfway through the Norman conquest of Sicily, and after the fall of Syracuse he relocated to Sfax in North Africa, before eventually making his way to al-Andalus, drawn by the reputation of its rulers as indefatigable patrons of the arts. It was during this period of exile in al-Andalus that Ibn Hamdis's Sicily finally fell to the Norman invaders for good. In one of the most complete fragments of his work still extant, Ibn Hamdis imagines Siqilliyat as a lost "paradise", the land of his "youth's mad joys", which has now become a "desert" he cannot bring himself to "bear witness to".

During the Tang Dynasty in China (620–905), exile was likely the most popular of the "five punishments", which included death by decapitation, a long sentence of hard labour or a beating with either a thin or a thick rod, compared to which banishment to remote, barbarous regions of the empire seemed like a far easier choice. Much like Ovid, the poet Bai Juyi (772–846) got himself in trouble at the Tang court over some controversial poems, which, as he explains in his preface to his poem "The Song of the Lute", led to him being "demoted to deputy governor and exiled to Jiujiang". The poem begins as Bai Juyi sees a friend off at the river, at which point he hears the sound of a lute being played by a woman, and, since finding refined music in distant provinces was uncommon, it reminds him of his old life in the sophisticated capital. With echoes of the interactions between Scheherazade and Shahryar in *The Thousand and One Nights*, Bai Juyi begins to ask the female musician a series of questions about her life, to which she answers:

My brother was drafted and my Madam died.
An evening passed, and when morning came my beauty was gone.
My door became desolate and horses seldom came,
and as I was getting old I married a merchant.
My merchant cared more about profit than being with me.
A month ago he went to Fuliang to buy tea.

Although the source of their loneliness is different, they are "both exiled to the edge of this world", and finally brought together by the sound of music, which is minutely described throughout the course of the poem.

While the Tang Dynasty's central government banished unpopular officials, the power to exile even the most influential citizens lay in the hands of Florence's masses, thereby truly earning its sobriquet as the "Athens of the Middle Ages". Failed wars, economic instability and unpopularity could easily get Florence's leaders exiled from their own city. In fact, a spell in exile caused by one's political allegiances occurred so often in Renaissance Italy that one had to have a sense of humour about it, as Niccolò Machiavelli (1469–1527) clearly did. In his *Florentine Histories*, Machiavelli gives us an anecdote involving two of the city's most famous sons, Rinaldo degli Albizzi (1370–1442) and Cosimo de' Medici (1389–1464), the patriarchs of two of Florence's most powerful families, who played an exilic game of cat and mouse with one another for much of their lives. "In 1435," Machiavelli tells us, "while Rinaldo degli Albizzi was in exile from Florence and scheming to start a war against the Florentines in the hope of returning home and chasing out Cosimo de' Medici, he sent this message to Medici: 'The hen is hatching her eggs.' Cosimo's reply was: 'Tell him she'll have a hard time hatching them outside the nest.'" Indeed, it was Cosimo the Elder who had the final laugh, given that, due to Cosimo's political perspicacity, Rinaldo's plot to have Florence invaded by Filippo Maria Visconti, the Duke of Milan, came to naught and Rinaldo never saw his native city again.

Long before Machiavelli's time, Dante Alighieri (1265–1321), another great Florentine, was chased out of his city, an episode from which we can perhaps draw most meaning by reading a few cantos situated roughly halfway through his *Paradiso*. Although Dante's journey through hell, purgatory and heaven throughout *The Divine Comedy* is studded with characters who appear incapable of speaking in anything but riddles, the poet is finally met by one of his ancestors, Cacciaguida, a warrior who was knighted during the Second Crusade (1147–49), and who, unlike anyone else in Dante's epic, does not mince his words. Cacciaguida tells Dante that his beloved Florence has been corrupted. Once a sturdy, honourable republic, its institutions have been polluted by the internecine warfare caused by greedy, competing clans — like the Albizzi and the Medici — who continually plotted and schemed to undermine the city's government to the detriment of its citizens' welfare. Before long, Cacciaguida warns his descendant that his own banishment won't be long in coming: "So you are destined to depart from Florence", he tells him, "You shall leave everything most dearly loved" and "You shall discover how salty is the savour / Of someone else's bread". Of course, luckily for Alighieri, this is paradise, where hope reigns supreme, and Cacciaguida tells his descendant that those who have exiled him will eventually be exiled themselves.

Some, of course, are fated to be exiled before they are even born, and the Byzantine poet Michael Marullus (1453–1500) was certainly one of them. Marullus was still inside his mother's womb as Constantine XI Palaiologos (1405–53) led the last desperate effort to keep the walls of the old imperial capital of Constantinople from being breached. An aristocrat with links to the former ruling family, Marullus came of age amidst the ashes of the Byzantine world, which had endured for 1,000 years after the end of the Roman Empire in the West. Growing up in the maritime Republic of Ragusa, an old Venetian vassal state, Marullus later moved to Italy, where he spent periods of time in Ancona, Padua, Venice and Naples. Aged seventeen, he took up arms as a mercenary and headed off to fight the Ottomans in the Black Sea region; but upon his return to Italy years later, he began to write poetry and forged a number of friendships with some of the peninsula's most distinguished inhabitants, including Pico della Mirandola and Sandro Botticelli, who painted his portrait. Regardless of where his dromomania led him, however, Marullus always betrayed his true roots by signing each poem with the word *Constantinopolitanus*.

There is no better statement of this exiled Greek poet's life and ideas than his "De exilio suo" — "On His Own Exile" — an intensely self-conscious lyric, apparently written while Marullus was serving as a mercenary, which contains some hard truths about life away from one's homeland:

> True, all dignity of birth and family is cast off
> As soon as you step on foreign land an exile.
> Nobility and virtuous lineage, a house which gleams
> With ancient honours — these are no help now.

Although Marullus acknowledges the loss of his world, he is obsessed with the warlike spirit he believes is necessary in order to reconquer it, a sentiment which shows its pagan roots in the line: "Liberty cannot be preserved except by our native Mars." Centuries ahead of his time — his belief in the need for violent rebellion would be proved right by the Greek War of Independence three centuries later — Marullus was nevertheless born astride two ages, although one could safely say that his death was squarely medieval. Attempting to cross the River Cecina atop his horse, Marullus drowned at the age of forty-seven, with a copy of Lucretius's *De rerum natura* stuffed in his pocket. Although praised by Pierre de Ronsard (1524–85), Marullus's poems may well have been lost to us had it not been for the efforts of the Italian philosopher Benedetto Croce (1866–1952), who translated his poems into Italian in 1938, a fortunate turn given that Marullus's books hadn't been reprinted since the sixteenth century.

THE DESERT FATHERS
Abba Longinus

Longinus, a friend and disciple of Lucius and later a famous abbot of the monastery of Enaton, led the monks in opposition to the Council of Chalcedon. Enaton was a leading monastery in Egypt; the Monophysite patriarchs took up residence there in the sixth century; it was sacked by the Persians in 611.

One day Abba Longinus questioned Abba Lucius about three thoughts, saying first, "I want to go into exile." The old man said to him, "If you cannot control your tongue, you will not be an exile anywhere. Therefore control your tongue here, and you will be an exile." Next he said to him, "I wish to fast." The old man replied, "Isaiah said, 'If you bend your neck like a rope or a bulrush that is not the fast I will accept; but rather, control your evil thoughts.'" (Isaiah 58.) He said to him the third time, "I wish to flee from men." The old man replied, "If you have not first of all lived rightly with men, you will not be able to live rightly in solitude."

Translated from Greek by Benedicta Ward

ABD AL-RAHMAN I
The Palm Tree

A palm tree stands in the middle of Rusafa, born in the West,
      Far from the land of palms.
I said to it: "How like me you are, far away and in exile,
      In long separation from family and friends.
You have sprung from soil in which you are a stranger;
      And I, like you, am far from home.
May dawn's clouds water you, streaming from the heavens
      In a grateful downpour."

Translated from Arabic by D.F. Ruggles

DU FU
from *Dreaming of Li Bai*

I've swallowed sobs of the lost dead,
but this live separation is chronic grief.
From the malarial south of the river
no news comes of the exiled traveller,
but you visit my dream, old friend,
knowing I ache for you.
Are you a ghost?
No way to tell with the long road between us.
Your spirit comes through green maple woods,
slips home past darkening border fortresses.
You are caught in the law's net,
so how can your spirit have wings?
The sinking moon pours onto the rafters
and your face glows in my mind.
The water is deep, the waves are wide.
Don't let the dragons snatch you!

Translated from Chinese by Tony Barnstone and Chou Ping

BAI JUYI
Song of the Lute

In the tenth year of the Yuanhe Period (815) I was demoted to deputy gov-
ernor and exiled to Jiujiang. In autumn the next year, I was seeing a friend
off at the Penpu ferry when I heard through the night someone playing
the lute in a boat. The tune, crisp and metallic, carried the flavour of the
music of the capital. I asked her who she was, and she told me she was
a prostitute from the capital, Changan, and had learnt to play the lute
from Master Mu and Master Cao. Now she was old and her beauty had
declined and therefore she had married a merchant. So I ordered wine and
asked her to play several tunes. We fell silent for a while. Then she told
me about the pleasure of her youth, though now she is low and withered,
drifting about on rivers and lakes. I had been assigned to posts outside
the capital for two years and had enjoyed myself in peace. But, touched
by her words, that evening I began to realize what I truly felt about being
exiled. So I wrote this long poem for her with a total of 612 characters,
entitled "Song of the Lute".

Seeing off a guest at night by the Xunyang River,
I felt autumn shivering on maple leaves and reed flowers.
I dismounted from my horse and my guest stepped on the boat;
we raised our cups for a drink without the music of pipes or strings.
We got drunk but not happy, mourning his departure.
When he embarked, the moon was half drowned in the river.
Suddenly we heard a lute sing across the water
and the host forgot to return home, and the guest stopped his boat.
Following the sound, we softly enquired who the musician was,
the lute fell silent and the answer came after a pause.
We steered our boat close and invited her to join us,

with wine refilled and lamp relit, our banquet opened again.
It took a thousand "please"s and ten thousand invitations before she appeared,
though with her lute she still hid half her face.
She plucked a few times to tune her strings.
Even before the melody formed one felt her emotions.
Each string sounded muted and each note meditative,
as if the music were narrating the sorrows of her life.
With eyebrows lowered she let her hands freely strum on and on,
pouring pent-up feelings out of her heart.
Softly strumming, plucking, sweeping and twanging the strings,
she played "Rainbow Garment" then "Green Waist".
The thick strings splattered like a rain shower,
the thin strings whispered privately like lovers.
Splattering and whispering back and forth,
big pearls and small pearls dropping into a jade plate.
Smooth the notes were, skylarks chirping under flowers.
Uneven the sound flowed like a spring under ice,
the spring water cold and strained, the strings congealing silence,
freezing to silence, till the sounds couldn't pass, and momentarily rest.
Now some other hidden sorrow and dark regret arose
and at this moment silence was better than sound.
Suddenly a silver vase exploded and the water splashed out,
iron horses galloped through and swords and spears clashed.
When the tune stopped, she struck the heart of the instrument,
all four strings together, like a piece of silk tearing.
Silence then in the east boat and the west.
All I could see in the river's heart was the autumn moon, so pale.

Silently she placed the pick between the strings,
straightened her garment and stood up with a serious face.
She told us, "I was a girl from the capital,

lived close to the Tombs of the Toad.
I finished studying lute at the age of thirteen,
and was first string in the Bureau of Women Musicians.
When my tunes stopped, the most talented players were humbled,
other girls were constantly jealous when they saw me made up,
the rich young city men competed to throw me brocade headscarves,
and I was given countless red silks after playing a tune.
My listeners broke hairpins and combs when they followed my rhythm.
I stained my blood-coloured silk skirt with wine
and laughed all year and laughed the next,
and autumn moon and spring wind passed unnoticed.
My brother was drafted and my Madam died.
An evening passed, and when morning came my beauty was gone.
My door became desolate and horses seldom came,
and as I was getting old I married a merchant.
My merchant cared more about profit than being with me.
A month ago he went to Fuliang to buy tea.
I am here to watch this empty boat at the mouth of the river.
The bright moon circles around the boat and the water is very cold.
Deep into the night I suddenly dreamt about my young days
and wept in dream as tears streaked through my rouge."

I was already sighing, listening to her lute,
but her story made me even sadder.
I said, "We both are exiled to the edge of this world
and our hearts meet though we've never met before.
Since I left the capital last year,
I was exiled to Xunyang and became sick.
Xunyang is too small to have any music;
all year round I heard no strings or pipes.
My home is close to the Pen River, low and damp,

yellow reeds and bitter bamboo surround the house.

What do you think I hear there day and night?

Cuckoos chirping blood and the sad howls of apes.

Spring river, blossoming morning and autumn moon night —

I often have my wine and drink by myself.

It is not that there are no folk songs or village flutes,

but their yawps and moans are just too noisy for my ear.

Tonight I heard your lute speak

and my ear pricked up, listening to fairy music.

Please don't decline, sit down to play another tune,

and I'll write a 'Song of the Lute' for you."

Touched by my words, she stood there for a long time,

then sat down and tuned up her strings and speeded up the rhythm.

Sad and touching, it was so different from her last song

and everyone started to weep.

If you ask, "Who shed most tears in this group?"

The Marshal of Jiangzhou's black gown was all wet.

Translated from Chinese by Tony Barnstone and Chou Ping

CHRISTOPHER OF MYTILENE

On the ex-emperor Michael Kalaphates, when he was arrested and blinded for having banished the Empress Zoe from imperial rule

So the thrice-hapless city of Byzas was to behold
the dreadful battle between the ship-caulker and the townsmen,
and the sun was to behold another disaster,
brought about by the exile of the fair empress
Zoe, the noble-born, whom, when she was still young,
the purple received, and the breast of an empress nursed;
Romanos thereafter obtained her as his wedded wife,
a high-bred man, they called him Argyropolos;
and it was he who loosened her maiden girdle.
Her exile bore the city many woes,
orphanhood for children, widowhood for women,
blood and wounds, strife and murder,
painful deaths, much sorrow and moaning,
all because of the infantile mind of her adopted child.
By a bad fate this man reigned over the great city.
Intent on evil, he quickly forgot the covenants,
and in his rashness he devised a wicked plan.
But in the middle of the city he lost his dear sight
by violating the truthful oaths with his offence.
He brought his crown to shame, he trampled upon truces,
this baneful emperor, by expelling the empress from the palace.
But foolishness and the unlawful violation of oaths
have terribly blinded him and taken away his sceptre.
Now this wicked creature sighs heavily, and cries out grief-stricken,
calling ruined "this empire that I ruled".

He lies now on the ground, the wretched one, who once held power,
an example of utter misery for future generations,
craving the light he lost with his foolish aspirations.

Translated from Greek by Floris Bernard and Christopher Livanos

IBN HAMDIS
Oh sea, you conceal my paradise

Oh sea, you conceal my paradise
on your other shore…
I recall Sicily — in my soul
pain resurrects her image,
land of youth's mad joys,
now desert, once alive like
the flower of noble minds.
Driven from paradise,
how can I bear witness to it?
If my tears were not so bitter
I could believe that they
were rivers of that holy place.

Translated from Arabic by Justin Vitiello

MOSES IBN EZRA
I am weary of roaming about the world

I am weary of roaming about the world,
Measuring its expanse, and I'm not yet done.
I walk with the beasts of the forest
And I hover like a bird of prey over the peaks of the mountains.
My feet run about like lightning to the far ends of the earth,
And I move from sea to sea.
Journey follows journey, but I find
No resting place, no calm repose.
How far must my feet, at Fate's behest,
Bear me o'er exile's path, and find no rest?
Oh, if indeed, the Lord would me restore
To beautiful Granada-land, my paths
Would be the paths of pleasantness once more
For in that land my life was very sweet —
A kindly Fate lay homage to my feet,
And deep I quaffed at Friendship's fount;
Though hope be long deferred, though heart be faint,
On God I wait,
Unto whose mercy there is no restraint —
And whose decree
Can break the shackles and unbar the gate,
And set the prisoner of exile free.

Translated from Hebrew by Salo Wittmayer Baron

ANNA KOMNENE
from *The Alexiad*

Here I must interrupt the thread of the story a while to relate how the emperor suppressed the Paulicians. He could not bear the thought of entering Constantinople without having first subdued these rebels, but, as though presiding over a second victory after a first, he caused the mass of the Manichæans to complete the cycle of his achievements. For it was not even right to allow those descendants of the Paulicians to be a blemish, as it were, on the brilliant trophy of his western victories. He did not wish to effect this by warfare, as in the clash of battle many lives on either side would be sacrificed; further, he knew from of old that these men were very spirited and breathed defiance against their enemies. For this reason he was eager only to punish the ringleaders, and to incorporate the rest in the body of his army. Hence he proceeded against them adroitly. He knew those men's love of danger and irrepressible courage in battle and therefore feared that, if they became desperate, they would commit some terrible outrage; and for the moment they were living quietly in their own country and so far had abstained from raids and other forms of devastation; therefore on his way back to Byzantium he asked them by letter to come and meet him and made them many promises. But the Manichæans had heard of his victory over the Franks and naturally suspected that those letters were misleading them by fair promises; nevertheless, though reluctant, they set out to meet him. Alexius halted close to Mosynopolis, pretending that he was waiting for other reasons, but in reality he was only awaiting their arrival. When they came he pretended that he wished to review them and write down each individual's name. So he presided with a grim face and commanded the chiefs of the Manichæans not to ride past promiscuously but in parties of ten, promising a general review shortly, and then, when their names had been inscribed, to enter the gates in that order. The men whose duty it was to take them captive were all ready, and, after taking away their horses and weapons, locked up the chiefs in the prisons assigned them. Those who came after were in complete ignorance of these doings and therefore entered the town little knowing the fate awaiting them. In this manner, then, he captured them, and their property he confiscated and distributed among the brave soldiers who had shared in the battles and dangers that had befallen him. The official who undertook this distribution went to Philippopolis and drove even the women from their homes and incarcerated them in the citadel. Within a short time the emperor took pity on the imprisoned Manichæans, and those who desired Christian baptism were not refused even this boon. So, having over-reached them by every kind of device, he discovered the authors of this terrible madness, and these he banished and imprisoned on islands. The rest he released, and he gave them permission to go whithersoever they wished. And they, preferring their mother country to any other, hastened back to it to put their affairs into what order they could.

Translated from Greek by Elizabeth A.S. Dawes

ATTAR
from *The Conference of the Birds*

A pauper fell in love with a famous Egyptian king. When news of it reached the royal ear, the king summoned the deluded lover. "Since you have fallen in love with a king," he said, "you have but two choices. Either leave this town and country, or give up your head for my love. Which do you choose: exile or decapitation?" The pauper in love was not a resolute man, so he chose banishment. When that indignant, penniless man left the royal presence, the king immediately commanded: "Cut off his head." A courtier said: "But your highness, the man is innocent; why do you order his death?" The king replied: "Because he loved me with insincerity. If he were a man truly in love, he would have chosen to stay and lose his head. If you value your head more than your love, then for you the practice of love is a crime. If the beggar had chosen execution, I would have bestowed upon him honours and would have myself put on the garb of servitude for him. In the face of such devotion even the world's monarch must become a slave to such a lover. However, since the beggar wavered in his love, his claim to love was false. He was double-dealing in love; beheading is what he deserves. If you say, 'I love' and then follow it with, 'but I want to keep my head too,' you are a liar and pretender. Let my subjects beware, so that no one dares to boast falsely of true love for me."

Leaving your self is annihilation.
When awareness of this annihilation
is annihilated, you'll find eternal life.
If your heart is anxious and panics

when it must cross the bridge over raging fire,
don't worry because that fire
is only a lamp's flame,
smoking soot, shadowy as a crow's feather.

When the oil burns, it loses itself,
and so emerges from its own self.
Yes, it burns, but it also yields charcoal
for ink to write the words of the Beloved.

Translated from Persian by Sholeh Wolpé

DANTE
Cacciaguida's Prophecy

"While I was in the company of Virgil
High on the mountain that heals many souls,
And while I climbed down through the world of death,

"Foreboding words were said to me concerning
My future life, although I feel myself
So squarely set to face the blows of chance

"That I willingly would be content to hear
What fortune now draws near for me, because
An arrow seen beforehand has less shock."

I spoke this answer to that same bright light
That previously had spoken to me, and so,
As Beatrice wished, my own wish was confessed.

Not in dark sayings, with which foolish people
Of old were once ensnared, before the Lamb
Of God who takes away our sins was slain,

But in clear words and with exact discourse
That fatherly love made his reply to me,
Contained in and shown out of his own smile:

"Contingency, which does not stretch beyond
The meagre volume of your world of matter,
Is fully pictured in the eternal vision;

"Yet thence it takes on no necessity,
No more than would a ship which sails downstream
Depend upon the eyes which mirror it;

"And thence, as to the ear sweet harmony
Comes from an organ, to my sight the time
Comes that already waits in store for you.

"As Hippolytus was driven out of Athens
Through the treachery and spite of his stepmother,
So you are destined to depart from Florence.

"Thus it was willed and thus already plotted,
And soon it shall be done by him who plans it
There where Christ every day is bought and sold.

"The common cry, as is the wont, will blame
The injured party, but the vengeance which
The truth demands will witness to the truth.

"You shall leave everything most dearly loved:
This is the first one of the arrows which
The bow of exile is prepared to shoot.

"You shall discover how salty is the savour
Of someone else's bread, and how hard the way
To come down and climb up another's stairs.

"And what will weigh down on your shoulders most
Will be the bad and brainless company
With whom you shall fall down into this ditch.

"For all shall turn ungrateful, all insane
And impious against you, but soon after
Their brows, and not your own, shall blush for it.

"Their own behaviour will prove their brutishness,
So that it shall enhance your reputation
To have become a party to yourself.

"First refuge and first place of rest for you
Shall be in the great Lombard's courtesy,
Who bears the sacred bird perched on the ladder

"And who shall hold you in such kind regard
That between you, in contrast with the others,
The granting will be first and asking last.

"With him you shall see one who at his birth
Was so imprinted by this star of strength
That men will take note of his noble deeds.

"Not yet have folk observed his worthiness
By reason of his age: these wheeling spheres
Have only for nine years revolved around him.

"But ere the Gascon cons high-riding Henry,
Some sparks of virtue shall show forth in him
By hard work and by caring naught for money.

53

"His bounty shall be so widespread hereafter
That the tongues, even of his enemies,
Will not be able to keep still about him.

"Look you to him and his beneficence.
Through him shall many folk find change of fortune,
Rich men and beggars shifting their positions.

"And you shall bear this written in your mind
Of him, but tell it not…" — and he told things
Beyond belief of those who witness them.

Then added, "Son, these are the glossaries
On what was told to you: behold the snares
Concealed by a few circlings of the sun!

"Yet be not envious against your neighbours,
For your life shall extend much longer than
The punishment of their perniciousness."

When this saintly soul showed by his silence
That he had set the woof across the warp
Which I had held in readiness for him,

I ventured, like someone who seeks advice,
In his confusion, from another person
Who sees and wills straightforwardly and loves:

"I clearly see, my father, how time spurs
Towards me to strike me such a blow as falls
The heaviest on him who heeds it least.

"So it is well I arm myself with foresight,
That if the dearest place be taken from me,
I'll not lose all the others, through my verse."

Translated from Italian by James Finn Cotter

JOHN BARBOUR
from *The Bruce of Bannockburn*

Bruce to his lodgings went anon.
The little respite he had won
You may be certain made him glad.
His steward instantly he bade
Provide his men in every way
Their entertainment for the day.
Himself would in his chamber be
A long while in strict privacy
Attended by his clerk alone.
As soon as e'er the steward had gone
To carry out his lord's behest,
The Bruce without a moment's rest,
Keeping his foemen in the dark,
Mounted on horseback with his clerk.
He rode by night, he rode by day,
Halting but little on the way,
Until, ere fifteen days were passed,
They saw Lochmaben's walls at last.
His brother Edward there they found,
Who viewed with wonder, I'll be bound,
This journey hasty and concealed.
The Bruce to him the cause revealed,
How, to escape King Edward's might,
He had resolved on sudden flight.
Now, as it happened, on that day
The Comyn was not far away:
'Twas at Dumfries he then abode.

The Bruce took horse and thither rode,
Firmly resolved to pay him well
For that which he had dared to tell.
From his resolve he did not falter:
Confronting Comyn at the altar
Of Gray Friars' Church with laughing face,
He showed him in that holy place
The fatal pact, and with a knife
Stabbed him and took away his life.
Sir Edmund Comyn also died,
And many mighty men beside.
However there are some who say
This happened in another way;
But, whatsoever caused the strife,
Thereby the Comyn lost his life,
And Bruce did evil to defy
The holy altar's sanctity,
For which such troubles him befell,
That no romance did ever tell
Of man that was so sore distressed
And was at last by fortune blessed.
Now going back, I must relate
How England's monarch sat in state
With all his peers in Parliament,
And for the Bruce a summons sent.
Knights, who the royal mandate bore,
Appear before the Bruce's door,
But call in vain. The servants say
That by command since yesterday
In his own room their lord had been
By all except his clerk unseen.

When, after knocking long in vain,
They found they could no answer gain,
They broke the door, but, though they sought
All through the room, discovered nought.
So they returned and told the King,
Why they had failed the Bruce to bring.
At his escape the King grieved sore,
And, filled with wrath, he stoutly swore
That Bruce both hanged and drawn should be.
He swore with confidence; but he,
The Bruce, hoped it might not be so,
And when, as ye already know,
In church he had the Comyn slain,
He to his castle went again.
Thence sent he messengers to ride
And carry letters far and wide
Bidding his friends come to his aid
And join the force he had arrayed,
For he now purposed to be crowned.

Translated from Scots by Michael MacMillan

MICHAEL MARULLUS
De exilio suo

So often I fled the enemy's chains,
And snatched my soul from fate. Why?
Not to stay here, the sole survivor of my bloodline
Cruel is the one willing to outlast his homeland!
And not because my mind loves the light so much
it would prefer death by slaughter to exile!
No, I did it for this: that I, ancient offspring of the Marulli,
Not be forced into slavery, snatched by the cruel enemy,
Just a child.
If, seized far from home in the land of Scythia,
I suffered the arrogant orders of a Bessian
And endured cruel commands and a mighty master,
My freedom nothing but an empty word,
It would have been more fitting to serve a harsh tyrant
And to endure with my native land
All grief to be endured.
It is something, at least, to see the ashes
And all the memorials of your people,
The authority of ancestors won by authority,
And to enjoy your native air while breath remains
And not be mocked and scorned far off in a foreign land.
True, all dignity of birth and family is cast off
As soon as you step on foreign land an exile.
Nobility and virtuous lineage, a house which gleams
With ancient honours — these are no help now.
But once, when the might of our country reigned,
The whole world was open to us as guests.

Then, ah then we should have exhaled our final breath
Young and old together. We should not have survived
that evil. Then we should have recalled
our ancestral spirit and the virtue we inherited
And rushed to be slaughtered by noble wounds.
Liberty cannot be preserved except by our native Mars.
That was the only path sure to bring salvation.
May he die who first exulted in arms!
If they are resolute, a small band of men is enough
However small, it is enough if the soldiers are fierce
When armed with their grandfathers' swords, and do not fear
To approach the enemy mass.
Thoughts of their wives, dear children and homes incite them to act,
And devoted care of their exhausted fathers.
What madness when surrounded by enemies
To entrust your city's defence to outside forces
And to confound your civic insignia with foreign hands,
To think Greek weapons insufficient for Greeks!

He, he was the enemy. He subdued the Greeks
That soldier, he tore apart their ruined wealth,
He gave their gods and temples to the wicked fire,
He handed over the Roman empire to the Turks.
It is not so much fate decreed by the gods
As our own guilt that must be atoned for
And the foolish intent of our leader.
And so we wretched men atone and we will always atone
As long as the Black Sea and our tears make us weak.

Translated from Greek by Amy S. Lewis

EXPULSIONS, EXPLORATIONS
AND MIGRATIONS

W ITH NEW KINGS COME new laws, and 1607 struck the death
knell for Gaelic Ireland. In that year, the Earls of Tyrconnel
and Tyrone fled to the Continent to seek Spanish aid against their
new English overlord, James I. The earls had been stripped of
much of their lands under the new freehold system as the Stuart
monarchy paved the path for the subsequent Plantation of Ulster.
It was, by all accounts, a tragic loss, leaving Ireland rudderless at a
critical juncture when the tide against foreign domination might
have been turned. Andrias MacMarcuis's (c.1570–c.1630) lament in
his poem "The Flight of the Earls" begins with the memorable line,
"Anocht is uaigneach Éire / This night sees Éire desolate", before
ending with the exact moment the Irish lords depart their beloved
Ireland with the hope of returning as conquering heroes:

Her chiefs are gone. There's none to bear
Her cross or lift her from despair;
The grieving lords take ship. With these
Our very souls pass overseas.

Of course, the Stuarts themselves would eventually be supplanted too. Ironically, the fate of the Irish earls would play out again in the shape of Bonnie Prince Charlie's (1720–88) escape to the Isle of Skye after the Battle of Culloden in 1746.

It is to Dante's first American translator, the poet Henry Wadsworth Longfellow (1807–82), that we owe one of the earliest popular chronicles of one of the first recorded acts of wholesale ethnic expulsion: that of *Le Grand Dérangement*. Also known as the expulsion of the Acadians, the term describes the British decision to deport 15,000 French colonists from their homes in Acadia (the modern Canadian Maritimes) and to ship them back to France, from where they were then resettled in Louisiana, becoming what we now call the Cajuns. Longfellow's *Evangeline: A Tale of Acadie* (1847) describes Evangeline Bellefontaine's efforts to find her beau Gabriel after the expulsion, no mean a task given the circumstances:

Scattered were they, like flakes of snow, when the wind from the
    north-east
Strikes aslant through the fogs that darken the Banks
    of Newfoundland
Friendless, homeless, hopeless, they wandered from city to city,
From the cold lakes of the North to sultry Southern savannas, —
From the bleak shores of the sea to the lands where the Father
    of Waters
Seizes the hills in his hands, and drags them down to the ocean

The techniques behind the expulsion of the Acadians would be repeated often in future chapters of American history, including the exile of the pro-British Iroquois to Canada, the Indian Removal of the 1830s and the Long Walk of the Navajo in 1864. Luci Tapahonso's (1953–) poem "In 1864" records the forced march of the Navajos to Bosque Redondo, where, as the poet notes in her preface, "they were held for four years until the US government declared the assimilation attempt a failure. More than 2,500 died of smallpox and other illnesses, depression, severe weather conditions, and starvation." As Tapahonso writes:

My aunt always started the story saying, "You are here
because of what happened to your great-grandmother long ago."

They began rounding up the people in the fall.
Some were lured into surrendering by offers of food, clothes,
and livestock. So many of us were starving and suffering
that year because the bilagáana kept attacking us.
Kit Carson and his army had burned all the fields,
and they killed our sheep right in front of us.

The literature of travel and exploration during the early modern period in the West is largely a blood-soaked chronicle of jingoism overseas, where animalistic natives are either exterminated or "civilized", or both. As outsider perspectives on the West during this period are quite rare, it is particularly interesting to pause on the reflections of Mirza Sheikh I'tesamuddin (c.1730–c.1800), who embarked on a diplomatic mission to Britain on behalf of the Mogul emperor in 1765. I'tesamuddin's memoirs of his trip, *The Wonders of Vilayet*, see him tour many parts of the world, including a visit to Oxford's renowned "madrassah", and his observations of the age-old Anglo-French dispute are engrossing for their deviation from white masochistic accounts of the "other":

> The French say that the present excellence of the English in the arts and sciences, trade and industry, is the result of French education; in the past, when they lacked this education, they were ignorant like the mass of Indians. However, even the French admit that the English have always been outstanding soldiers. The French say that the lower classes of Englishmen do not go to foreign countries to seek trade or employment because, being stupid and without any skills or business acumen, they would fail to earn a decent livelihood. The French, on the other hand, are skilled in all the arts and sciences, and wherever they go they are cordially received and acquire dignity and honour in diverse professions. I realized clearly that the French are a conceited race, whose conversation was always an attempt to display their own superiority and to unfairly belittle other nations.

It is in earlier chapters of *The Wonders of Vilayet*, however, that we come across a fine description of the slaveocracy of French Mauritius (1715–1810), where the *Code Noir* ruled supreme:

> The French notables live in mansions built on stockaded plots of a couple of bighas in the middle of their estates, which are cultivated with the help of a hundred or so male and female slaves. Oranges, Indian corn and vegetables are grown for the market. One half of the proceeds goes to the landlord, the other half is divided among the slaves. These slaves are brought as adolescents from Bengal, Malabar,

the Deccan and other regions and sold for fifty to sixty rupees each [...] It is reported that the Portuguese were the island's first colonizers, but they found it so heavily infested with snakes, serpents, scorpions and other noxious creatures that they were soon forced to abandon it. After them the French moved in and had better luck. French priests, using a kind of necromancy, caught the dangerous creatures, took them out to sea and drowned them. Since then there is no sign of them on the island. Of course, Allah alone knows how far the story is true.

As technological advancement shortened distances, economic migration accordingly increased, and in a time of renewed xenophobia, as the West raises it drawbridge to keep out the rabble of its present and past empires, many would benefit from turning to the words of Mary Antin (1881–1949), a Jew who emigrated from Czarist Russia at the age of ten and who in 1912 penned a famous memoir of her journey from immigrant to citizen, appositely entitled *The Promised Land*. In a lesser-known work published only two years later, *They Who Knock at Our Gates*, Antin posed an increasingly important question that continues to divide opinion around the world to this day: do our beliefs in fundamental human rights truly afford anyone a say over restricting new arrivals into a country? As Antin says:

Let any man who lays claim to any portion of the territory of the United States produce his title deed. Are not most of us squatters here, and squatters of recent date at that? The rights of a squatter are limited to the plot he actually occupies and cultivates. The portion of the United States territory that is covered by squatters' claims is only a fraction, albeit a respectable fraction, of the land we govern. In the name of what moral law do we wield a watchman's club over the vast regions that are still waiting to be staked out? The number of American citizens who can boast of ancestral acres is not sufficient to swing a presidential election.

While nativists across the world spew their hatred, the death toll continues to rise as increasing numbers of people put themselves at risk in order to seek better lives. The 2017 UN Migration report noted that just over 170,000 migrants illegally entered Europe by sea that year, with "70 per cent arriving in Italy". "In Lampedusa", a poem written by the Italo-Eritrean Ribka Sibhatu (1962–), records one of the many forgotten episodes of the crisis, when a ship carrying 518 passengers sank taking 368 victims with it, almost all of whom were Eritreans fleeing the dictatorship of the People's Front for Democracy and Justice. Sibhatu's realism is unsparing:

> To send a distress call,
>   they set a sail on fire, and as the
>   flames began to spread, some frightened people
>   jumped overboard and tipped the boat.
> They were all adrift in the freezing sea!
> Amidst that storm, some died right away,
> some beat the odds and cheated death,
> some who could swim tried to help
> some drowned using their last breath
> to send messages back to their native land.

WILLIAM SHAKESPEARE
from *Coriolanus,* Act III, Scene 3

BRUTUS

There's no more to be said, but he is banished,
As enemy to the people and his country.
It shall be so.

CITIZENS

It shall be so, it shall be so.

CORIOLANUS

You common cry of curs, whose breath I hate
As reek o'th' rotten fens, whose loves I prize
As the dead carcasses of unburied men
That do corrupt my air: I banish you!
And here remain with your uncertainty.
Let every feeble rumour shake your hearts;
Your enemies, with nodding of their plumes,
Fan you into despair! Have the power still
To banish your defenders, till at length
Your ignorance — which finds not till it feels
Making but reservation of yourselves,
Still your own foes, deliver you
As most abated captives to some nation
That won you without blows! Despising
For you the city, thus I turn my back.
There is a world elsewhere.

ANDRIAS MACMARCUIS
The Flight of the Earls

This night sees Éire desolate,
Her chiefs are cast out of their state;
Her men, her maidens weep to see
Her desolate that should peopled be.

How desolate is Connla's plain,
Though aliens swarm in her domain;
Her rich bright soil had joy in these
That now are scattered overseas.

Man after man, day after day
Her noblest princes pass away
And leave to all the rabble rest
A land dispeopled of her best.

O'Donnell goes. In that stern strait
Sore-stricken Ulster mourns her fate,
And all the northern shore makes moan
To hear that Aodh of Annagh's gone.

Men smile at childhood's play no more
Music and song, their day is o'er;
At wine, at Mass the kingdom's heirs
Are seen no more; changed hearts are theirs.

They feast no more, they gamble not,
All goodly pastime is forgot,
They barter not, they race no steeds,
They take no joy in stirring deeds.

No praise in builded song expressed
They hear, no tales before they rest;
None care for books and none take glee
To hear the long-traced pedigree.

The packs are silent, there's no sound
Of the old strain on Bregian ground.
A foreign flood holds all the shore,
And the great wolf-dog barks no more.

Woe to the Gael in this sore plight!
Hence forth they shall not know delight.
No tidings now their woe relieves,
Too close the gnawing sorrow cleaves.

These the examples of their woe:
Israel in Egypt long ago,
Troy that the Greek hosts set on flame,
And Babylon that to ruin came.

Sundered from hope, what friendly hand
Can save the sea-surrounded land?
The clan of Conn no Moses see
To lead them from captivity.

Her chiefs are gone. There's none to bear
Her cross or lift her from despair;
The grieving lords take ship. With these
Our very souls pass overseas.

Translated from Irish Gaelic by Robin Flower

HENRY WADSWORTH LONGFELLOW
from *Evangeline: A Tale of Acadie*

Many a weary year had passed since the burning of Grand-Pré,
When on the falling tide the freighted vessels departed,
Bearing a nation, with all its household gods, into exile,
Exile without an end, and without an example in story.
Far asunder, on separate coasts, the Acadians landed;
Scattered were they, like flakes of snow, when the wind from the north-east
Strikes aslant through the fogs that darken the Banks of Newfoundland.
Friendless, homeless, hopeless, they wandered from city to city,
From the cold lakes of the North to sultry Southern savannas, —
From the bleak shores of the sea to the lands where the Father of Waters
Seizes the hills in his hands, and drags them down to the ocean,
Deep in their sands to bury the scattered bones of the mammoth.
Friends they sought and homes; and many, despairing, heart-broken,
Asked of the earth but a grave, and no longer a friend nor a fireside.
Written their history stands on tablets of stone in the churchyards.
Long among them was seen a maiden who waited and wandered,
Lowly and meek in spirit, and patiently suffering all things.
Fair was she and young; but, alas! before her extended,
Dreary and vast and silent, the desert of life, with its pathway
Marked by the graves of those who had sorrowed and suffered before her,
Passions long extinguished, and hopes long dead and abandoned,
As the emigrant's way o'er the Western desert is marked by
Camp-fires long consumed, and bones that bleach in the sunshine.
Something there was in her life incomplete, imperfect, unfinished;
As if a morning of June, with all its music and sunshine,
Suddenly paused in the sky, and, fading, slowly descended
Into the east again, from whence it late had arisen.

Sometimes she lingered in towns, till, urged by the fever within her,
Urged by a restless longing, the hunger and thirst of the spirit,
She would commence again her endless search and endeavor;
Sometimes in churchyards strayed, and gazed on the crosses and tombstones,
Sat by some nameless grave, and thought that perhaps in its bosom
He was already at rest, and she longed to slumber beside him.
Sometimes a rumor, a hearsay, an inarticulate whisper,
Came with its airy hand to point and beckon her forward.
Sometimes she spake with those who had seen her beloved and known him,
But it was long ago, in some far-off place or forgotten.
"Gabriel Lajeunesse!" they said; "Oh yes! we have seen him.
He was with Basil the blacksmith, and both have gone to the prairies;
Coureurs-des-Bois are they, and famous hunters and trappers."
"Gabriel Lajeunesse!" said others; "Oh yes! we have seen him.
He is a Voyageur in the lowlands of Louisiana."
Then would they say, "Dear child! Why dream and wait for him longer?
Are there not other youths as fair as Gabriel? Others
Who have hearts as tender and true, and spirits as loyal?
Here is Baptiste Leblanc, the notary's son, who has loved thee
Many a tedious year; come, give him thy hand and be happy!
Thou art too fair to be left to braid St Catherine's tresses."
Then would Evangeline answer, serenely but sadly, "I cannot!
Whither my heart has gone, there follows my hand, and not elsewhere.
For when the heart goes before, like a lamp, and illumines the pathway,
Many things are made clear, that else lie hidden in darkness."
Thereupon the priest, her friend and father-confessor,
Said, with a smile, "O daughter! Thy God thus speaketh within thee!
Talk not of wasted affection, affection never was wasted;
If it enrich not the heart of another, its waters, returning
Back to their springs, like the rain, shall fill them full of refreshment;
That which the fountain sends forth returns again to the fountain.

Patience; accomplish thy labour; accomplish thy work of affection!
Sorrow and silence are strong, and patient endurance is godlike.
Therefore accomplish thy labour of love, till the heart is made godlike,
Purified, strengthened, perfected, and rendered more worthy of heaven!"
Cheered by the good man's words, Evangeline laboured and waited.
Still in her heart she heard the funeral dirge of the ocean,
But with its sound there was mingled a voice that whispered, "Despair not!"
Thus did that poor soul wander in want and cheerless discomfort,
Bleeding, barefooted, over the shards and thorns of existence.
Let me essay, O Muse! to follow the wanderer's footsteps; —
Not through each devious path, each changeful year of existence,
But as a traveller follows a streamlet's course through the valley:
Far from its margin at times, and seeing the gleam of its water
Here and there, in some open space, and at intervals only;
Then drawing nearer its banks, through sylvan glooms that conceal it,
Though he behold it not, he can hear its continuous murmur;
Happy, at length, if he find the spot where it reaches an outlet.

OLAUDAH EQUIANO
The Middle Passage

At last, when the ship we were in had got in all her cargo, they made ready with many fearful noises, and we were all put under deck, so that we could not see how they managed the vessel. But this disappointment was the least of my sorrow. The stench of the hold while we were on the coast was so intolerably loathsome, that it was dangerous to remain there for any time, and some of us had been permitted to stay on the deck for the fresh air; but now that the whole ship's cargo were confined together, it became absolutely pestilential. The closeness of the place, and the heat of the climate, added to the number in the ship, which was so crowded that each had scarcely room to turn himself, almost suffocated us. This produced copious perspirations, so that the air soon became unfit for respiration, from a variety of loathsome smells, and brought on a sickness among the slaves, of which many died, thus falling victims to the improvident avarice, as I may call it, of their purchasers. This wretched situation was again aggravated by the galling of the chains, now become insupportable; and the filth of the necessary tubs, into which the children often fell, and were almost suffocated. The shrieks of the women, and the groans of the dying, rendered the whole a scene of horror almost inconceivable. Happily perhaps for myself I was soon reduced so low here that it was thought necessary to keep me almost always on deck; and from my extreme youth I was not put in fetters. In this situation I expected every hour to share the fate of my companions, some of whom were almost daily brought upon deck at the point of death, which I began to hope would soon put an end to my miseries. Often did I think many of the inhabitants of the deep much more happy than myself; I envied them the freedom they enjoyed, and as often wished I could change my condition for theirs. Every circumstance I met with served only to render my state more painful, and heighten my apprehensions, and my opinion of the cruelty of the whites. One day they had taken a number of fishes; and when they had killed and satisfied themselves with as many as they thought fit, to our astonishment who were on the deck, rather than give any of them to us to eat, as we expected, they tossed the remaining fish into the sea again, although we begged and prayed for some as well we could, but in vain; and some of my countrymen, being pressed by hunger, took an opportunity, when they thought no one saw them, of trying to get a little privately; but they were discovered, and the attempt procured them some very severe floggings.

MIRZA SHEIKH I'TESAMUDDIN
from *The Wonders of Vilayet*

It was late March when we arrived in Mauritius. There I met a Sareng — a lascar officer — from Chittagong and seven other Muslim lascars from Hooghly, Vellore and Shahpur. They had come to the port city to pray at the Eid congregation that marks the end of Ramadan. They had all settled on the island and had no inclination to return to their own country, having, so to speak, married into slavery. Their wives were slaves of French masters who wouldn't in any case allow them to leave the island. I was glad to meet my countrymen, whose hospitality ensured my comfort during the sixteen days we stayed there. But I also grieved inwardly because they had forsaken their own land. Mauritius has a perimeter of 600 miles. The central part is taken up by hills, woods and wild tracts, but the eastern coast has 2,000–3,000 bighas of cultivated land and a small city where the French have built a factory and a fort.

The French notables live in mansions built on stockaded plots of a couple of bighas in the middle of their estates, which are cultivated with the help of a hundred or so male and female slaves. Oranges, Indian corn and vegetables are grown for the market. One half of the proceeds goes to the landlord, the other half is divided among the slaves. These slaves are brought as adolescents from Bengal, Malabar, the Deccan and other regions and sold for fifty to sixty rupees each. The wealthy Mauritians eat fine wheat and rice imported from Bengal, Malabar or Europe, and the poor natives live on Indian corn, the only grain produced on the island. They also pound a radish-like root plant into flour and bake bread with it. I found it utterly insipid — neither sweet nor sour not salty nor bitter.

With the help of my lascar acquaintances, who acted as my interpreters, I purchased mangoes, watermelons, cucumbers, musk-melons and several other varieties of fruits peculiar to the Bengali summer. The mangoes weighed from half to one pound, were free of fibres and had an excellent flavour. There was one species of mango rarely seen in Bengal, green on the outside, blue inside, firm of flesh and sweet to taste. The small, thin-skinned lime, kagazi nimboo, and the red chilli grow wild in the hills and are picked by the poor and sold in the bazaar. Copper coins and cowries are not used in Mauritius, but there is a paper currency in denominations ranging from one to 100 rupees, which is the sole medium of exchange.

The air is humid, rainfall heavy, and soil sandy; consequently mud houses are impractical. Houses here are entirely of wood, and built on stilts one or two cubits high. The walls are of wooden planks and the roofs, grass or straw being rare, are made of planks overlapping like tiles and are fixed in place with iron nails. Not a drop of rainwater can get through. These houses will stand without any repairs for fifty to 100 years. As they are on stilts they can be easily put on wheels and transported to another site. Mauritius is difficult of access. Coastal hills deny landing to ships except in the east, where the island's only harbour is situated. Even this has to be approached by a six-mile-long channel, which is quite hazardous. Those unfamiliar with its course may find it well nigh impossible to negotiate. So it is hardly surprising that it is the only French island in this region that the British failed to take during the recent war between the two countries. An English force under Captain Weatherburn launched a number of attacks on it, without success.

It is reported that the Portuguese were the island's first colonizers, but they found it so heavily infested with snakes, serpents, scorpions and other noxious creatures that they were soon forced to abandon it. After them the French moved in and had better luck. French priests, using a kind of necromancy, caught the dangerous creatures, took them out to sea and drowned them. Since then there is no sign of them on the island. Of course, Allah alone knows how far the story is true. Fish abound in the waters around the island and are caught by the islanders with hook, spear and net. A few species resemble Bengali fish, though they aren't exactly the same. One is like the anabas, but with a wider mouth; another resembled our puti. It too had a wide mouth. It was also attractively coloured (white, with red spots) and was excellent to taste. Other fish resembled the kholisa and the boal, and these too were quite good to eat. The day after we landed in Mauritius a violent cyclone struck. For three days the wind raged and rain fell in torrents. Two heavily laden French merchantmen dragged anchor and were wrecked on the treacherous rocks to the east of the harbour. Our ship was also driven in that direction and was run foul of by a Spanish man-of-war. We suffered serious damage, but thanks to Allah's mercy and the efforts of our sailors we returned safely to our anchorage. One of our outer planks broke, causing a huge leak, and a couple of telescopes mounted on the top deck were smashed. This necessitated time-consuming repairs, which is why we had to spend so many days there.

Among the vessels wrecked in this storm was a French ship that had started with us from Hooghly; it was caught in the storm before it could reach Mauritius and was swept far and wrecked. Later, when we neared the Cape, we saw its wreckage. If the storm had caught us in the high sea, our fate would have been the same. We thanked Allah for saving us from such an end. Mercifully there were no more storms of such severity, nor any other misfortune, till we reached Europe. One day Captain Swinton and Mr Peacock, another passenger, said to me jokingly, "It is owing to the presence of your prosperous foot that we have survived the danger." They were referring to the belief in lucky feet, which, like the belief in the evil eye, is prevalent among Muslim and Hindu Indians alike. I replied, "I am an impure creature from whom no advantage will come. It is owing to the mercy of Allah the Preserver that his servants aboard this ship are safe and can hope to see green fields once again."

On our way to Mauritius we had passed by many interesting islands and coasts on the Indian Ocean. To the south-east of Bengal there is a Portuguese island called Batavia, whose inhabitants include Muslims, Dutchmen, Englishmen and dark-complexioned natives, besides Portuguese colonists. Chillies, pepper, cinnamon, cardamom and other spices grow in abundance here, as also do varieties of fruits. Farther in the same direction, about two months' journey from Bengal, is an island which is a part of the Chinese kingdom and is famous for its Chinaware.

Pegu and Malacca

These are populous countries lying to the south-east of Bengal at a distance of half a month's voyage. Tahir Mohammed, an emir at the court of Badshah Akbar, during a long stint as ambassador to the court of Adil Shah, Sultan of Bijapur in the Deccan, wrote a book called the *Rowza-t-ut-fahereen*, or *Garden of the Immaculate*, where there are accounts of all the countries in the region, including Pegu. According to Tahir, in former times the people of Pegu had no religion and were ignorant of the distinction between right and wrong, the lawful and the forbidden. Among them went a Sayyid — a descendant of the Prophet Mohammed — from Bengal.

He introduced these people to Islam in the following manner. He was in the habit of reciting loudly and mellifluously from the Koran. The natives were charmed by the recitation and began gathering regularly to listen to him. Gradually they started emulating his religious practices — praying, fasting, giving the azan, or call to prayer — and were soon received into Islam. At the request of native leaders, the Sayyid became their imam and king, that is, both their religious and secular chief. To this day his descendants are the nobles among the population of Pegu, who still follow Islam. Tahir narrates an extraordinary tale, well known in Bengal, about this Sayyid. He is said to have captured a fairy, who lived with him for seven years and bore him children. But at last the fairy's true nature triumphed. She became faithless and, deserting husband and children, returned to her native realm.

Translated from Persian by Kaiser Haq

PHILLIS WHEATLEY
A Farewell to America

I.

Adieu, New-England's smiling meads,
Adieu, th' flow'ry plain:
I leave thine op'ning charms, O spring,
And tempt the roaring main.

II.

In vain for me the flow'rets rise,
And boast their gaudy pride,
While here beneath the northern skies
I mourn for health deny'd.

III.

Celestial maid of rosy hue,
Oh let me feel thy reign!
I languish till thy face I view,
Thy vanish'd joys regain.

IV.

Susannah mourns, nor can I bear
To see the crystal shower
Or mark the tender falling tear
At sad departure's hour;

V.

Not regarding can I see
Her soul with grief opprest
But let no sighs, no groans for me
Steal from her pensive breast.

VI.

In vain the feather'd warblers sing
In vain the garden blooms
And on the bosom of the spring
Breathes out her sweet perfumes.

VII.

While for Britannia's distant shore
We weep the liquid plain,
And with astonish'd eyes explore
The wide-extended main.

VIII.

Lo! Health appears! celestial dame!
Complacent and serene,
With Hebe's mantle o'er her frame,
With soul-delighting mien.

IX.

To mark the vale where London lies
With misty vapors crown'd
Which cloud Aurora's thousand dyes,
And veil her charms around.

X.

Why, Phoebus, moves thy car so slow?
So slow thy rising ray?
Give us the famous town to view,
Thou glorious King of day!

XI.

For thee, Britannia, I resign
New-England's smiling fields;
To view again her charms divine,
What joy the prospect yields!

XII.

But thou! Temptation hence away,
With all thy fatal train,
Nor once seduce my soul away,
By thine enchanting strain.

XIII.

Thrice happy they, whose heavenly shield
Secures their souls from harm,
And fell Temptation on the field
Of all its pow'r disarms.

FRANCIS BAILY
The First Discoverer of Kentucky

Sunday, the 9th of April — we started by daylight. We had observed a canoe ahead of us the preceding day, and for the sake of company wished we could have overtaken it; but as the person who was in it did not seem disposed to stop for us, we soon lost sight of him, as he proceeded along much faster than we. However, this morning we observed the same vessel behind us, and in a short time it came alongside. It contained but one old man, accompanied by his dog and his gun, and a few things lying at the bottom of the canoe. We called to him to come into our boat, which he accordingly did; and after a little conversation, our guest proved to be old Colonel Boon, the first discoverer of the now flourishing state of Kentucky. I was extremely happy in having an opportunity of conversing with the hero of so many adventures, a relation of which is drawn up and published in Imlay's *A Topographical Description of the Western Territory of North America.* Happening to have this account by me, I read it over to him, and he confirmed all that was there related of him. I could observe the old man's face brighten up at the mention of any of those transactions in which he had taken so active a part; and upon my adverting particularly to his adventure in August 1778, with the Indians at Boonsborough (a considerable town, so called from the remarkableness of the transaction, and the fame of its founder,) where they, with most barefaced deceit, endeavoured to take him and his men prisoners, he entered upon the subject with all the minuteness imaginable, and as descriptively as if it had recently happened. He then made us follow him in his narration, — how he was taken prisoner by the Indians, and carried a tour round the lakes with them; and the old man interspersed his tale with many a pleasing anecdote and interesting observation. He took (in truly an Indian style) a drop of water, and on a board he marked out the whole course of his travels; and, though I showed him a map, he continued on, after barely looking at it, and would not be diverted from the one which he had formed with his own finger. Upon asking him whether it did not give him a secret satisfaction to behold a province (in the discovery and settlement of which he held so conspicuous part) rise from a desert wilderness, and at once to flourish in arts and sciences and the conveniences of life, in all the maturity of old age, he shook his head, and with a significant frown, said they were got too proud; and then began to enter into the disadvantages of great improvements of society. I easily conceived his meaning, and soon found that he was one of that class of men who, from nature and habit, was nearly allied in disposition and manners to an Indian, and may be ranked under those who form the first class of settlers in a country. He said he had a great deal of land given him on the first settlement of the country; but that when societies began to form around him, he moved off, and divided his lands among his relations, unwilling (as he expressed himself) to live among men who were shackled in their habits, and would not enjoy uncontrolled the free blessings which nature had bestowed upon them. Since this time, he told me he had spent his time a great deal on the frontiers; and at this present moment he said he was going to hunt for beavers in some unfrequented corner of the woods, where undisturbed he might pursue this amusement, and enjoy the pleasures arising from a secluded and solitary life.

MARY SHELLEY
Voltaire

One day, dining at the table of the duke de Sully, one of his warmest friends, Voltaire was treated impertinently by the chevalier de Rohan, a man of high birth, but disreputable character. The chevalier asked, Who he was? Voltaire replied that he did not inherit a great name, but would never dishonour that which he bore. The chevalier angrily left the room, and took his revenge by causing him to be seized and struck with a cane by his servants. Such were the prejudices then existent in the minds of the French noblesse, that though the duke de Sully esteemed and even loved Voltaire, and held the chevalier de Rohan in contempt, yet the bourgeois birth of the former, and noble blood of the latter, caused him to show himself perfectly indifferent to the insult. Voltaire resolved to avenge himself. He secluded himself from all society, and practised fencing carefully. As soon as he considered himself a match for his enemy, he sought him out at the opera, and demanded satisfaction. The chevalier appointed time and place for a duel, and then acquainted his family. The consequence was, the instant arrest of his antagonist, and his imprisonment for six months in the Bastille; to which was added the further injustice of an order of exile after his liberation from prison. Voltaire took this opportunity to visit England. He had been acquainted with lady Bolingbroke in France. He appreciated the talents of the illustrious Englishman, admired his various knowledge, and was fascinated by the charms of his conversation. Although he never appears to have at all understood the real foundations of English liberty, yet he appreciated its effects, especially at a moment when he was suffering so grievously from an act of despotism. Liberty of thought was in his eyes a blessing superior to every other. He read the works of Locke with enthusiasm; and while he lamented that such disquisitions were not tolerated in France, he became eager to impart to his countrymen the new range of ideas he acquired from the perusal. The discoveries of Newton also attracted his attention. He exchanged the frivolities of Paris for serious philosophy. He became aware that freedom from prejudice and the acquirement of knowledge were not mere luxuries intended for the few, but a blessing for the many; to confer and extend which was the duty of the enlightened. From that moment he resolved to turn his chief endeavours to liberate his country from priestly thraldom and antique prejudices. He felt his powers; his industry was equal to his wit, and enabled him to use a vast variety of literary weapons. What his countrymen deemed poetry, the drama, history, philosophy, and all slighter compositions, animated by wit and fancy, were put in use by turns for this great end. He published his *Henriade* while in England. It was better received than it deserved; and the profits he gained were the foundation of his future opulence. He wrote the tragedy of *Brutus*, in which he imagined that he developed a truly republican spirit, and a love of liberty worthy of the Romans.

He spent three years in exile. He became eager to return to his country, to his friends, and to a public which naturally understood him better, and could sympathise more truly with him than the English. He ventured over to Paris. For a time his return was known only to a few friends, and he resided in an obscure quarter of the capital. By degrees he took courage; and the success of various tragedies which he brought out raised him high in public favour, and promised greater security for the future. He was regarded as the pride of France by the majority of his countrymen. The priesthood — accustomed to persecute on the most frivolous pretexts of difference of opinion — who had excited Louis XIV to banish the Jansenists and suppress their convents — to exile the virtuous Fénélon — to massacre the Huguenots, who had long wielded religion as a weapon of offence and destruction, and had risen to a bad height of power by its misuse — held him in the sincerest hatred; while his attacks, excited by, and founded on, their crimes, unveiled to the world a scene which, had it not been rife with human suffering, had been worthy only of ridicule. A couplet in *Oedipus* first awakened their suspicion and hatred: *"Nos prêtres ne sont point ce qu'un vain peuple pense, / Notre credulité fait tout leur science."* [1] From that moment they lay in wait to crush him. It needed all his prudence to evade the effects of their enmity.

---

1   "Priests aren't what we assume them to be / Their artfulness lies in our credulity."

EMMA LAZARUS
The New Colossus

Not like the brazen giant of Greek fame,
With conquering limbs astride from land to land;
Here at our sea-washed, sunset gates shall stand
A mighty woman with a torch, whose flame
Is the imprisoned lightning, and her name
Mother of Exiles. From her beacon-hand
Glows world-wide welcome; her mild eyes command
The air-bridged harbor that twin cities frame.
"Keep, ancient lands, your storied pomp!" cries she
With silent lips. "Give me your tired, your poor,
Your huddled masses yearning to breathe free,
The wretched refuse of your teeming shore.
Send these, the homeless, tempest-tost to me,
I lift my lamp beside the golden door!"

ROBERT W. SERVICE
The Spell of the Yukon

I wanted the gold, and I sought it;
    I scrabbled and mucked like a slave.
Was it famine or scurvy — I fought it;
    I hurled my youth into a grave.
I wanted the gold, and I got it —
    Came out with a fortune last fall, —
Yet somehow life's not what I thought it,
    And somehow the gold isn't all.

No! There's the land. (Have you seen it?)
    It's the cussedest land that I know,
From the big, dizzy mountains that screen it
    To the deep, deathlike valleys below.
Some say God was tired when He made it;
    Some say it's a fine land to shun;
Maybe; but there's some as would trade it
    For no land on earth — and I'm one.

You come to get rich (damned good reason);
    You feel like an exile at first;
You hate it like hell for a season,
    And then you are worse than the worst.
It grips you like some kinds of sinning;
    It twists you from foe to a friend;
It seems it's been since the beginning;
    It seems it will be to the end.

I've stood in some mighty-mouthed hollow
    That's plumb-full of hush to the brim;
I've watched the big, husky sun wallow
    In crimson and gold, and grow dim,
Till the moon set the pearly peaks gleaming,
    And the stars tumbled out, neck and crop;
And I've thought that I surely was dreaming,
    With the peace o' the world piled on top.

The summer — no sweeter was ever;
    The sunshiny woods all athrill;
The grayling aleap in the river,
    The bighorn asleep on the hill.
The strong life that never knows harness;
    The wilds where the caribou call;
The freshness, the freedom, the farness —
    O God! how I'm stuck on it all.

The winter! the brightness that blinds you,
    The white land locked tight as a drum,
The cold fear that follows and finds you,
    The silence that bludgeons you dumb.
The snows that are older than history,
    The woods where the weird shadows slant;
The stillness, the moonlight, the mystery,
    I've bade 'em good-by — but I can't.

There's a land where the mountains are nameless,
    And the rivers all run God knows where;
There are lives that are erring and aimless,
    And deaths that just hang by a hair;

There are hardships that nobody reckons;
　　There are valleys unpeopled and still;
There's a land — oh, it beckons and beckons,
　　And I want to go back — and I will.

They're making my money diminish;
　　I'm sick of the taste of champagne.
Thank God! when I'm skinned to a finish
　　I'll pike to the Yukon again.
I'll fight — and you bet it's no sham-fight;
　　It's hell! — but I've been there before;
And it's better than this by a damsite —
　　So me for the Yukon once more.

There's gold, and it's haunting and haunting;
　　It's luring me on as of old;
Yet it isn't the gold that I'm wanting
　　So much as just finding the gold.
It's the great, big, broad land 'way up yonder,
　　It's the forests where silence has lease;
It's the beauty that thrills me with wonder,
　　It's the stillness that fills me with peace.

SOL PLAATJE

from *Native Life in South Africa*

"Man's inhumanity to man makes countless thousands mourn."
Burns

Thaba Ncho (Mount Black) takes its name from the hill below which the town is situated. Formerly this part of Africa was peopled by Bushmen and subsequently by Basutos. The Barolong, a section of the Bechuana, came here from Motlhanapitse, a place in the Western "Free" State, to which place they had been driven by Mzilikasi's hordes from over the Vaal in the early 'twenties. The Barolongs settled in Thaba Ncho during the early 'thirties under an agreement with Chief Mosheshe. The Seleka branch of the Barolong nation, under Chief Moroka, after settling here, befriended the immigrant Boers who were on their way to the north country from the south and from Natal during the 'thirties. A party of immigrant Boers had an encounter with Mzilikasi's forces of Matabele. Up in Bechuanaland the powerful Matabele had scattered the other Barolong tribes and forced them to move south and join their brethren under Moroka. Thus during the 'thirties circumstances had formed a bond of sympathy between the Boers and Barolongs in their mutual regard of the terrible Matabele as a common foe.

But the story of the relations between the Boers and the Barolong needs no comment: it is consistent with the general policy of the Boers, which, as far as Natives are concerned, draws no distinction between friend and foe. It was thus that Hendrik Potgieter's Voortrekkers forsook the more equitable laws of Cape

Colony, particularly that relating to the emancipation of the slaves, and journeyed north to establish a social condition in the interior under which they might enslave the Natives without British interference. The fact that Great Britain gave monetary compensation for the liberated slaves did not apparently assuage their strong feelings on the subject of slavery; hence they were anxious to get beyond the hateful reach of British sway. They were sweeping through the country with their wagons, their families, their cattle, and their other belongings, when in the course of their march, Potgieter met the Matabele far away in the Northern Free State near a place called Vecht-kop. The trekkers made use of their firearms, but this did not prevent them from being severely punished by the Matabele, who marched off with their horses and livestock and left the Boers in a hopeless condition, with their families still exposed to further attacks. Potgieter sent back word to Chief Moroka asking for assistance, and it was immediately granted.

Chief Moroka made a general collection of draught oxen from among his tribe, and these with a party of Barolong warriors were sent to the relief of the defeated Boers, and to bring them back to a place of safety behind Thaba Ncho Hill, a regular refugee camp, which the Boers named "Moroka's Hoek". But the wayfarers were now threatened with starvation; and as they were guests of honour among his people, the Chief Moroka made a second collection of cattle, and the Barolong responded with unheard-of liberality. Enough milch cows, and sheep, and goats were thus obtained for a liberal distribution among the Boer families, who, compared with the large numbers of their hospitable hosts, were relatively few. Hides and skins were also collected from the tribesmen, and their tanners were set to work to assist in making veldschoens (shoes), velbroeks (skin trousers), and karosses (sheepskin rugs) for the tattered and footsore Boers and their children. The oxen which they received at Vechtkop they were allowed to keep, and these came in very handy for ploughing and transport purposes. No doubt the Rev. Mr Archbell, the Wesleyan Methodist missionary and apostle to the Barolong, played an active part on the Barolong Relief Committee, and, at that time, there were no more grateful people on earth than Hendrik Potgieter and his party of stricken Voortrekkers.

After a rest of many moons and communicating with friends at Cape Colony and Natal, the Dutch leader held a council of war with the Barolong chiefs. He asked them to reinforce his punitive expedition against the Matabele. Of course they were to use their own materials and munitions and, as a reward, they were to retain whatever stock they might capture from the Matabele; but the Barolongs did not quite like the terms. Tauana especially told Potgieter that he himself was a refugee in the land of his brother Moroka. His country was Bechuanaland, and he could only accompany the expedition on condition that the Matabele stronghold at Coenyane (now Western Transvaal) be smashed up, Mzilikasi driven from the neighbourhood and the Barolong returned to their homes in the land of the Bechuana, the Boers themselves retaining the country to the east and the south (now the "Free" State and the Transvaal). That this could be done Tauana had no doubt, for since they came to Thaba Ncho, the Barolong had acquired the use of firearms — long-range weapons — which were still unknown to the Matabele, who only used hand spears. This was agreed to, and a vow was made accordingly. To make assurance doubly sure, Tauana sent his son Motshegare to enlist the co-operation of a Griqua by the name of Pieter Dout, who also had a bone to pick with the Matabele.

Pieter Dout consented, and joined the expedition with a number of mounted men, and for the time being the Boer-Barolong-Griqua combination proved a happy one. The expedition was successful beyond the most sanguine expectations of its promoters. The Matabele were routed, and King Mzilikasi was driven north, where he founded the kingdom of Matabeleland — now Southern Rhodesia — having left the allies to share his old haunts in the south.

This successful expedition was the immediate outcome of the friendly alliance between the Boers in the "Free" State and Moroka's Barolong at Thaba Ncho. But Boers make bad neighbours in Africa, and, on that account, the Government of the "Free" State thereafter proved a continual menace to the Basuto, their neighbours to the east. Pretexts were readily found and hostile inroads constantly engineered against the Basuto for purposes of aggression, and the friendliness of the Barolong was frequently exploited by the Boers in their raids, undertaken to drive the Basuto farther back into the mountains. This, however, must be said to the honour of the mid-nineteenth century "Free" Staters, in contrast to the "Free" Staters of later date: that the earlier "Free" Staters rewarded the loyalty of their Barolong allies by recognizing and respecting Thaba Ncho as a friendly native State; but it must also be stated that the bargain was all in the favour of one side; thereby all the land captured from the Basuto was annexed to the "Free" State, while the dusky warriors of Moroka, who bore the brunt of the battles, got nothing for their pains. So much was this the case that Thaba Ncho, which formerly lay between the "Free" State and Basutoland, was subsequently entirely surrounded by "Free" State territory.

Eventually Chief Moroka died, and a dispute ensued between his sons concerning the chieftainship. Some Boers took sides in this dispute and accentuated the differences. In 1884, Chief Tsipinare, Moroka's successor, was murdered after a night attack by followers of his brother Samuel, assisted by a party of "Free" State Boers. It is definitely stated that the unfortunate chief valiantly defended himself. He kept his assailants at bay for the best part of the day by shooting at them through the windows of his house, which they had surrounded; and it was only by setting fire to the house that they managed to get the chief out, and shoot him. As a matter of fact the house was set on fire by the advice of one of the Boers, and it is said that it was a bullet from the rifle of one of these Boers that killed Chief Tsipinare.

President Brand, the faithful ally of the dead chieftain, called out the burghers who reached Thaba Ncho after the strife was over. He annexed Thaba Ncho to the "Free" State, and banished the rival chief from "Free" State territory, with all his followers. The Dutch members of the party which assassinated the chief were put upon a kind of trial, and discharged by a white jury at Bloemfontein.

MARY ANTIN
from *They Who Knock at Our Gates*

We Americans, disciples of the goddess Liberty, are saved the trouble of carrying our gospel to the nations, because the nations come to us. Right royally have we welcomed them, and lavishly entertained them at the feast of freedom, whenever our genuine national impulses have shaped our immigration policy. But from time to time the national impulse has been clogged by selfish fears and foolish alarms parading under the guise of civic prudence. Ignoring entirely the rights of the case, the immigration debate has raged about questions of expediency, as if convenience and not justice were our first concern. At times the debate has been led by men on whom the responsibilities of American citizenship sat lightly, who treated immigration as a question of the division of spoils.

A little attention to the principles involved would have convinced us long ago that an American citizen who preaches wholesale restriction of immigration is guilty of political heresy. The Declaration of Independence accords to all men an equal share in the inherent rights of humanity. When we go contrary to that principle, we are not acting as Americans; for, by definition, an American is one who lives by the principles of the Declaration. And we surely violate the Declaration when we attempt to exclude aliens on account of race, nationality, or economic status. "All men" means yellow men as well as white men, men from the South of Europe as well as men from the North of Europe, men who hold kingdoms in pawn, and men who owe for their dinner. We shall have to recall officially the Declaration of Independence before we can lawfully limit the application of its principles to this or that group of men.

Americans of refined civic conscience have always accepted our national gospel in its literal sense. "What becomes of the rights of the excluded?" demanded the younger Garrison, in a noble scolding administered to the restrictionists in 1896.

If a nation has a right to keep out aliens, tell us how many people constitute a nation, and what geographical area they have a right to claim. In the United States, where a thousand millions can live in peace and plenty under just conditions, who gives to seventy millions the right to monopolize the territory? How few can justly own the earth, and deprive those who are landless of the right to life, liberty, and the pursuit of happiness? And what becomes of the rights of the excluded?

If we took our mission seriously, — as seriously, say, as the Jews take theirs, — we should live with a copy of our law at our side, and oblige every man who opened his mouth to teach us, to square his doctrine with the gospel of liberty; and him should we follow to the end who spoke to us in the name of our duties, rather than in the name of our privileges.

The sins we have been guilty of in our conduct of the immigration debate have had their roots in a misconception of our own position in the land. We have argued the matter as though we owned the land, and were, therefore, at liberty to receive or reject the unbidden guests who came to us by thousands. Let any man who lays claim to any portion of the territory of the United States produce his title deed. Are not most of us squatters here, and squatters of recent date at that? The rights of a squatter are limited to the plot he actually occupies and cultivates. The portion of the United States territory that is covered by squatters' claims is only a fraction, albeit a respectable fraction, of the land we govern. In the name of what moral law do we wield a watchman's club over the vast regions that are still waiting to be staked out? The number of American citizens who can boast of ancestral acres is not sufficient to swing a presidential election. For that matter, those whose claims are founded on ancestral tenure should be the very ones to dread an examination of titles. For it would be shown that these few got their lands by stepping into dead men's shoes, while the majority wrenched their estates from the wilderness by the labor of their own hands. In the face of the sturdy American preference for an aristocracy of brain and brawn, the wisest thing the man with a pedigree can do is to scrape the lichens off his family tree. Think of having it shown that he owes the ancestral farmhouse to the deathbed favoritism of some grouchy uncle! Or, worse still, think of tracing the family title to some canny deal with a band of unsophisticated Indians!

No, it will not do to lay claim to the land on the ground of priority of occupation, as long as there is a red man left on the Indian reservations. If it comes to calling names, usurper is an uglier name than alien. And a squatter is a tenant who doesn't pay any rent, while an immigrant who occupies a tenement in the slums pays his rent regularly or gets out.

A.C. JACOBS
Immigration

I.
It wasn't easy getting out of the Tsar's Russia.
They had to bribe and lie.

And it was terrible on the ship.
They couldn't go up deck,
Someone stole all their luggage,
And the children were sick with fever.

Still, she came through it, my young grandmother,
And travelled to Manchester,
Where my grandfather was waiting, with a new language,
In Cheetham Hill.

II.
Really, they'd wanted to reach America,
But never saved enough for the tickets,
Or perhaps it was just that their hearts were in the east,
And they could go no farther west.
However it was, when Hitler went hunting,
We found that luckily
They had come far enough.

NGŨGĨ WA THIONG'O
A Colonial Affair!

In 1967, just before returning home from a three-year stay in England, I had signed a contract with William Heinemann to write a book focusing on the social life of European settlers in Kenya. The literary agent who negotiated the contract — he was also the originator of the idea — put it this way: "Theirs is a world which has for ever vanished, but for that very reason, many readers will find an account of it still interesting." The title? *A Colonial Affair!* I had agreed to do the book because I strongly held that the settlers were part of the history of Kenya: the seventy years of this destructive alien presence could not be ignored by Kenyans. Heaven knows, as they would say, that I tried hard to come to terms with the task. I dug up old newspapers and settlers' memoirs to get an authentic feel of the times as the settlers lived it. A writer must be honest. But in the end I was unable to write the book. I could not quite find the right tone. The difficulty lay in more than my uncertainty as to whether or not "their world" had really vanished. An account of their social life would have to include a section on culture, and I was by then convinced that a Draculan idle class could never produce a culture.

For the settlers in Kenya were really parasites in paradise. Kenya, to them, was a huge winter home for aristocrats, which of course meant big-game hunting and living it up on the backs of a million field and domestic slaves, the Watu as they called them. Coming ashore in Mombasa, as was clearly shown by the photographic evidence in the 1939 edition of Lord Cranworth's book, *Kenya Chronicles*, was literally on the backs of Kenyan workers. "No one coming into a new country," he writes, "could desire a more attractive welcome. We were rowed ashore in a small boat and came to land on the shoulders of sturdy Swahili natives." This was in 1906.

By 1956, Sir Evelyn Baring, the governor, could still get himself photographed being carried, like a big baby, in the arms of a Kenyan worker. Thus by setting foot on Kenyan soil at Mombasa, every European was instantly transformed into a blue-blooded aristocrat. An attractive welcome: before him, stretching beyond the ken of his eyes, lay a vast valley garden of endless physical leisure and pleasure that he must have once read about in the *Arabian Nights* stories. The dream in fairy tales was now his in practice. No work, no winter, no physical or mental exertion. Here he would set up his own fiefdom. Life in these fiefdoms is well captured in Gerald Henley's novels *Consul at Sunset* and *Drinkers of Darkness*. Whoring, hunting, drinking, why worry? Work on the land was carried out by gangs of African "boys". Both *Consul at Sunset* and *Drinkers of Darkness* are fiction. Observed evidence comes from the diaries of a traveller. In her 1929–30 diaries, now brought out together under the title *East African Journey*, Margery Perham described the same life in minute detail:

> We drove out past the last scattered houses of suburban Nairobi, houses very much like their opposite numbers in England. But here ordinary people can live in sunlight; get their golf and their tennis more easily and cheaply than at home; keep three or four black servants; revel in a social freedom that often turns, by all accounts, into licence, and have the intoxicating sense of belonging to a small ruling aristocracy... certainly, on the surface, life is very charming in Nairobi, and very sociable with unlimited entertaining; all the shooting, games and bridge

anyone could want. And in many houses a table loaded with drinks, upon which you can begin at any hour from 10.00 A.M. onwards, and with real concentration from 6.00 P.M.

And, so, beyond drinking whisky and whoring each other's wives and natives (what Margery Perham prudishly calls social freedom turned "by all accounts, into licence") and gunning natives for pleasure in this vast happy valley — oh, yes, are you married or do you live in Kenya? — the settlers produced little. No art, no literature, no culture, just the making of a little dominion marred only by niggers too many to exterminate, the way they did in New Zealand, and threatened by upstart "Gikuyu agitators".

The highest they reached in creative literature was perhaps Elspeth Huxley and she is really a scribbler of tourist guides and anaemic settler polemics blown up to the size of books. The most creative things about her writing are her titles — *The Flame Trees of Thika* and *The Mottled Lizard*, for instance — because in them she lets herself be inspired by native life and landscape. Beyond the title and the glossy covers, there is only emptiness, and emptiness as a defence of oppression has never made a great subject for literature. Their theatre, professional and amateur, never went beyond crude imitation and desperate attempts to keep up with the West End or Broadway. This theatre never inspired a single original script or actor or critic. In science, they could of course display Leakey. But Leakey's speciality was in digging up, dating and classifying old skulls. Like George Eliot's Casaubon, he was happier living with the dead. To the Leakeys, it often seems that the archaeological ancestors of Africans were more lovable and noble than the current ones — an apparent case of regressive evolution. Colonel Leakey, and even Lewis Leakey, hated Africans and proposed ways of killing off nationalism, while praising skulls of dead Africans as precursors of humanity. The evidence is there in black and white: L.S.B. Leakey is the author of two anti-Mau Mau books — *Mau Mau and the Kikuyu* and *Defeating Mau Mau*.

In art, their highest achievement was the mural paintings on the walls of the Lord Delamere bar in the Norfolk Hotel, Nairobi.[2] The murals stand to this day and they still attract hordes of tourists who come to enjoy racist aesthetics in art. But the murals in their artistic mediocrity possess a revealing historical realism. On one wall are depicted scenes drawn from the English countryside: four-teen different postures for the proper deportment of an English gentleman; fox-hunting with gentlemen and ladies on horseback surrounded on all sides by well-fed hounds panting and wagging tails in anticipation of the kill to come; and of course the different pubs, from the White Hart to the Royal Oak, waiting to quench the thirst of the ladies and the gentlemen after their blood sports. Kenya is England away from England, with this difference: Kenya is an England of endless summer tempered by an eternal spring or sprouting green life.

On another wall are two murals depicting aspects of settler life in that Kenya. One shows the Norfolk — the House of Lords as it was then known — in 1904. Here again are English ladies and gentlemen — some on horseback, others sitting or standing on the verandah — but all drinking hard liquor served them by an African waiter wearing the servant's uniform of white kanzu, red fez, and a red band over his shoulder and front. In the foreground is an ox-wagon with two Africans: one, the driver, lashing at the dumb

---

2   On 31st December 1980 the Norfolk Hotel was bombed, reportedly by rev-olutionaries. But the Lord Delamere bar remained intact.

oxen; and the other, the pilot, pulling them along the right paths. The ribs of the "pushing boy" and the "pulling boy" are protruding, in contrast to the fully fleshed oxen and members of the House of Lords. But the most prominent feature in this mural is "a rickshaw boy" with grinning teeth holding up this human-powered carriage for a finely dressed English lady to enter. Oxen-powered wagons for English survival goods; African-powered carriages for English lords and ladies. Eleanor Cole, in her 1975 random recollections of pioneer settler life in Kenya, writes: "Transport in Nairobi in those days was by rickshaw, one man in front between the shafts and one behind, either pushing or acting as a brake. People had their private rickshaws and put their rickshaw men in uniform. There were also public ones for hire."

The other mural depicts the same type of royal crowd at Nairobi railway station. At the forefront, is a well-fed dog wagging its tail before its lord and master. But amidst the different groups chatting or walking stands a lone bull-necked, bull-faced settler in riding breeches with a hat covering bushy eyebrows and a grey moustache. He could have been a Colonel Grogan or a Lord Delamere or any other settler. The most representative feature about him is the sjambok he is firmly holding in his hands.

The rickshaw. The dog. The sjambok. The ubiquitous underfed, wide-eyed, uniformed native slave.

In March 1907, Colonel Grogan and four associates flogged three "rickshaw boys" outside a Nairobi court-house. The "boys" were later taken to hospital with lacerated backs and faces. Their crime? They had had the intention of alarming two white ladies by raising the rickshaw shafts an inch too high! The rhetoric of the magistrate when later Grogan, Bowkes, Gray, Fichat, and Low were summoned before him for being members of an unlawful assembly, left not the slightest doubt about the sadistic brutality of the deeds of these sons of English nobility and graduates of Cambridge:

> From the first to the last it appears to me that out of all the people present assisting at the flogging of these men, there was no one of that number who ever took the trouble to satisfy himself as to whether these natives had ever done anything deserving of punishment at all. There was no trial of any sort nor any form or pretence of trial. These boys were neither asked whether they had any defence or explanation to give, nor does it appear that they ever had any opportunity of making one. Grogan, who ordered the flogging, has himself stated that no plea or defence which they might have made would have diverted him from his purpose. This is a very unpleasant feature in the case and I consider it about as bad as it can be. Yet, in my opinion, it is further aggravated by the fact that the place selected for this unlawful act was directly in front of a courthouse.

Sweet rhetoric versus bitter reality: the culprits, all found guilty, were given prison terms ranging from seven to thirty days. Prison? Their own houses where they were free to receive and entertain guests! Elsewhere, in the plantations and estates, the "bwana" would simply have shot them and buried them, or fed them to his dogs. In 1960, Peter Harold Poole shot and killed Kamame Musunge for throwing stones at Poole's dogs in self-defence. To the settlers, dogs ranked infinitely higher than Kenyans; and Kenyans were either children (to be paternalistically loved but not appreciated, like dogs) or mindless scoundrels (to be whipped or killed). In his autobiography, *The Words* (1963), Sartre has made the apt comment that "when you love children and dogs too much, you love them instead of adults". The settlers' real love was for dogs and puppies. Thus, to hit an attacking dog was a worse crime than killing a Kenyan. And when Poole was sentenced to death, the whole colonial Herrenvolk cried in unison against this "miscarriage of justice". Peter Harold Poole had done what had been the daily norm since 1895. In 1918, for instance, two British peers flogged a Kenyan to death and later burnt his body. His crime? He was suspected of having an intention to steal property. The two murderers were found guilty of a "simple hurt" and were fined two thousand shillings each. The governor later appointed one of them a member of a district committee to dispense justice among the "natives". The gory details are there in Macgregor Ross's book *Kenya From Within*. Justice in a sjambok!

I thought about this in my cell at Kamin prison and suddenly realized that I had been wrong about the British settlers. I should have written that book. For the colonial system did produce a culture. But it was the culture of legalized brutality, a ruling-class culture of fear, the culture of an oppressing minority desperately trying to impose total silence on a restive oppressed majority. This culture was sanctified in the colonial administration of P.C., D.C., D.O., Chiefs, right down to the askari. At Kamlti, we called it the Mbwa Kali[3] culture.

---

3   Mad Dogs.

SARGON BOULUS
Du Fu in Exile

"The smoke of war is blue
Human bones are white"

Du Fu reaches a village
A fire is about to go out
He arrives knowing that the word
like his dying horse
might not stay in bloom
after all these catastrophes
without a handful of grass

How many battlefields did he pass through
In which the wind howled
The rider's bones mixed
with those of his own horse
and soon thereafter the grass hid the rest

A fire warming two hands
the head droops
the heart is firewood

He started wandering at twenty
and never found a place to settle until the end

Wherever he went, war and its burdens were there
his daughter died in a famine

It is said in China that he wrote like the gods

Du Fu reaches another village
The smoke billows from its kitchens
The hungry wait at the door of a bakery
the bakers' sweaty faces are mirrors
attesting to the fire's ferocity.

Du Fu is you, sir
The master of exile

Translated from Arabic by Sinan Antoon

JUSUF NAOUM
As a Dog

As a dog living in Berlin this long,
I'd already be naturalized and wouldn't need
to beg for a residence permit every year.

As a dog living in Berlin this long,
I'd already have the rights of a German human
and nobody would want to deport me.

As a dog living in Berlin this long,
I wouldn't be barred from the pub
instead I'd be welcomed in every house.

As a dog living in Berlin this long,
I'd have a respectable, warm home
and not have to squat in a condemned building.

As a dog living in Berlin this long,
I wouldn't have to feel ashamed
of having many children.

As a dog living in Berlin this long,
nobody would call me Kanake
or Kameltreiber.

Yes, if I were a dog
and had lived in Berlin this long,

a pretty collar would decorate my neck
and I could shit wherever I pleased.

Translated from German by Martin Kratz

LUCI TAPAHONSO
In 1864

In 1864, 8,354 Navajos were forced to walk from Dinetah to Bosque Redondo in southern New Mexico, a distance of 300 miles. They were held for four years until the US government declared the assimilation attempt a failure. More than 2,500 died of smallpox and other illnesses, depression, severe weather conditions, and starvation. The survivors returned to Dinetah in June of 1868.

While the younger daughter slept, she dreamt of mountains,
the wide blue sky above, and friends laughing.

We talked as the day wore on. The stories and highway
beneath became a steady hum. The center lines were a blurred guide.
As we neared the turn to Fort Sumner, I remembered this story:

A few winters ago, he worked as an electrician on a crew
installing power lines on the western plains of New Mexico.
He stayed in his pickup camper, which was connected to a generator.
The crew parked their trucks together and built a fire in the center.
The nights were cold and there weren't any trees to break the wind.
It snowed off and on, a quiet, still blanket. The land was like
he had imagined it from the old stories — flat and dotted with shrubs.
The arroyos and washes cut through the soft dirt.
They were unsuspectingly deep.
During the day, the work was hard and the men were exhausted.
In the evenings, some went into the nearby town to eat and drink
a few beers. He fixed a small meal for himself and tried to relax.
Then at night, he heard cries and moans carried by the wind

and blowing snow. He heard the voices wavering and rising
in the darkness. He would turn over and pray, humming songs
he remembered from his childhood. The songs returned to him
as easily as if he had heard them that very afternoon.
He sang for himself, his family, and the people whose spirits
lingered on the plains, in the arroyos, and in the old windswept plants.
No one else heard the thin wailing.
After the third night, he unhooked his camper, signed his time card,
and started the drive north to home. He told the guys,
"Sure, the money's good. But I miss my kids and it sure gets lonely
out here for a family man." He couldn't stay there any longer.
The place contained the pain and cries of his relatives,
the confused and battered spirits of his own existence.
After we stopped for a Coke and chips, the storytelling resumed:

My aunt always started the story saying, "You are here
because of what happened to your great-grandmother long ago."

They began rounding up the people in the fall.
Some were lured into surrendering by offers of food, clothes,
and livestock. So many of us were starving and suffering
that year because the bilagáana kept attacking us.
Kit Carson and his army had burned all the fields,
and they killed our sheep right in front of us.
We couldn't believe it. I covered my face and cried.
All my life, we had sheep. They were like our family.
It was then I knew our lives were in great danger.
We were all so afraid of that man, Redshirt,[4] and his army.

---

4   Kit Carson's Navajo name.

114

Some people hid in the foothills of the Chuska Mountains
and in Canyon de Chelly. Our family talked it over,
and we decided to go to this place. What would our lives
be like without sheep, crops, and land? At least, we thought
we would be safe from gun fire and our family would not starve.

The journey began, and the soldiers were all around us.
All of us walked, some carried babies. Little children and the elderly
stayed in the middle of the group. We walked steadily each day,
stopping only when the soldiers wanted to eat or rest.
We talked among ourselves and cried quietly.
We didn't know how far it was or even where we were going.
All that was certain was that we were leaving Dinetah, our home.
As the days went by, we grew more tired, and soon,
the journey was difficult for all of us, even the military.
And it was they who thought all of this up.

We had such a long distance to cover.
Some old people fell behind, and they wouldn't let us go back to help them.
It was the saddest thing to see — my heart hurts so to remember that.
Two women were near the time of the births of their babies,
and they had a hard time keeping up with the rest.
Some army men pulled them behind a huge rock, and we screamed out loud
when we heard the gunshots. The women didn't make a sound,
but we cried out loud for them and their babies.
I felt then that I would not live through everything.

When we crossed the Rio Grande, many people drowned.
We didn't know how to swim — there was hardly any water deep enough
to swim in at home. Some babies, children, and some of the older men
and women were swept away by the river current.
We must not ever forget their screams and the last we saw of them —
hands, a leg, or strands of hair floating.

There were many who died on the way to Hwééldi.[5] All the way
we told each other, "We will be strong, as long as we are together."
I think that was what kept us alive. We believed in ourselves
and the old stories that the holy people had given us.
"This is why," she would say to us. "This is why we are here.
Because our grandparents prayed and grieved for us."

The car hums steadily, and my daughter is crying softly.
Tears stream down her face. She cannot speak. Then I tell her that
it was at Bosque Redondo the people learnt to use flour and now
fry bread is considered to be the "traditional" Navajo bread.
It was there that we acquired a deep appreciation for strong coffee.
The women began to make long, tiered calico skirts
and fine velvet shirts for the men. They decorated their dark velvet
blouses with silver dimes, nickels, and quarters.
They had no use for money then.
It is always something to see — silver flashing in the sun
against dark velvet and black, black hair.

---

5   Navajo name for Fort Sumner.

ADNAN AL-SAYEGH
Iraq

Iraq disappears with
every step its exiles take
and contracts whenever
a window's left half-shut
and trembles wherever
shadows cross its path.
Maybe some gun-muzzle
was eyeing me up an alley.
The Iraq that's gone: half
its history was kohl and song
its other half evil, wrong.

Translated from Arabic by Stephen Watts and Marga Burgui-Artajo

RIBKA SIBHATU
In Lampedusa

On 3rd October
a barge carrying 518 people
arrived in Lampedusa
    Having survived a brutal dictatorship
    and a journey full of pitfalls
    they stood atop their raft in the dead of night
    and saw the lights of the promised land
Believing their suffering had reached an end,
they raised a chorus and praised the Virgin Mary.
While waiting for those ships to rescue them,
men and women, children and grown-ups,
the sick and the healthy began to sing hymns!
    ስምኪ ጸዊዐ መዓስ ሓፈረ፣
    I wasn't ashamed when I called out Your name,
    ማርያም ኢለ ኣበይ ወዲቐ:
    I called out to Mary and didn't fall
    ስምኪ እዩእ'ሞ ስንቄ ኮይኑኒ:
    Your name sustained me throughout my journey
    እንሆ ምስጋናይ ተቐበልኒ!
    and here is the grateful echo of the song I raise to thank you!
Suddenly the raft
started filling with water;
they began flashing
red lights to sound the alarm;
switched their lanterns on and off!
Alas, all was quiet on the island.
Meanwhile the water rose, stoking fears the ship would sink.

118

To send a distress call,
they set a sail on fire, and as the
flames began to spread, some frightened people
jumped overboard and tipped the boat.
They were all adrift in the freezing sea!
Amidst that storm, some died right away,
some beat the odds and cheated death,
some who could swim tried to help
some drowned using their last breath
to send messages back to their native land,
some called out their names and countries of origin
before succumbing to their fate!
Among the floating corpses
Mebrahtom raised a desperate cry
Yohanna! Yohanna! Yohanna!
But Yohanna didn't answer;
all alone, and in
an extreme act of love,
she brought her son into the world,
birthing him into the fish-filled sea:
yet nobody in Lampedusa
heard the seven ululations welcoming his birth!
ሀ ስ ስ ስ ስ ስ ስ ስ ስ ስ ስ ስ ስ ስ ስ
Because after a superhuman struggle
Yohanna died alongside her son,
who never saw the light of day
and perished without even . . . drawing his first breath!
A baby died
drowned in the salty sea!
The baby was born and died
with its umbilical cord still unsevered!

119

A woman died while giving birth!
368 people died! 357 Eritreans died!
On 3rd October
3,000 feet from Rabbit Island,
in the heart of the Mediterranean,
a tragedy struck the Eritrean people,
only one of many they've endured.

Translated from Italian by André Naffis-Sahely

DYNASTIES, MERCENARIES
AND NATIONS

A S THE WORLD GREW smaller, the possibility of soldiers and mercenaries finding themselves farther from home than they could have possibly imagined became an everyday reality. Among the many anecdotes assembled and published by Percy Sholto (1868–1920), brother of Lord Alfred Douglas, Oscar Wilde's lover, we find the story of Richard Grace (c.1612–91), an Irish Royalist who fought for the last three Stuart kings of England. When his first monarch, Charles I, lost his head, Grace was labelled a fugitive criminal by Cromwell's Commonwealth, which may have contributed to Grace's decision to serve under other governments in Continental Europe, first Spain's, then France's; yet whoever wished to gain Richard Grace's loyalty had to consent to a chief condition, namely that he should be "permitted to go and serve" his own king, Charles II (1630–85), whenever required by the latter.

While kings, princes and petty potentates rose and fell across Europe, in 1795 the Polish-Lithuanian Commonwealth, Europe's largest nation, was dissolved and partitioned for the third and final time between Austria, Russia and Prussia, unleashing a wave of Polish emigration that would last for decades. Indeed, long before the famous *Légion étrangère* was founded, France sent the Polish Legion to Haiti. Assembled by Napoléon Bonaparte (1769–1821) from captured Austrian regiments composed of conscripted Poles eager to turn on their new oppressors, the Polish Legion was sent by the French emperor to put down the rebellion in the sugarcane paradise of Saint-Domingue. Setting off from Italy, the Legion reached the island we now know as Haiti in January 1802, carrying with it thousands of men, among them Władysław Franciszek Jabłonowski (1769–1802), an officer of mixed Polish and African heritage. Nevertheless, surrounded by a British blockade, plagued by illnesses and starved of supplies, the Legion proved unable to hold back the tide against Toussaint Louverture (1743–1803). Missives from these Polish soldiers of misfortune spell out the horrifying extent of their mission's blunder: "I cannot forgive myself the naïvety and stupidity that drove me to seek my fortune in America." As Józef Zador's letter home to a friend confesses, "I do not wish such a fate on my worst enemy. It is better to beg for bread in Europe than to seek one's fortune here, amidst a thousand diseases". Those who didn't die or flee back to France eventually switched sides and joined the rebels, becoming the ancestors of a community of Polish Haitians who claim direct descent from Napoleon's soldiers.

Although it took only twenty years for Poland to be partitioned, it would require over 120 years to be put back together.[6] As the translator Boris Dralyuk has noted, the result of those invasions was that "the story of modern Polish literature to a large extent" became "a story of exile", and that while Poland died as a political entity, it survived in the works of Adam Mickiewicz (1798–1855), who was born in what became Russian Lithuania in the year of the Third Partition and who died in Constantinople. A poem penned by Mickiewicz in either 1839 or 1840, but never published, shows him having grown listless to his surroundings after spending years wandering around Russia, Germany, Italy, Switzerland and France, nevertheless retaining a hold on the spiritual Poland in his heart:

I have a country, homeland of my thoughts,
where my heart has innumerable kin:
a land more fair than what I see before me,
a family more dear than anything.

The legacies of the American and French revolutions towards the close of the eighteenth century are difficult to overestimate. Not only did they inspire the nationalist revolutionaries of the nineteenth century and the ethnic self-determination movements among Germans, Italians and Poles, among many others, but they also provided the kindling for the idea-oriented Russian revolutions of 1905 and 1917, the last of which sent over two million Russians into exile. While the new nation states triumphed, the old pluralistic empires collapsed, one by one.

Since the downfall of the Ottoman Empire and the Balfour Declaration of 1917, the Middle East's near-continuous

---

6   This occurred after World War I.

fragmentation has ensured its writers have endured violent retaliation owing to their work in a way perhaps almost entirely unknown in other parts of the world. Naguib Mahfouz (1911–2006) was stabbed in the neck, the Palestinian writer Ghassan al-Kanafani (1936–72) was murdered by the Mossad, the Egyptian intellectual Nawal El Saadawi (1931–) has been imprisoned and has lived much of her life under police protection, Kateb Yacine (1929–89) was sent into internal exile, while the great Abdelrahman Munif (1933–2004) was stripped of his Saudi citizenship and banished to Syria.

At the age of seven, Mahmoud Darwish's (1941–2008) native village of al-Birwa in the Galilee was razed to the ground, for ever shaping the man who would become the voice of Palestinians in exile and one of the world's most famous poets. Although Darwish's compatriot Edward Said (1935–2003) considered exile an "unhealable rift", a loss that would permanently undermine all achievements in its wake, Darwish took a very different view, which he arguably elaborated best in his prose book, *In The Presence of Absence*, which he wrote only two years prior to his untimely death: "Exile is not journeying, it is not moving back and forth. Nor is it to dwell in longing. It may be a visit, or a waiting room — what time does to you, or a departure of the self for another, to know and be in harmony with, or for the self to return to its skin. Each exile has its character and every exile his characteristics. In exile you train yourself to contemplate and admire what is not yours." Darwish's poems would have a great effect on the young Moroccan poet Abdellatif Laâbi (1942–), who founded the magazine *Souffles* in 1966, helping to launch a generation of writers such as Mohammed Khaïr-Eddine, Mustafa Nissaboury, Tahar Ben Jelloun and Abdelkebir Khatibi, leaving an indelible mark on North African literature.

As Laâbi wrote in his editorial in the first issue of *Souffles*: "Poetry is the only means left to man to proclaim his dignity, to be more than just a number, so that his breath will remain forever imprinted and attested to by his cry." In January 1972, Laâbi was arrested by the Moroccan security services of Hassan II's brutal regime and savagely tortured. Student demonstrations ensued, which eventually forced the authorities to release him, but he was rearrested a month later, at which point he began serving an eight-and-a-half-year sentence at the infamous Kénitra penitentiary for distributing political pamphlets. During his stay in Kénitra as prisoner number 18611, Laâbi penned a long poem entitled "Lettre à mes amis d'outre-mer", or "Letter to My Friends Overseas", to whom he says:

you've become
one of those beacons of light
who help to defend me
from the forceps of the night
You find your way to me
through the mercy of the poem
and I'll see you again
beyond the barbed wire of exile.

This poem was first published in *La Nouvelle Critique* in August 1978, after being smuggled out of prison piecemeal to friends of Laâbi's in France and later reassembled. A truncated and transliterated English version appeared in *Index on Censorship* in 1980, in order to bring attention to Laâbi's worsening medical condition, by which time he had served seven years of his sentence. Laâbi was unexpectedly released shortly afterwards, largely thanks to the behind-the-scenes efforts of various international committees and Danielle Mitterrand, at the time the wife of the French President François Mitterrand.

PERCY SHOLTO
An Irish Colonel

An Irish colonel, of the name of Richard Grace, after serving Charles I till the surrender of Oxford, withdrew to Ireland, where he continued to maintain the cause of Charles II as long as any part of that island held out for him. When the royal cause became hopeless, Grace had still influence enough with the predominant party to obtain permission to carry along with him into the Spanish service, a regiment of his own countrymen, consisting of twelve hundred men. The colonel procured a very honourable and favourable engagement for himself and his men, from the Spanish government; but as soon as they arrived in Spain, the Spaniards forgot all their promises, and used them so ill, that before they reached Catalonia, they were reduced to one half of their original number. Notwithstanding this cruel treatment, Grace and his Irish followers served in the Spanish army with great reputation, till the end of the campaign of 1656; when they were left to garrison a castle on the frontiers, of considerable importance. Colonel Grace reflecting here on the ill usage which he had received, and was still likely to receive; and learning, at the same time, how differently several Irish regiments in the French service were treated, he felt strongly tempted to go and join them; but though the Spaniards had broken their engagements with him, he had too much regard to his own character, to quit them in any other but the fairest and most honourable manner. He sent a message to Marshal D'Hocquincourt, who, at that time, commanded the French army in Catalonia, to let him know, that on a certain day named, he would march off with his regiment, and join him on these conditions; that his regiment should be upon the same footing with the Irish regiments then in the French service; and that they should be permitted to go and serve their own king, whenever his affairs required their service. These conditions were readily assented to by the French Marshal, who added the most tempting offers to Colonel Grace, to induce him to deliver up the castle at the same time. Grace, however, would not on any account consent to such a breach of faith; and would only allow the marshal to have a party of horse in waiting near the castle, to cover his retreat. When the day appointed for the evacuation arrived, Colonel Grace sent to the commander of the nearest Spanish garrison, and gave him notice of his intention, in order that he might instantly despatch some of his men, to take possession of the castle as he marched out of it, warning him, at the same time, not to send more than two hundred, for in case he gave him any reason to suspect that he intended to betray him, he would give up the castle to the French. The Spaniards did not offer to infringe this condition; and as soon as their detachment of two hundred approached the place, Grace permitted them to enter at one gate, while he marched out at the other, and went off to the French, who were waiting for him.

POLISH LEGION IN HAITI
Letters Home

"General! The First Consul has rewarded the brave Polish Legions that have shed so much blood for France... by sending them to Saint-Domingue; but here too, fighting a savage, barbarous nation, the Poles have demonstrated to ungrateful France that they fulfill their duties. We are surrounded by 3,000 Negroes. Unable to hold them off and not wanting to fall into the hands of savages who are fighting for their independence, I take my life."

From a letter sent by Battalion Chief Jasinski to General Philibert Fressinet, 1803.

"This is likely my last letter. Only 300 men from the Third Brigade remain [...] The others are dead, among them your brother, whose destiny was to die a few months after arriving. I cannot forgive myself the naïvety and stupidity that drove me to seek my fortune in America. I do not wish such a fate on my worst enemy. It is better to beg for bread in Europe than to seek one's fortune here, amidst a thousand diseases [...] and the blacks, who commit the greatest atrocities against their prisoners. Night and day, I dream of returning to Europe [...] I am begging you, for God's sake, do not let [my brother] Teodor follow me, because both of us will end our lives here."

From a letter sent by Józef Zador to a friend at home, 1803.

Translated from Polish by Boris Dralyuk

MADAME DE STAËL
from *Ten Years' Exile*

I was at Geneva, living from taste and from circumstances in the society of the English, when the news of the declaration of war reached us. The rumour immediately spread that the English travellers would all be made prisoners: as nothing similar had ever been heard of in the law of European nations, I gave no credit to it, and my security was nearly proving injurious to my friends: they contrived, however, to save themselves. But persons entirely unconnected with political affairs, among whom was Lord Beverley, the father of eleven children, returning from Italy with his wife and daughters, and a hundred other persons provided with French passports, some of them repairing to different universities for education, others to the South for the recovery of their health, all travelling under the safeguard of laws recognised by all nations, were arrested, and have been languishing for ten years in country towns, leading the most miserable life that the imagination can conceive. This scandalous act was productive of no advantage; scarcely two thousand English, including very few military, became the victims of this caprice of the tyrant, making a few poor individuals suffer, to gratify his spleen against the invincible nation to which they belong.

During the summer of 1803 began the great farce of the invasion of England; flat-bottomed boats were ordered to be built from one end of France to the other; they were even constructed in the forests on the borders of the great roads. The French, who have in all things a very strong rage for imitation, cut out deal upon deal, and heaped phrase upon phrase: while in Picardy some erected a triumphal arch, on which was inscribed, "the road to London", others wrote, "To Bonaparte the Great. We request you will admit us on board the vessel which will bear you to England, and with you the destiny and the vengeance of the French people." This vessel, on board of which Bonaparte was to embark, has had time to wear herself out in harbour. Others put, as a device for their flags in the roadstead, "a good wind, and thirty hours". In short, all France resounded with gasconades, of which Bonaparte alone knew perfectly the secret.

Towards the autumn I believed myself forgotten by Bonaparte: I heard from Paris that he was completely absorbed in his English expedition, that he was preparing to set out for the coast, and to embark himself to direct the descent. I put no faith in this project; but I flattered myself that he would be satisfied if I lived at a few leagues distance from Paris, with the small number of friends who would come that distance to visit a person in disgrace. I thought also that, being sufficiently well known to make my banishment talked of all over Europe, the first consul would wish to avoid this éclat. I had calculated according to my own wishes; but I was not yet thoroughly acquainted with the character of the man who was to domineer over Europe. Far from wishing to keep upon terms with persons who had distinguished themselves, in whatever line that was, he wished to make all such merely a pedestal for his own statue, either by treading them underfoot, or by making them subservient to his designs.

I arrived at a little country seat, I had at ten leagues from Paris, with the project of establishing myself during the winter in this retreat, as long as the system of tyranny lasted. I only wished to see my friends there, and to go occasionally to the theatre, and to the museum. This was all the residence I wished in Paris, in the state of distrust and espionnage which had begun to be established, and I confess I cannot see what inconsistency there would have been in the first consul allowing me to remain in this state of voluntary exile. I had been there peaceably for a month, when a female, of that description which is so numerous, endeavouring to make herself of consequence at the expense of another female, more distinguished than herself, went and told the first consul that the roads were covered with people going to visit me. Nothing certainly could be more false. The exiles whom the world went to see, were those who in the eighteenth century were almost as powerful as the monarchs who banished them; but when power is resisted, it is because it is not tyrannical; for it can only be so by the general submission. Be that as it may, Bonaparte immediately seized the pretext, or the motive that was given him to banish me, and I was apprized by one of my friends, that a gendarme would be with me in a few days with an order for me to depart. One has no idea, in countries where routine at least secures individuals from any act of injustice, of the terror which the sudden news of arbitrary acts of this nature inspires. It is besides extremely easy to shake me; my imagination more readily lays hold of trouble than hope, and although I have often found my chagrin dissipated by the occurrence of novel circumstances, it always appears to me, when it does come, that nothing can deliver me from it. In fact it is very easy to be unhappy, especially when we aspire to the privileged lots of existence.

I withdrew immediately on receiving the above intimation to the house of a most excellent and intelligent lady, to whom I ought to acknowledge I was recommended by a person who held an important office in the government; I shall never forget the courage with which he offered me an asylum himself: but he would have the same good intentions at present, when he could not act in that manner without completely endangering his existence. In proportion as tyranny is allowed to advance, it grows, as we look at it, like a phantom, but it seizes with the strength of a real being. I arrived then, at the country seat of a person whom I scarcely knew, in the midst of a society to which I was an entire stranger, and bearing in my heart the most cutting chagrin, which I made every effort to disguise. During the night, when alone with a female who had been for several years devoted to my service, I sat listening at the window, in expectation of hearing every moment the steps of a horse gendarme; during the day I endeavoured to make myself agreeable, in order to conceal my situation. I wrote a letter from this place to Joseph Bonaparte, in which I described with perfect truth the extent of my unhappiness. A retreat at ten leagues distance from Paris, was the sole object of my ambition, and I felt despairingly, that if I was once banished, it would be for a great length of time, perhaps for ever. Joseph and his brother Lucien generously used all their efforts to save me, and they were not the only ones, as will presently be seen.

Madame de Latour — Regnault de Saint-Jean-d'Angely

Madame Recamier, so celebrated for her beauty, and whose character is even expressed in her beauty, proposed to me to come and live at her country seat at St. Brice, at two leagues from Paris. I accepted her offer, for I had no idea that I could thereby injure a person so much a stranger to political affairs; I believed her protected against every thing, notwithstanding the generosity of her character. I found collected there a most delightful society, and there I enjoyed for the last time, all that I was about to quit. It was during this stormy period of my existence, that I received the speech of Mr. Mackintosh; there I read those pages, where he gives us the portrait of a Jacobin, who had made himself an object of terror during the revolution to children, women and old men, and who is now bending himself double under the rod of the Corsican, who ravishes from him, even to the last atom of that liberty, for which he pretended to have taken arms. This morceau of the finest eloquence touched me to my very soul; it is the privilege of superior writers sometimes, unwittingly, to solace the unfortunate in all countries, and at all times. France was in a state of such complete silence around me, that this voice which suddenly responded to my soul, seemed to me to come down from heaven; it came from a land of liberty. After having passed a few days with Madame Recamier, without hearing my banishment at all spoken of, I persuaded myself that Bonaparte had renounced it. Nothing is more common than to tranquillize ourselves against a threatened danger, when we see no symptoms of it around us. I felt so little disposition to enter into any hostile plan or action against this man, that I thought it impossible for him not to leave me in peace; and after some days longer, I returned to my own country seat, satisfied that he had adjourned his resolution against me, and was contented with having frightened me. In truth I had been sufficiently so, not to make me change my opinion, or oblige me to deny it, but to repress completely that remnant of republican habit which had led me the year before, to speak with too much openness.

I was at table with three of my friends, in a room which commanded a view of the high road, and the entrance gate; it was now the end of September. At four o'clock, a man in a brown coat, on horseback, stops at the gate and rings: I was then certain of my fate. He asked for me, and I went to receive him in the garden. In walking towards him, the perfume of the flowers, and the beauty of the sun particularly struck me. How different are the sensations which affect us from the combinations of society, from those of nature! This man informed me, that he was the commandant of the gendarmerie of Versailles; but that his orders were to go out of uniform, that he might not alarm me; he shewed me a letter signed by Bonaparte, which contained the order to banish me to forty leagues distance from Paris, with an injunction to make me depart within four and twenty hours; at the same time, to treat me with all the respect due to a lady of distinction. He pretended to consider me as a foreigner, and as such, subject to the police: this respect for individual liberty did not last long, as very soon afterwards, other Frenchmen and Frenchwomen were banished without any form of trial. I told the gendarme officer, that to depart within twenty-four hours, might be convenient to conscripts, but not to a woman and children, and in consequence, I proposed to him to accompany me to Paris, where I had occasion to pass three days to make the necessary arrangements for my journey. I got into my carriage with my children and this officer, who had been selected for this occasion, as the most literary of the gendarmes. In truth, he began complimenting me upon my writings. "You see," said I to him, "the consequences of being a woman of intellect, and I would recommend you, if there is occasion, to dissuade any females of your family from attempting it." I endeavoured to keep up my spirits by boldness, but I felt the barb in my heart.

I stopped for a few minutes at Madame Recamier's; I found there General Junot, who from regard to her, promised to go next morning to speak to the first consul in my behalf; and he certainly did so with the greatest warmth. One would have thought, that a man so useful from his military ardour to the power of Bonaparte, would have had influence enough with him, to make him spare a female; but the generals of Bonaparte, even when obtaining numberless favours for themselves, have no influence with him. When they ask for money or places, Bonaparte finds that in character; they are in a manner then in his power, as they place themselves in his dependance; but if, what rarely happens to them, they should think of defending an unfortunate person, or opposing an act of injustice, he would make them feel very quickly, that they are only arms employed to support slavery, by submitting to it themselves.

I got to Paris to a house I had recently hired, but not yet inhabited; I had selected it with care in the quarter and exposition which pleased me; and had already in imagination set myself down in the drawing room with some friends, whose conversation is in my opinion, the greatest pleasure the human mind can enjoy. Now, I only entered this house, with the certainty of quitting it, and I passed whole nights in traversing the apartments, in which I regretted the deprivation of still more happiness than I could have hoped for in it. My gendarme returned every morning, like the man in *Blue-beard*, to press me to set out on the following day, and every day I was weak enough to ask for one more day. My friends came to dine with me, and sometimes we were gay, as if to drain the cup of sorrow, in exhibiting ourselves in the most amiable light to each other, at the moment of separating perhaps for ever. They told me that this man, who came every day to summon me to depart, reminded them of those times of terror, when the gendarmes came to summon their victims to the scaffold.

Some persons may perhaps be surprised at my comparing exile to death; but there have been great men, both in ancient and modern times, who have sunk under this punishment. We meet with more persons brave against the scaffold, than against the loss of country. In all codes of law, perpetual banishment is regarded as one of the severest punishments; and the caprice of one man inflicts in France, as an amusement, what conscientious judges only condemn criminals to with regret. Private circumstances offered me an asylum, and resources of fortune, in Switzerland, the country of my parents; in those respects, I was less to be pitied than many others, and yet I have suffered cruelly. I consider it, therefore, to be doing a service to the world, to signalize the reasons, why no sovereign should ever be allowed to possess the arbitrary power of banishment. No deputy, no writer, will ever express his thoughts freely, if he can be banished when his frankness has displeased; no man will dare to speak with sincerity, if the happiness of his whole family is to suffer for it. Women particularly, who are destined to be the support and reward of enthusiasm, will endeavour to stifle generous feelings in themselves, if they find that the result of their expression will be, either to have themselves torn from the objects of their affection, or their own existence sacrificed, by accompanying them in their exile.

Anonymous translation from French

UGO FOSCOLO
To Zakynthos

Never again will I touch the sacred shores
where my youthful body once lay,
Zakynthos, whose reflection rises from the waves
of the Greek sea, from whose waters

virgin Venus arose, turning those islands fertile
with her first smile, that even he did not fail
to mention your limpid clouds and leafage
in his illustrious verses, he who sang

of these fatals waters, and of the various
exiles that made Ulysses, adorned by fame
and misfortune, kiss his rocky Ithaca.

Your sons will give you nothing but their song,
my beloved homeland, for fate has dealt us
a grave forevermore devoid of tears.

Translated from Italian by André Naffis-Sahely

GIACOMO LEOPARDI
On the Monument to Dante Being Erected in Florence

Although Peace is gathering
our people under her white wings,
Italian minds will not be freed
from their age-old drowsiness
if this great land will not return
to the examples our forefathers set.
O Italy, let it be in your heart
to honour the ancients; for this land
has no such men today
and no one to honour.
Turn back, my country,
look back on that infinity of immortals,
and weep with shame;
for grieving without shame is senseless:
turn back and be ashamed and shake yourself awake
and let the memory of those ancestors
and what feebly followed stab you.

A stranger, singular in attitude
and cast of mind and speech,
travelled through Tuscany
seeking the tomb of the poet thanks to whom
Homer doesn't stand alone.
And to our shame he learned
that since the poet's death
his ashes and his bones still lie
in exile, and, incredibly,

not a single monument was raised
within your walls to him whose greatness, Florence,
means the whole world honours you.
Oh patriots, who will set
our country free from this disgrace!
You undertake a noble task,
generous and noble band, and anyone
who loves Italy will love you for it.

Love of Italy, my friends — let love
for this unhappy country triumph in you
since loyalty to her otherwise has gone,
for after her bright day
came bitter ones.
Let mercy give you energy
and bless your work, you patriots,
who know so well how Italy's misery
floods her cheeks and veil with tears.
But how to sing your praises, citizens,
for the noble work you do,
the care and wisdom that you showed,
and the genius and gifts
that will always bring you honour?
What else can I say
to strike a new spark in your heart
that will inspire you?

This greatest of all themes will spur you on
and pierce your heart;
who can tell the wave and whirlwind
of your fury and enormous love?

Who imagines your impassioned look,
the lightning in your eyes?
What human voice does justice
describing something that's celestial?
Away, profane spirit. How many tears
will Italy shed for this great monument!
How or when
will time erase your glory?
You still live, O divine arts
to console us in our misery,
comfort for our luckless people,
bent on celebrating
Italian greatness in the ruins of Italy.

Look: I want
to honour our grieving mother, too;
I bring what I have,
and sing my song beside you as you work,
sitting where your chisel brings the stone alive.
O noble father of Tuscan poetry,
if you hear some news of things on earth,
or about the woman you so loved,
I know that for yourself you feel no joy,
that bronze and marble are less permanent
than wax or sand next to the fame
you left behind; and if you ever
vanish from our minds again,
may our unhappiness,
if possible, increase
and your descendants weep,
unknown to the whole world, in endless misery.

But not you; you'll rejoice
for your poor country,
if the example of their ancestors
ever gives its drowsy, sickly sons
the courage to lift their eyes for once.
You can tell
what endless trouble worried her,
she who so unhappily said farewell
when you rose to paradise again!
She is so reduced today
that next to what you see she was a queen.
Such misery assails her
you won't believe it, seeing her.
I'll ignore her other enemies and hardships;
but not the newest and most cruel,
because of which your country feared
her final evening had arrived.

You were lucky fate did not condemn you
to live among these horrors;
you didn't see Italian wives
in barbarian soldiers' arms;
you didn't see the angry enemy
lay waste to our cities and our fields,
or divine works of Italian genius
carted across the Alps to abject slavery,
or the highway blocked by groaning wagons,
the sharp looks and the insolent commands;
you didn't hear the insults
and the abused word "freedom"
they mocked us with

amidst chains and whipping.
Who doesn't grieve? What have we not suffered?
What did those felons leave untouched —
what temple, altar, crime?

How did we come to these corrupted times?
Bitter fate, why give us life,
or else why not an earlier death,
when you see our country
enslaved by profane foreigners,
her virtue cut to ribbons
by their biting steel?
No help or comfort: we weren't given
any way of lessening
the relentless pain that tore at her.
Alas, you didn't take our blood or life,
beloved country,
and I haven't died for your cruel fate.
So rage and pity overwhelm the heart,
for many of us also fought and fell,
but not for dying Italy:
for her tyrants.

Father (that is, if you don't disdain us),
you're no longer what you were on earth.
Brave Italians who deserved another death
fell on the lonely Russian steppe,
and the freezing weather
pitilessly attacked both men and beasts.
Squad after squad they fell,
half naked, mangled, bloodied,

and the ice became a bed for their poor bodies.
And as they breathed their painful last
they recalled the mother they had longed for,
saying: Not clouds and wind, but iron
should have killed us, and for you, our country.
Here, so far away from you,
while time smiles most benevolently on us,
unknown to all the world, we die
for those who are murdering you.

The northern wasteland hears them cry,
and the whispering woods were witness too.
So their moment came,
and wild beasts
tore up their deserted corpses
on that enormous, horrid sea of snow.
And the stragglers and malingerers
will always be remembered
with the noble and the strong. Beloved spirits,
though your agony will never end,
be at peace, and let it comfort you
that you will have no comfort
now or in any future time.
Rest on the breast
of your unmeasured pain,
O true sons of her whose final ruin
only yours resembles.

Your country doesn't grieve for you
but for him
who made you fight against her;

so she weeps as bitterly as ever
and her tears are mixed with yours.
If only pity for her whose glory
excelled all others' came alive
in those who love her and can save her,
exhausted and lethargic as she is,
from such abyssal darkness! Glorious spirit,
tell me: Has your love for your Italy died?
Has the fire that gave you life gone cold?
Will the myrtle that assuaged our sadness for so long
never turn green again?
Have all our crowns been scattered on the ground?
Will she never rise again
to resemble you in any way?

Did we die for all eternity?
Will our shame never end?
I, while I'm alive, shall keep exhorting,
turn back to your ancestors, corrupted sons.
Look at these ruins,
these pages, canvases, these stones and temples.
Think what earth you walk on. And if the light
of these examples fails to inspire you,
what are you waiting for? Arise and go.
Such low behaviour is unworthy
of this nurse and teacher of great spirits.
If she is the home of cowards,
better she be a widow and alone.

Translated from Italian by Jonathan Galassi

ADAM MICKIEWICZ
While my corpse is here, sitting among you

While my corpse is here, sitting among you,
while it looks you in the eye, and even speaks,
my soul is far, so very far away —
it wanders and it weeps, oh, how it weeps.

I have a country, homeland of my thoughts,
where my heart has innumerable kin:
a land more fair than what I see before me,
a family more dear than anything.

There, amidst work and worry and amusements,
I run away to rest beneath the pines,
to lie about in lush and fragrant grasses,
to chase the sparrows and the butterflies.

I see her there — in white, descending from the porch,
flying towards us from the meadows green,
bathing in grain as in the deepest waters,
shining from mountains like the light of dawn.

Translated from Polish by Boris Dralyuk

PIERRE FALCON
General Dickson's Song

Red River's just had news
all citizens draw near;
an army general's
recruiting soldiers here.

Enlistments he does seek
of many Bois-Brûlés,
and now as soldiers brave
he's led a group away.

These silver epaulettes,
to you I would present,
dear Mr. Cuthbert Grant,
chief of the regiment.

For I'm a general
and Dickson is my name;
in the land of Mexico,
a crown I go to claim.

When you reach Mexico,
right in the chiefest town,
generals and cannoneers
will greet you with a crown.

My officers, farewell,
you've all deserted me;
unhappy Dickson's tale
will soon be history.

I thank you one and all,
men of the company,
for you have brought me back
to Fort Mackenzie.

I know I owe you thanks,
your money goes to pay
the service of two guides,
two hardy Bois-Brûlés.

Who is the district bard,
that this song composed?
If you wait for the end,
his name will be disclosed.

At table we will sit,
one day, to sing and drink;
to sing the whole song through,
and let the glasses clink!

Now, friends, let's have a toast,
let us salute the song!
Sung by our prairie bard,
the poet, Pierre Falcon.

Translated from French by Robert L. Walters

GEORGE W. CABLE
from *Café des Exilés*

That which in 1835 — I think he said thirty-five — was a reality in the Rue Burgundy — I think he said Burgundy — is now but a reminiscence. Yet so vividly was its story told me, that at this moment the old Café des Exilés appears before my eye, floating in the clouds of revery, and I doubt not I see it just as it was in the old times.

An antiquated story-and-a-half Creole cottage sitting right down on the banquette, as do the Choctaw squaws who sell bay and sassafras and life-everlasting, with a high, close board-fence shutting out of view the diminutive garden on the southern side. An ancient willow droops over the roof of round tiles, and partly hides the discolored stucco, which keeps dropping off into the garden as though the old café was stripping for the plunge into oblivion — disrobing for its execution. I see, well up in the angle of the broad side gable, shaded by its rude awning of clapboards, as the eyes of an old dame are shaded by her wrinkled hand, the window of Pauline. Oh for the image of the maiden, were it but for one moment, leaning out of the casement to hang her mocking-bird and looking down into the garden, — where, above the barrier of old boards, I see the top of the fig-tree, the pale green clump of bananas, the tall palmetto with its jagged crown, Pauline's own two orange-trees holding up their bands towards the window, heavy with the promises of autumn; the broad, crimson mass of the many-stemmed oleander, and the crisp boughs of the pomegranate loaded with freckled apples, and with here and there a lingering scarlet blossom.

The Café des Exilés, to use a figure, flowered, bore fruit, and dropped it long ago — or rather Time and Fate, like some uncursed Adam and Eve, came side by side and cut away its clusters, as we sever the golden burden of the banana from its stem; then, like a banana which has borne its fruit, it was razed to the ground and made way for a newer, brighter growth. I believe it would set every tooth on edge should I go by there now, — now that I have heard the story, — and see the old site covered by the "Shoo-fly Coffee-house". Pleasanter far to close my eyes and call to view the unpretentious portals of the old café, with her children — for such those exiles seem to me — dragging their rocking-chairs out, and sitting in their wonted group under the long, out-reaching eaves which shaded the banquette of the Rue Burgundy.

It was in 1835 that the Café des Exilés was, as one might say, in full blossom. Old M. D'Hemecourt, father of Pauline and host of the café, himself a refugee from San Domingo, was the cause — at least the human cause — of its opening. As its white-curtained, glazed doors expanded, emitting a little puff of his own cigarette smoke, it was like the bursting of catalpa blossoms, and the exiles came like bees, pushing into the tiny room to sip its rich variety of tropical sirups, its lemonades, its orangeades, its orgeats, its barley-waters, and its outlandish wines, while they talked of dear home — that is to say, of Barbadoes, of Martinique, of San Domingo, and of Cuba.

There were Pedro and Benigno, and Fernandez and Francisco, and Benito. Benito was a tall, swarthy man, with immense gray moustachios, and hair as harsh as tropical grass and gray as ashes. When he could spare his cigarette from his lips, he would tell you in a cavernous voice, and with a wrinkled smile that he was "a-t-thorty-seveng".

There was Martinez of San Domingo, yellow as a canary, always sitting with one leg curled under him and holding the back of his head in his knitted fingers against the back of his rocking-chair. Father, mother, brother, sisters, all, had been massacred in the struggle of '21 and '22; he alone was left to tell the tale, and told it often, with that strange, infantile insensibility to the solemnity of his bereavement so peculiar to Latin people.

But, besides these, and many who need no mention, there were two in particular, around whom all the story of the Café des Exilés, of old M. D'Hemecourt and of Pauline, turns as on a double centre. First, Manuel Mazaro, whose small, restless eyes were as black and bright as those of a mouse, whose light talk became his dark girlish face, and whose redundant locks curled so prettily and so wonderfully black under the fine white brim of his jaunty Panama. He had the hands of a woman, save that the nails were stained with the smoke of cigarettes. He could play the guitar delightfully, and wore his knife down behind his coat-collar.

The second was "Major" Galahad Shaughnessy. I imagine I can see him, in his white duck, brass-buttoned roundabout, with his sabreless belt peeping out beneath, all his boyishness in his sea-blue eyes, leaning lightly against the door-post of the Café des Exilés as a child leans against his mother, running his fingers over a basketful of fragrant limes, and watching his chance to strike some solemn Creole under the fifth rib with a good old Irish joke.

Old D'Hemecourt drew him close to his bosom. The Spanish Creoles were, as the old man termed it, both cold and hot, but never warm. Major Shaughnessy was warm, and it was no uncommon thing to find those two apart from the others, talking in an undertone, and playing at confidantes like two schoolgirls. The kind old man was at this time drifting close up to his sixtieth year. There was much he could tell of San Domingo, whither he had been carried from Martinique in his childhood, whence he had become a refugee to Cuba, and thence to New Orleans in the flight of 1809.

It fell one day to Manuel Mazaro's lot to discover, by sauntering within earshot, that to Galahad Shaughnessy only, of all the children of the Café des Exilés, the good host spoke long and confidentially concerning his daughter. The words, half heard and magnified like objects seem in a fog, meaning Manuel Mazaro knew not what, but made portentous by his suspicious nature, were but the old man's recital of the grinding he had got between the millstones of his poverty and his pride, in trying so long to sustain, for little Pauline's sake, that attitude before society which earns respect from a surface-viewing world. It was while he was telling this that Manuel Mazaro drew near; the old man paused in an embarrassed way; the Major, sitting sidewise in his chair, lifted his cheek from its resting-place on his elbow; and Mazaro, after standing an awkward moment, turned away with such an inward feeling as one may guess would arise in a heart full of Cuban blood, not unmixed with Indian.

As he moved off, M. D'Hemecourt resumed: that in a last extremity he had opened, partly from dire want, partly for very love to homeless souls, the Café des Exilés. He had hoped that, as strong drink and high words were to be alike unknown to it, it might not prejudice sensible people; but it had. He had no doubt they said among themselves, "She is an excellent and beautiful girl and deserving all respect"; and respect they accorded, but their respects they never came to pay.

"A café is a café," said the old gentleman. "It is nod possib' to ezcape him, aldough de Café des Exilés is differen from de rez."

"It's different from the Café des Réfugiés," suggested the Irishman.

"Differen' as possib'," replied M. D'Hemecourt. He looked about upon the walls. The shelves were luscious with ranks of cooling sirups which he alone knew how to make. The expression of his face changed from sadness to a gentle pride, which spoke without words, saying — and let our story pause a moment to hear it say:

"If any poor exile, from any island where guavas or mangoes or plantains grow, wants a draught which will make him see his home among the cocoa-palms, behold the Café des Exilés ready to take the poor child up and give him the breast! And if gold or silver he has them not, why Heaven and Santa Maria, and Saint Christopher bless him! It makes no difference. Here is a rocking-chair, here a cigarette, and here a light from the host's own tinder. He will pay when he can."

ROMAIN ROLLAND

from *Jean-Christophe in Paris*

Following on a sequence of apparently insignificant events, relations between France and Germany suddenly became strained:
and, in a few days, the usual neighbourly attitude of banal courtesy
passed into the provocative mood which precedes war. There was
nothing surprising in this, except to those who were living under
the illusion that the world is governed by reason. But there were
many such in France: and numbers of people were amazed from
day to day to see the vehement Gallophobia of the German press
becoming rampant with the usual quasi-unanimity. Certain of
those newspapers which, in the two countries, arrogate to themselves a monopoly of patriotism, and speak in the nation's name,
and dictate to the State, sometimes with the secret complicity
of the State, the policy it should follow, launched forth insulting
ultimatums to France. There was a dispute between Germany
and England; and Germany did not admit the right of France not
to interfere: the insolent newspapers called upon her to declare for
Germany, or else threatened to make her pay the chief expenses
of the war: they presumed that they could wrest alliance from
her fears, and already regarded her as a conquered and contented
vassal, — to be frank, like Austria. It only showed the insane vanity
of German Imperialism, drunk with victory, and the absolute
incapacity of German statesmen to understand other races, so that
they were always applying the simple common measure which was
law for themselves: Force, the supreme reason. Naturally, such a
brutal demand, made of an ancient nation, rich in its past ages of
a glory and a supremacy in Europe, such as Germany had never
known, had had exactly the opposite effect to that which Germany

expected. It had provoked their slumbering pride; France was shaken from top to base; and even the most diffident of the French roared with anger.

The great mass of the German people had nothing at all to do with the provocation: they were shocked by it: the honest men of every country ask only to be allowed to live in peace: and the people of Germany are particularly peaceful, affectionate, anxious to be on good terms with everybody, and much more inclined to admire and emulate other nations than to go to war with them. But the honest men of a nation are not asked for their opinion: and they are not bold enough to give it. Those who are not virile enough to take public action are inevitably condemned to be its pawns. They are the magnificent and unthinking echo which casts back the snarling cries of the press and the defiance of their leaders, and swells them into the "Marseillaise", or the "Wacht am Rhein".

It was a terrible blow to Christophe and Olivier. They were so used to living in mutual love that they could not understand why their countries did not do the same. Neither of them could grasp the reasons for the persistent hostility, which was now so suddenly brought to the surface, especially Christophe, who, being a German, had no sort of ground for ill-feeling against the people whom his own people had conquered. Although he himself was shocked by the intolerable vanity of some of his fellow-countrymen, and, up to a certain point, was entirely with the French against such a high-handed Brunswicker demand, he could not understand why France should, after all, be unwilling to enter into an alliance with Germany. The two countries seemed to him to have so many deep-seated reasons for being united, so many ideas in common, and such great tasks to accomplish together, that it annoyed him to see them persisting in their wasteful, sterile ill-feeling. Like all Germans, he regarded France as the most to blame for the misunderstanding: for, though he was quite ready to admit that it was painful for her to sit still under the memory of her defeat, yet that was, after all, only a matter of vanity, which should be set aside in the higher interests of civilization and of France herself. He had never taken the trouble to think out the problem of Alsace and Lorraine. At school he had been taught to regard the annexation of those countries as an act of justice, by which, after centuries of foreign subjection, a German province had been restored to the German flag. And so, he was brought down with a run, and he discovered that his friend regarded the annexation as a crime. He had never even spoken to him about these things, so convinced was he that they were of the same opinion: and now he found Olivier, of whose good faith and broad-mindedness he was certain, telling him, dispassionately, without anger and with profound sadness, that it was possible for a great people to renounce the thought of vengeance for such a crime, but quite impossible for them to subscribe to it without dishonour.

They had great difficulty in understanding each other. Olivier's historical argument, alleging the right of France to claim Alsace as a Latin country, made no impression on Christophe: there were just as good arguments to the contrary: history can provide politics with every sort of argument in every sort of cause. Christophe was much more accessible to the human, and not only French, aspect of the problem. Whether the Alsatians were or were not Germans was not the question. They did not wish to be Germans: and that was all that mattered. What nation has the right to say: "These people are mine: for they are my brothers"? If the brothers in question renounce that nation, though they be a thousand times in the wrong, the consequences of the breach must always be borne by the party who has failed to win the love of the other, and therefore has lost the right to presume to bind the other's fortunes up with his own. After forty years of strained relations, vexations, patent or disguised, and even of real advantage gained from the exact and intelligent administration of Germany, the Alsatians persist in their refusal to become Germans: and, though they might give in from sheer exhaustion, nothing could ever wipe out the memory of the sufferings of the generations, forced to live in exile from their native land, or, what is even more pitiful, unable to leave it, and compelled to bend under a yoke which was hateful to them, and to submit to the seizure of their country and the slavery of their people.

Christophe naïvely confessed that he had never seen the matter in that light; and he was considerably perturbed by it. And honest Germans always bring to a discussion an integrity which does not always go with the passionate self-esteem of a Latin, however sincere he may be. It never occurred to Christophe to support his argument by the citation of similar crimes perpetrated by all nations all through the history of the world. He was too proud to fall back upon any such humiliating excuse: he knew that, as humanity advances, its crimes become more odious, for they stand in a clearer light. But he knew also that if France were victorious in her turn she would be no more moderate in the hour of victory than Germany had been, and that yet another link would be added to the chain of the crimes of the nations. So the tragic conflict would drag on for ever, in which the best elements of European civilization were in danger of being lost.

Translated from French by Gilbert Cannan

KHUSHWANT SINGH
from *Train to Pakistan*

Mr Hukum Chand, magistrate and deputy commissioner of the district, heaved his corpulent frame out of the car. He had been travelling all morning and was somewhat tired and stiff. A cigarette perched on his lower lip sent a thin stream of smoke into his eyes. In his right hand he held a cigarette tin and a box of matches. He ambled up to the subinspector and gave him a friendly slap on the back while the other still stood at attention.

"Come along, Inspector Sahib, come in," said Hukum Chand. He took the inspector's right hand and led him into the room. The bearer and the deputy commissioner's personal servant followed. The constables helped the chauffeur to take the luggage out of the car. Hukum Chand went straight into the bathroom and washed the dust off his face. He came back still wiping his face with a towel. The subinspector stood up again.

"Sit down, sit down," he commanded.

He flung the towel on his bed and sank into an armchair. The punkah began to flap forward and backward to the grating sound of the rope moving in the hole in the wall. One of the orderlies undid the magistrate's shoes and took off his socks and began to rub his feet. Hukum Chand opened the cigarette tin and held it out to the subinspector. The subinspector lit the magistrate's cigarette and then his own. Hukum Chand's style of smoking betrayed his lower-middle-class origin. He sucked noisily, his mouth glued to his clenched fist. He dropped cigarette ash by snapping his fingers with a flourish. The subinspector, who was a younger man, had a more sophisticated manner.

"Well, Inspector Sahib, how are things?"

The subinspector joined his hands. "God is merciful. We only pray for your kindness."

"No communal trouble in this area?"

"We have escaped it so far, sir. Convoys of Sikh and Hindu refugees from Pakistan have come through and some Muslims have gone out, but we have had no incidents."

"You haven't had convoys of dead Sikhs this side of the frontier. They have been coming through at Amritsar. Not one person living! There has been killing over there." Hukum Chand held up both his hands and let them drop heavily on his thighs in a gesture of resignation. Sparks flew off his cigarette and fell on his trousers. The subinspector slapped them to extinction with obsequious haste.

"Do you know," continued the magistrate, "the Sikhs retaliated by attacking a Muslim refugee train and sending it across the border with over a thousand corpses? They wrote on the engine 'Gift to Pakistan!'"

The subinspector looked down thoughtfully and answered: "They say that is the only way to stop killings on the other side. Man for man, woman for woman, child for child. But we Hindus are not like that. We cannot really play this stabbing game. When it comes to an open fight, we can be a match for any people. I believe our RSS boys beat up Muslim gangs in all the cities. The Sikhs are not doing their share. They have lost their manliness. They just talk big. Here we are on the border with Muslims living in Sikh villages as if nothing had happened. Every morning and evening the muezzin calls for prayer in the heart of a village like Mano Majra. You ask the Sikhs why they allow it and they answer that the Muslims are their brothers. I am sure they are getting money from them."

Hukum Chand ran his fingers across his receding forehead into his hair.

"Any of the Muslims in this area well-to-do?"

"Not many, sir. Most of them are weavers or potters."

"But Chundunnugger is said to be a good police station. There are so many murders, so much illicit distilling, and the Sikh peasants are prosperous. Your predecessors have built themselves houses in the city."

"Your honour is making fun of me."

"I don't mind your taking whatever you do take, within reason of course — everyone does that — only, be careful. This new government is talking very loudly of stamping out all this. After a few months in office their enthusiasm will cool and things will go on as before. It is no use trying to change things overnight."

"They are not the ones to talk. Ask anyone coming from Delhi and he will tell you that all these Gandhi disciples are minting money. They are as good saints as the crane. They shut their eyes piously and stand on one leg like a yogi doing penance; as soon as a fish comes near — hurrup."

Hukum Chand ordered the servant rubbing his feet to get some beer. As soon as they were alone, he put a friendly hand on the subinspector's knee.

"You talk rashly like a child. It will get you into trouble one day. Your principle should be to see everything and say nothing. The world changes so rapidly that if you want to get on you cannot afford to align yourself with any person or point of view. Even if you feel strongly about something, learn to keep silent."

The subinspector's heart warmed with gratitude. He wanted to provoke more paternal advice by irresponsible criticism. He knew that Hukum Chand agreed with him.

"Sometimes, sir, one cannot restrain oneself. What do the Gandhi-caps in Delhi know about the Punjab? What is happening on the other side in Pakistan does not matter to them. They have not lost their homes and belongings; they haven't had their mothers, wives, sisters and daughters raped and murdered in the streets. Did your honour hear what the Muslim mobs did to Hindu and Sikh refugees in the marketplaces at Sheikhupura and Gujranwala? Pakistan police and the army took part in the killings. Not a soul was left alive. Women killed their own children and jumped into wells that filled to the brim with corpses."

"Harey Ram, Harey Ram," rejoined Hukum Chand with a deep sigh. "I know it all. Our Hindu women are like that: so pure that they would rather commit suicide than let a stranger touch them. We Hindus never raise our hands to strike women, but these Muslims have no respect for the weaker sex. But what are we to do about it? How long will it be before it starts here?"

"I hope we do not get trains with corpses coming through Mano Majra. It will be impossible to prevent retaliation. We have hundreds of small Muslim villages all around, and there are some Muslim families in every Sikh village like Mano Majra," said the subinspector, throwing a feeler.

Hukum Chand sucked his cigarette noisily and snapped his fingers.

"We must maintain law and order," he answered after a pause. "If possible, get the Muslims to go out peacefully. Nobody really benefits by bloodshed. Bad characters will get all the loot and the government will blame us for the killing. No, Inspector Sahib, whatever our views — and God alone knows what I would have done to these Pakistanis if I were not a government servant — we must not let there be any killing or destruction of property. Let them get out, but be careful they do not take too much with them. Hindus from Pakistan were stripped of all their belongings before they were allowed to leave. Pakistani magistrates have become millionaires overnight. Some on our side have not done too badly either. Only where there was killing or burning the government suspended or transferred them. There must be no killing. Just peaceful evacuation."

The bearer brought a bottle of beer and put two glasses before Hukum Chand and the subinspector. The subinspector picked up his glass and put his hand over it, protesting, "No, sir, I could not be impertinent and drink in your presence."

The magistrate dismissed the protest peremptorily. "You will have to join me. It is an order. Bearer, fill the Inspector sahib's glass and lay out lunch for him."

The subinspector held out his glass for the bearer to fill. "If you order me to, I cannot disobey." He began to relax. He took off his turban and put it on the table. It was not like a Sikh turban which needed re-tying each time it was taken off; it was just three yards of starched khaki muslin wrapped round a blue skullcap which could be put on and off like a hat.

"What is the situation in Mano Majra?"

"All is well so far. The lambardar reports regularly. No refugees have come through the village yet. I am sure no one in Mano Majra even knows that the British have left and the country is divided into Pakistan and Hindustan. Some of them know about Gandhi but I doubt if anyone has ever heard of Jinnah."

TIN MOE
Meeting with the Buddha

Not for anything in particular —
even me the very Buddha
along with other antiques
they've put up for sale
here in Europe,
they have such a sharp eye for business —
what business brings you here?
asks the Buddha

You may not know it
but if you were in Burma
you would surely receive
all kinds of veneration,
but
telling only untruths and preaching only falsehoods
Your Holiness would exclaim "Buddha!"
and long to flee
Telling untruths
you tire yourself out
on the rounds of births
A scandal to the whole world
the generals delivering all kinds of orders
engaging in all kinds of impropriety
what if they bind you hand and foot
and put you under lock and key?

These hare-brained guys
don't know the truth
they don't keep promises
all kinds of lies
come out of their foul mouths
they have no respect for the nation
with their childish mentality
they're too dirty

An army exists to oppress the people
who flatter them they ask them
to sharpen the swords
it's a haven for thugs
the king of the master gangsters
Bo Ne Win's army
only knows how to shoot and cheat

The people are paupers now
the monks are beggars now
the scoundrels are monsters
weapons matter most
weapons are paramount
weapons reign supreme — that's militarism

For you
to sit in peace
here in a European supermarket
is much safer
far from all the mishaps
fame growing a million-fold

and the name Buddha bandied about
don't feel uncomfortable

With all the crimes of the Burmese military
the Buddha will never leave prison
will always be in trouble
then you'll really be uncomfortable

Don't think such an ignoramus as me
was lecturing you
I've come to think like this
because so many lay disciples in my country
have been victimized —
excuse me, Venerable Sir!

Translated from Burmese by Maung Tha Noe and Christopher Merrill

MICHÈLE LALONDE
Speak White

speak white
it's so nice to hear you
talk about Paradise Lost
or the gracious, anonymous profile who trembles in Shakespeare's sonnets

we are an uncultivated, stuttering people
but we're not deaf to geniuses in other languages
speak with Milton's, Byron's, Shelley's, Keats's accent
speak white
and forgive us for making no reply
except the husky cries of our ancestors
and Émile Nelligan's melancholy

speak white
speak of this and that
tell us about the Magna Carta
or the Lincoln Monument
or the Thames's greyish charms
the Potomac's pinkish waters
speak to us about your traditions
we're a dull-minded people
but we can still appreciate
the importance of crumpets
or that of the Boston Tea Party
but when you *really speak white*
when you *get down to brass tacks*
to talk about *gracious living*

and talk of standards of life
and of the Great Society
speak white a little louder then
raise your petty supervisor voices
we're a little hard of hearing
we live too close to the machines
and can barely hear our breaths above the din

speak white and loud
so we'll hear you
from Saint-Henri to Saint-Domingue
yes what an admirable language
to hire workers in
to give orders in
to fix the time of death at work
and the break that refreshes
and reinvigorates the dollar

speak white
tell us that God is a great big shot
and that we're paid to trust him
speak white
tell us about productivity profits and percentages
speak white
it's a rich language
when it's time to buy
but when it's time to sell
but when it's time to sell until your soul is lost
but when it's time to sell

ah!

speak white
big deal
but how to describe
the infiniteness of a day spent on picket lines
how to describe
the lives of a janitor-people
as we go back home at night
when the sun plummets over the back-alleys
how to tell you that the sun is setting yes
each day of our lives to the east of your empires
languages rife with swearwords are peerless
our slang is fairly dirty
stained with grease and oil

speak white
be at ease within your words
we're a bitter people
yet let's not reproach anyone
for exercising a monopoly
over the correctness of language

using Longfellow's accent
and in Shakespeare's sweet tongue
speak a French that is pure and atrociously white
like in Vietnam like in the Congo
speak an impeccable German
a yellow star between your teeth
speak Russian speak call to order speak repression
speak white
it's a universal language
we were born to understand it

with its teargas words
its truncheon words
speak white
tell us again about Freedom and Democracy
we know that liberty is a black word
just like misery is black
just like the blood mixing with dust in the streets of Algiers or Little Rock

speak white
take turns doing it from Westminster to Washington
speak white like on Wall Street
white like in Watts
be civilized
and listen good when we speak about circumstances
when you lot politely ask us
how do you do
and you can hear us tell you
we're doing all right
we're doing fine
we
are not alone

we know
that we're not alone

Translated from French by André Naffis-Sahely

168

MAHMOUD DARWISH
from *A State of Siege*

In a land preparing for its dawn,
in a while
the planets will sleep in the language of poetry.

In a while
we will bid this hard road farewell,
and ask: Where shall we begin?

In a while
we will warn the young mountain daffodils
their beauty will be eclipsed when our young women pass by.

*

I raise a glass
to those who share my vision
of a butterfly's joyful iridescence
in this interminable tunnel of night.

*

I raise a glass
to the one who shares a glass with me
in the pitch black of this night,
a night so thick we're both in the dark.
I raise a glass to my ghost.

*

Peace for the traveller on the other side
is to hear a traveller talking to himself.

Peace is the sound of a dove in flight
heard by two strangers standing together.

*

Peace is the longing of two enemies
to be left to themselves till they die of boredom.

Peace is two lovers
swimming in moonlight.

*

Peace is the apology of the strong
to the weak,
agreeing strength lies in vision.

Peace is the disarming of arms
before beauty —
iron turns to rust when left out in the dew.

*

Peace means a full and honest confession
of what was done to the ghost of the murdered.

Peace means returning to dig up the garden
to plan all the crops we will plant.

*

Peace is the anguish
in the music of Andalusia
weeping from the heart of a guitar.

*

Peace is an elegy said over a young man
whose heart's been torn open
by neither bullet nor bomb,
but the beauty-spot of his beloved.

*

Peace sings of life — here, in the midst of life,
wind running free through fields ripe with wheat.

Ramallah, 2002

Translated from Arabic by Sarah Maguire and Sabry Hafez

ABDELLATIF LAÂBI

from *Letter to My Friends Overseas*

Kind friends
usually when I write
I barely have the time
to feel your warmth
and sit amongst you
(a cigarette in my lips, the same tune in my head)
and must leave you
before I've reached the end of the page
You see, here they ration out
even the stationery
The request form that I fill
only allows correspondence
between the prisoner
and his family
They'll never understand
that family to me
doesn't mean ancestry
or heredity
or villages or IDs
I've never been able to estimate
the size of my family
It stretches out
as far the sunrise in our eyes
as far as our newly born continent
tears down the walls erected inside us

Friends
I've got so much to tell you:
it's just that usually
I keep my mouth shut not wanting to risk
the censors putting a stop
to these acts of presence
in fact I censor myself
fearing the briefness of my answers
might twist my thoughts
out of shape for you
or warp what this humble letter
this gradual rediscovery of ourselves
these simultaneously peaceful upsetting accounts
of the other through dialogue
have to say

Friends
I grow more convinced
that the poem
can only ever be
a dialogue
made of live flesh and sound
that stares you straight in the eyes
even if the poem has to cross
the cold wastes of distance
to finally reach you
in the creases created by absence
This is why
you no longer hear me speaking alone
in the trances of exorcism
in my tragic haemorrhages

as I extricate myself from this quagmire
and call out to the earthquake survivors
to heap my distress calls and curses on them
A long time ago
I wrote those poems
about the infernos of solitude
about my desperate climb back to my fellow human beings
and I'm not quite ready to disown them
those bitter fruits
of the murderous twilight
where I struggled
as I sought the roots
of a voice I knew was my own
of a human face that reflected
the exact image of my truth
Those violent poems were healthy
and without them
maybe my voice
would be empty today
devoid of what gave it
its vital intensity
But the problem
is that I can't write like that any more
Nowadays
my life's taken a different path
and so has my style
I'm not alone any more
My ordeal has placed me
on the road of encounters
My body has learned
to be pushed to the limits and curl up

like a scalding hot steel plate
to endure the lacerations
and to resist
to translate humiliation and pain
into their literal opposites
and inside this lead-sealed arena
where they condemned me to shuffle
for ten whole years
I have started to dig
entire tunnels
and underground passages
even into my veins
even into my mind's vital parts
and I heard other people were digging
in all the directions towards which
I was piercing through my aphasia
until the day when the first hand broke through
and I felt the willowy vines of embraces

Translated from French by André Naffis-Sahely

VALDEMAR KALININ
And a Romani Set Off

Once upon a time, many thousands of years ago, all sorts of people lived in the Garden of Eden. It was the most beautiful garden. Do you know what I mean by Paradise? It's a sophisticated sort of place where truthful people lived in great comfort. They worked hard and had plenty of everything.

Now, one day, believing his people were ready for it, God decided to give them all their own countries and scatter them to the four corners of the earth. He announced a day on which they should present themselves before him to claim their title deeds bearing God's own seal. But since, as you know, God lives in inaccessible light, it was his angels who dealt with people.

On the appointed day, the weather was exceptionally lovely, the morning was warm and the birds were singing. Ah, if only we knew what those birds looked like and the sound of their song . . .

Anyway, the Romani man was so soundly asleep he overslept his appointment. One can only imagine the profound sleep induced by that Garden, shadowed as it must have been by sweetly scented flowers and lulled by the quiet murmuring of distant streams. Suddenly, he was abruptly woken by the sound of joyful singing nearby; indeed, it was only when some Gadzo tripped over him that he sat up.

"Why are you all so happy?" he asked.

"Because I was given my land and I am going to cultivate it. Hurry up, Rom! Otherwise you might be given barren land!" and he hurried on his way.

The Rom set off to the Paradise Palace. On his way, he met different Gadze neighbors who told him the good news of their newly inherited land. The Rom realized that by the time he reached the Palace, there'd be nothing left for him, so decided it would be better not to ask. When he arrived at the Palace, everyone was busy discussing the technicalities of settling their lands and dividing up the countries with the Angels. The Senior Angel asked the Rom what he wanted.

"Nothing special," said the Rom, "I just want to thank God and his Angels for this wonderful life in the Garden of Eden."

"But what country would you like?" asked the Angel.

"I'm happy to stay here," said the Rom. "Let me once again express my gratitude on behalf of all these people. However, there is one small thing: maybe you would let me visit my neighbors from time to time in their new countries?"

"Because you are the only one who asked God for nothing, you are given the right to wander the face of the earth, to visit all its countries and stay there as long as you like," replied the Angel.

The Romani thanked the Angel and set off on a long journey across the countries of his neighbors. And that is why he continues to roam to this day.

SOUÉLOUM DIAGHO
Exile gnaws at me

Exile gnaws at me, the world's negligence irks me.

So distant from my memories, my people fight, their eyes tanned by the sun, their gazes fixed on the desert encampments, the perfume of nostalgia weighs down my thoughts, pain desiccates my heart, like a flower you try to keep alive despite the lack of its mother's sap. Worries have carved deep grooves into my brow, like the ripples the wind leaves on the sand-dunes. Miracles and equality lie far from our valleys, what remains is the hardest of ordeals, like travelling along cliff-edges, or enduring the suave bitterness that lingers in the mouth of an abandoned invalid. Hundreds of steps are left on the journey to where the demon first emerged, the demon who cast a shadow over nomadic life, like the darkness swallows the light of day. This journey isn't over, brothers, anguish binds us, fear strips us naked, like dead leaves torn during a savage storm. Pain is my mantle, I dance in the flames that devour my dreams before they surge out of my soul. So many tears have been shed to water the plant that refuses to grow. I searched through endless universes for answers to questions put to me, yet nothing could soothe my sorrow or stifle the groans of my overwhelming journey, nothing except for promises written in air which lingered unsolved. The voices of boys and girls intertwined with the wind lost themselves in oblivion, words of praise blended with the perfume of warriors brandishing their swords are now nothing but a nightmare. Only fragments of poetic license remain to keep a few memories alive. Life is nothing but a mirage, my friends, nothing is absolute except for the face of the all-powerful master.

Translated from French by André Naffis-Sahely

AHMATJAN OSMAN
Uyghurland, the Farthest Exile

In my early isolation, I'd often withdraw
homeward into my heart. Then, as my grief
subsided, my eyes would quickly close
not giving me a chance
to say, "I am alone..."

After days of staring
at lit candles (the flame
no longer burns in the corner
of the old house in the land of memory)
a strange feeling woke me up
to the time of searching
for the birds
who pronounced the words of the Wandering Angel
between lines of buried books,
"Uyghurland,
the farthest exile!"

Now I wish to forget
what emerged from the tongues of birds
and accept a land of darkness
where my feet bleed. To stop
thinking of the ancient things I've heard
for the voices have shifted direction in me
so that am I indeed what the birds pronounced?
Here, the mysterious moon
falls, heavy twilight on my shut eyes

as if embracing a stray thought
in the springtime of reincarnation
"Come towards me," the candle beckons,
"you must leave this extinguished land
to shout freely with a vital voice,
'Uyghurland!' "

From within the folds of speech
I recovered the ancient sun.
Perhaps time
was measure without day
as it leapt towards us like a wolf
for no reason
impossible to comprehend
from the moment we arrived here
the moment I questioned myself,
"What land could that be?"
I listen to the cries of suffering there
far away, waking inside me a nostalgic distance
like the caws of crows
on bare branches in a cemetery.
Thus the widening sea
of exile within me
where the guardian birds
signal the next island.
Perhaps the immobile winds around you
O distant outliers
were a fated certainty, a futility
in the depths of death and of being
purely one's self,
one's pure self.

Whatever space the great birds fly through
I wake beneath the wings
of the famous ode
the place I am in, in
silence, disturbed
I watch
everything revolve around me
in darkness…

The body searches
circles like a ghost in blue fog
to discern the direction of what was foretold
as suffering
and form a dream
it can reside in
and name.

Later in sorrow, the birds
would often withdraw
homeward into my heart. Their eyes,
as my thoughts
subsided, would quickly close
not giving me a chance to say,
"That day
was the most beautiful day."
O the terror —
as the bells of your footsteps break
at the border of each country,
and the echo
of sun shines through a window
onto a woman's rusted bosom —

that repeats around you without disruption,
"Uyghurland,
the farthest exile!"

Translated from Uyghur by Jeffrey Yang

KAJAL AHMAD
Birds

According to the latest classification, Kurds
now belong to a species of bird
which is why, across the torn, yellowing pages
of history, they are nomads spotted by their caravans.
Yes, Kurds are birds! And even when
there's nowhere left, no refuge for their pain,
they turn to the illusion of travelling
between the warm and the cold climes
of their homeland. So naturally,
I don't think it strange that Kurds can fly.
They go from country to country
and still never realise their dreams of settling,
of forming a colony. They build no nests
and not even on their final landing
do they visit Mewlana to enquire of his health,
or bow down to the dust in the gentle wind, like Nali.

Translated from Kurdish by Choman Hardi and Mimi Khalvati

OMNATH POKHAREL
from *The Short-Lived Trek*

The problem in Bhutan had started in a rather unique way. The slight misunderstanding in the multi-lingual, multicultural and multi-ethnic country between the people's demand for respect for human rights and the government's refusal to grant them should have been resolved with level-headedness. Nevertheless, it had ultimately led to the abuse of the law, while a great deal of land had been appropriated by a handful of opportunists. That's why many people, like Muktinath, are compelled to sneak into their own land at night, carrying a heavy burden of fear and apprehension.

This is how Muktinath would have justified his midnight odyssey.

Muktinath still trusted his friend, Dorji. Apart from being close, the two of them were related by marriage. Dorji's youngest daughter was married to Muktinath's nephew, who lived in Dorji's village.

"Should I go and meet him in his house?" he asked himself, laughing into the dark, lonesome morning. He had re-entered Bhutan feeling a mixture of fear and desire. He scraped fear from the package and made up his mind to visit Dorji the following night.

Muktinath had seen a cave at the base of Chhachay cliff. He would first go to his house, pick a handful of soil and walk down to the cave before dawn.

He would stay inside the cave the whole day and sneak out at dusk. He knew it would be a Herculean feat; still, he decided to take the risk for the sake of his friendship with Dorji.

"Will Dorji look the same? Will he recognize me? Will he

embrace me? What if he forced me to stay in Bhutan? Or, what if he pointed a dagger at me?" he asked a series of questions, feeling the touch of his khukuri.

He stripped some corn from the tall ears and shoved it into the pockets of his poncho.

"This will be my memento," he said to himself.

He stood up and walked towards the bamboo dumps that stood as old as a hill at the north-western flank of the paddy field. He remembered a python that dwelt betwixt the huge rocks beneath the bamboo canopy.

He also remembered how it used to hiss very loudly, alerting the people if there was an imminent danger in the village. He reminisced over how a flock of mynahs use to nestle in their nests at nights.

The bamboo dumps stood there looking exactly as they had two decades earlier. Muktinath stood in silence and waited to see if there was any sign of movement. There wasn't; nor the hiss of the ancient python, that used to be revered by the village folks.

"The python may have migrated and flown to a foreign jungle looking for peace and love," he whispered, consoling himself. He walked up towards the range which had once been part of his ancestral land. Fruits had begun to change colours. Just a few more months left before harvest. He walked around touching each tree, whispering to them that he had returned. Did the trees understand their lost master's plight?

He picked a large orange and peeled it in the chill, late October dawn. He was exhilarated. He picked two more oranges and shoved them into the pockets.

"These are for my youngest daughter back in the camp," he whispered. The orchard had an important story to tell. Dorji had given him three dozen saplings as a present. Muktinath had brought eight dozen from Suntalay, a village that boasted the highest quality mandarins. He had also raised a couple of dozen saplings in his own nursery. He laughed a euphoric, ephemeral and tearful laugh in the silence of the ripening darkness.

"Who could have benefited from my harvests these last fifteen years?" he murmured, massaging and caressing a tree trunk.

He thought seeing his orchard had been a Pyrrhic victory. His mind was weighed down by the thought of how much he had toiled, laboured and sacrificed to bring that orchard to its existing shape and form. Muktinath hadn't committed any crimes. The entire orchard witnessed the tears streaming down his face.

The age-old pear tree stood in the same spot where it had been when he'd been evicted fifteen years earlier. The pomegranate tree, however, was nowhere to be seen. It looked like it had been cut down. He remembered bringing it to his land as a foot-tall sapling from Sarpang thirty years ago. The damson tree that stood beside the banana grove wasn't there, either.

All of a sudden, Muktinath experienced a difficulty in breathing, accompanied by a slight pain in his chest. He staggered to his feet. He sat on the chill soil of his clandestine mission, took out the khukuri from its sheath, and, with its tip, dug out some soil from the forecourt. He clenched a handful of it and heaved a sigh of relief and satisfaction.

Muktinath realized that his three-storied house had been dismantled. He could see a clay-walled hut beside the hummock of ruins. People could be heard snoring inside the hut. Piglets could be heard grunting and squealing in the pen a few meters away from where he sat. A few cows were tethered in a row of poles under a pen. A heifer could be seen roaming around. Its rope had probably snapped.

Muktinath decided to take a risk. He pulled out his torch.

"I must get a proper view of my house, even though it's in ruins, and the hut, as well." He flashed the torch around the house. A dog sprinted towards him barking in an unusual tone. He recognized it. It was his dog — Bhaloo Kukoor.

"Bhaloo, are you still alive? I was on a quest to find you, too," he told him. Bhaloo had grown old and much of his fur had fallen out. His tail resembled a scabied snake. The dog wagged its tail and sat beside its master. It listened to the story of its master, shedding blissful tears.

"Bhaloo, can I get some water to drink?" he asked the dog. Bhaloo clutched one of the hands of its master between the jaws and led him to the faucet. Muktinath drank the euphoric elixir of life at the sound of the rooster's first cock-a-doodle-doo.

Would the villagers recognize Muktinath if they happened upon him? Though feeling unwell, Muktinath was happy beside his dog. Although old and decrepit, the faithful beast could still recognize its old master.

"I'm pleased with you, Bhaloo. You recognized me and gave what comfort you could. I wonder if anyone from the village would extend a similar helping hand," he said, expressing a sense of satisfaction. He patted the dog on its head. The dog responded with a torrent of tears rolling down its cheeks.

"I will soon leave this place," he said, "and I ask you to keep guarding my land, the way you have done until now."

Bhaloo nodded his head and licked his master's legs.

Muktinath's body had frozen when the door of the house was pushed open. The time was 5:30 A.M. A middle-aged woman had stepped out into the dust-laden patio, looking shabbily dressed. Her hair hung from her pumpkin-shaped head like a bunch of wilting catkins and a long uncared-for and mangy robe was flung from an elasticated waistband. She stood still for a while. From the way she looked at the ghastly scene on the porch, it was clear she'd been born with a squint. She approached the corpse. *"Ajai! Ani Gaachi Mo?* Oh! What's this?"* she shrieked at the top of her voice.

Her children rushed out like startled squirrels. She spoke to the children in a language that the Lhotsampas found difficult to understand.

Soon, the forecourt was flooded by the villagers. Muktinath's body lay as still as a willow bough. Bhaloo Kukoor kept watch over his dead master, shedding tears profusely. He licked his master's dead face and looked at the throng. The rivulets of tears showed that he wanted to convey a message to the crowd. Yet what genius could ever understand an animal's tears?

A man in a Buddhist robe tried to chase the dog away. It didn't move an inch; instead, it bared its teeth at him — a warning, probably. He licked his dead master's face a second time. Penjor, the headman of the village, asked if anyone in the crowd could identify the body. Nobody answered. However, the look on people's faces made it clear that many of them recognized the dead person. Their lips moved in an attempt to disclose the body's identity to the newly settled non-Lhotsampas, but in the end they feigned ignorance.

Novin Thapa, the deceased's closest neighbour, almost fainted when he came across the scene. His blistered legs, blood-clotted nose and the ears of corn said much about how far he had walked and how he'd died.

He remembered how the two of them had grown up together and lived alongside one another for more than five decades before the innocent Muktinath had been evicted. Novin Thapa looked at Muktinath's hands, which were still clutching a handful of soil, while a pair of oranges had tumbled out of his pockets and onto the ground.

"You won in the end, Muktinath," Novin Thapa muttered. "You used to tell me that one day you would be buried in your own soil — and, you won the bet. You're a winner. Today, I'm alive and standing on top of my land, but I don't know where I'll die. You're lucky — you don't know you're being buried in your own soil," he muttered in a whisper, still looking at Muktinath's pale corpse.

Poor Muktinath lay asleep on his own soil . . . finally at peace, for ever. Bhaloo Kukoor sobbed by his side.

"What a lucky man! He looks so happy," Novin Thapa mumbled.

REVOLUTIONS,
COUNTER-REVOLUTIONS
AND PERSECUTIONS

G OING BY NEWTON'S THIRD LAW, it is little wonder that the Age of Nations would produce the internationalist socialist movement, and it is even less surprising that the cosmopolitan component of that progressive ideology would attract the spleen of patriots and jingoists everywhere. On 11th July 1917, executives of the Phelps Dodge corporation, which ran the copper mines and border town of Bisbee, Arizona, like a medieval fief, colluded with Harry Wheeler, the local sheriff, to deport over 1,000 miners who had been on a peaceful week-long strike for better working conditions. Many of the strikers belonged to the Industrial Workers of the World (IWW). Bolshevik-inspired paranoia was in the air and, facing a sharp drop in copper prices,

Phelps Dodge executives decided to break the strike by any means necessary. Their plan was ruthlessly ambitious: roughly an eighth of Bisbee's population was to be exiled in a single morning. In order to arrange this mammoth expulsion, the sheriff deputized 2,000 local gunmen from the surrounding areas of Cochise County, gave them white armbands and weapons and unleashed them on the unsuspecting miners. The El Paso and Southwestern Railroad provided a dozen cattle cars for the operation, and, following six hours of mayhem, from early morning to noon, 1,186 men, women and children were loaded onto trains under armed guard and sent to Hermanas, New Mexico, 200 miles to the east.

To suppress all news of the deportation, Bisbee was placed under a communications lockdown: the telegraph office was seized by the sheriff's thugs, who also erected checkpoints on all roads leading in or out. Although lists of names had been handed out to the posse, many of the deportees didn't belong to the IWW. Some were innocent bystanders, others were business-owners who sympathized with the miners. Although Harry Wheeler and a dozen of his Phelps Dodge paymasters were later indicted on kidnapping charges by the federal government, the Supreme Court ultimately decided Washington had no right to interfere and referred the matter back to the state of Arizona in the ruling *United States v. Wheeler* (1920), since kidnapping wasn't a federal crime at the time. When questioned by Arizona's Attorney General as to the legality of his actions, Sheriff Wheeler replied that it had nothing to do with the law, but rather with whether the striking miners were "American, or not". As Wheeler told the Attorney General: "I would repeat the operation any time I find my own people endangered by a mob composed of eighty per cent aliens and enemies of my government."

None of those involved in the Bisbee deportation of 1917 were ever imprisoned for their actions, and Phelps Dodge's rule over Bisbee actually tightened. Deportees who returned were denied work, while the unions were effectively shut out of mining operations. Further underscoring the company's influence, all talk of the deportation was squashed until the 1980s, when most mining operations ceased. Fortunately, however, a poem survives. It was published in the IWW's *One Big Union Monthly* in August 1919: "We are waiting, brother, waiting / Tho' the night be dark and long" the poem begins, before detailing the experience of that terrible day:

> We were herded into cars
> And it seemed our lungs were bursting
> With the odor of the Yards.
>
> Floors were inches deep in refuse
> Left there from the Western herds.
> Good enough for miners. Damn them.
> May they soon be food for birds.

The poem was unsigned; the only indication to the author's identity was his union card number, 512210.

A mere two years following the deportation, the same violent hysteria led to Emma Goldman's expatriation to Russia aboard the USS *Buford* on 21st December, 1919. Like the Bisbee strikers, Goldman had dared to question the validity of the American Dream, and, despite her thirty-four years in the US, her belief that the Dream was nothing more than a pyramid scheme, made it clear that she was still a foreigner. The supposed foreignness of Goldman's political beliefs therefore came to justify, in the eyes of

American conservatives, her denaturalization and exile. Indeed, although American nativists denounced progressives and proponents of social and economic reform as dangerous foreigners out to destroy America's uniqueness, it was overwhelmingly clear to observers like Goldman that, by so doing, America was becoming as tyrannical as the rest of the world:

> I looked at my watch. It was 4:20 A.M. on the day of our Lord, December 21, 1919. On the deck above us I could hear the men tramping up and down in the wintry blast. I felt dizzy, visioning a transport of politicals doomed to Siberia, the étape of former Russian days. Russia of the past rose before me and I saw the revolutionary martyrs being driven into exile. But no, it was New York, it was America, the land of liberty! Through the port-hole I could see the great city receding into the distance, its sky-line of buildings traceable by their rearing heads. It was my beloved city, the metropolis of the New World. It was America, indeed, America repeating the terrible scenes of tsarist Russia! I glanced up — the Statue of Liberty!

The sad fates of Nicola Sacco (1891–1927) and Bartolomeo Vanzetti (1888–1927), two working-class immigrant anarchists who were wrongfully convicted of violent armed robbery due to their unpopular political beliefs, were eulogized by the Filipino-American writer and labour activist Carlos Bulosan (1913–56) in his poem "American History", which fashions the final scene of both men's lives into a haunting portrait as Vanzetti, "the dreamy fish-peddler", and Sacco," the good shoemaker", dream of a "future […] that never was":

in spheres of tragic light, dreaming of the world that never was, as each tragic moment passed in streams of vivid light, to radiate a harmony of thought and action that never came to pass.

Oppression at home usually paled in comparison to oppression abroad, and the stories and novels of the Syro-Libyan Alessandro Spina, né Basili Shafik Khouzam (1927–2013), are fuelled by the intensity of the horrors of the Italian colonial experience in Libya. In 1939, when Spina was twelve, Italy officially annexed Libya, by which time Italian settlers constituted 12 per cent of the population and over a third of the inhabitants of Tripoli and Benghazi, the epicentres of Italian power. Nevertheless, what had been expected to be an easy conquest in 1911 had instead turned into a twenty-year insurgency that was quelled only when the Fascists took power in Rome and Mussolini, in a quest to solve Italy's emigration problem, dispatched one of his most ruthless generals, the hated Rodolfo Graziani (1882–1955), to bring the *quarta sponda* to heel and "make room" for colonists. Genocide ensued: a third of Libya's population was killed; tens of thousands were interned in concentration camps; a 300-kilometre barbed-wire fence was erected on the Egyptian border to block rebels from receiving supplies and reinforcements; and the leader of the resistance, a venerable Koranic teacher named Omar Mukhtar (1858–1931), was hunted down and summarily hanged.

Alessandro Spina's "The Fort at Régima" is set in the mid-1930s, when an Italian officer, Captain Valentini, is ordered south of Benghazi to take command of a garrison stationed in an old Ottoman fortress that "recalled the castles the knights had built in Greece during the Fourth Crusade". Valentini is glad to leave Benghazi and its tiresome military parades behind, but as he's driven to his new posting, his mind is suddenly flooded with the names of famous Crusaders who had "conquered Constantinople, made and unmade emperors, and had carved the vast empire into feuds; they had scrambled hither and thither throughout the lengths of the Empire vainly trying to sustain an order, which, lacking any roots in that country, was ultimately fated to die". Employing only a few hundred words, Spina slices across seven hundred years, showing the inanity of the concept of conquest as well as the existential vacuum it inevitably leaves in its wake: "As the Captain bounced around in his armoured car, it struck him that repeating the same sequence of events so many centuries later was both cruel and unbearable."

As the Peruvian journalist José Carlos Mariátegui (1894–1930) noted, while Leon Trotsky (1879–1940) was known as one of the chief engineers of the Soviet takeover of Russia, he was above all "a man of the cosmopolis" and that, as such, his exile from Russia had been inevitable: "The Russian revolution is in a period of national organization", Mariátegui noted,

It is not a matter, at the moment, of establishing socialism internationally, but of realizing it in a nation that, while being a territory populated by 130 million inhabitants that overflows onto two continents, does not yet constitute a geographical and historical unit. It is logical that, in this stage, the Russian revolution is represented by men who more deeply sense its national character and problems. Stalin, a pure Slav, is one of these men. He belongs to a phalanx of revolutionaries who always remained rooted in the Russian soil, while Trotsky, Radek and Rakovsky belong to a phalanx that passed the larger part of their lives in exile. They were apprenticed as international revolutionaries in exile, an apprenticeship that has given the Russian revolution its universalist language and its ecumenical vision. For now, alone with its problems, Russia prefers more simply and purely Russian men.

Although the Russian poet Elena Shvarts (1948–2010) is now generally considered among her generation's most important voices, her translator Sasha Dugdale noted that "she was not adequately recognized in Russia", and that while she "received more critical attention and admiration elsewhere, like many unofficial Soviet poets, she was denied the opportunity to travel abroad until 1989". Shvarts's essay "Why, Let the Stricken Deer Go Weep" is about her mother, Dina, who studied at the Leningrad Theatre Institute during World War II and the infamous Siege of Leningrad, and who was evacuated in 1942 to Pyatigorsk. As the essay begins, the Germans have advanced so rapidly that the soldiers and the town's administration all flee again, this time south to Tbilisi. "While Shvarts barely sketches the scene," Dugdale elucidated,

> Any Russian reader would understand immediately the contrast between starving Leningrad and the beautiful southern spa town of Pyatigorsk, where the poet Lermontov was killed in a duel, with its mountain air, mineral springs and sanatoriums, which were operating as war hospitals until the German invasion in August 1942. When the Germans invade Pyatigorsk, not everyone leaves. With our gift of hindsight the reluctance to flee may seem suicidal, but if you consider the suffering and fearful confusion that was Soviet Russia at the time, German occupation and staying put may have seemed the lesser of a number of evils. Radlov's decision to remain,

and his tour of *Hamlet* in Germany, is a curious legend which I first heard quite recently from the theatre critic Alyona Karas. Shvarts maintains that Radlov chose not to evacuate his theatre south to Tbilisi when the Germans approached. I have read elsewhere that the theatre troupe left and Radlov and his wife remained. Other versions of the story describe how Radlov simply did not manage to evacuate his theatre from Pyatigorsk in time. But all seem to agree on the fact that Radlov's theatre was moved by the Germans to Zaporozhye, where the theatre premiered *Hamlet*, and then, in September 1943, to Berlin. Part of the theatre subsequently went to France, where it performed Ostrovskii's *Guilty Without Guilt*: an example of rarely bettered theatrical irony."

Not long before the events described in Shvarts's essay, Mussolini's Fascists had busied themselves with invading and oppressing Ethiopia, the only African country to survive Europe's bloodthirsty scramble for its territories in the eighteenth and nineteenth centuries. In the words of her translator, Aaron Robertson, Martha Nasibù's (1931–) sole literary production, *Memories of an Ethiopian Princess*, was produced by the "daughter of Nasibù Zamanuel, one of the most significant political and military figures of twentieth-century Ethiopia, who served as mayor of Addis Ababa in the 1920s and early 1930s and who commanded the Ethiopian armed forces under the last emperor, Haile Selassie, during the Second Italo–Ethiopian War (1935–37)". In the excerpt featured in this anthology, Nasibù produces an atmosphere of constant deracination, as we watch the Italian authorities displace these exiled Ethiopian aristocrats from Rhodes to Naples and finally to Tripoli, all in the space of slightly under a year, a narrative where "time is more elliptical than linear; because the exilic element is always changing where the 'center' is located . . . and where the future is a horrific ellipsis with no intention of becoming anything else".

VICTOR HUGO
To Octave Lacroix

30th June 1862

Dear Sir, — I readily answer your letter, for I recognize in you a valiant combatant for truth and right, and I greet a noble mind. After having, like you, fought against the Second of December, I was banished from France. I wrote *Napoléon le Petit* at Brussels; I had to leave Belgium. I went to Jersey, and there fought for three years against the common enemy; the English government was subjected to the same pressure as the Belgian government, and I had to leave Jersey. I have been in Guernsey for seven years. I have bought a house here, which gives me the right of citizenship and protects my person; here I am safe from a fourth expulsion. However, I am bound to say that Jersey two years ago, and Belgium a year ago, spontaneously reopened their doors to me. I live near the sea in a house built sixty years ago by an English privateer and called Hauteville House. I, a representative of the people and an exiled soldier of the French Republic, pay *droit de poulage*[7] every year to the Queen of England, sovereign lady of the Channel Islands, as Duchess of Normandy and my feudal suzerain. This is one of the curious results of exile. I live a retired life here, with my wife, my daughter, and my two sons, Charles and François. A few exiles have joined me, and we make a family party. Every Tuesday I give a dinner to fifteen little children, chosen from among the most poverty-stricken of the island, and my family and I wait on them; I try by this means to give this feudal country an idea of equality and fraternity. Every now and then a friend crosses the sea and pays me

---

7   The payment of two hens a year to the British monarch.

a visit. These are our gala-days. I have some dogs, some birds, some flowers. I hope next year to have a small carriage and a horse. My pecuniary circumstances, which had been brought to a very low ebb by the coup d'état, have been somewhat improved by my book *Les Misérables*. I get up early, I go to bed early, I work all day, I walk by the sea, I have a sort of natural armchair in a rock for writing at a beautiful spot called Firmain Bay; I do not read the seven hundred and forty articles published against me during the last three months (and counted by my publishers) in the Catholic newspapers of Belgium, Italy, Austria, and Spain. I am very fond of the worthy, hard-working little people among whom I live, and I think they are rather fond of me, too. I do not smoke, I eat roast beef like an Englishman, and I drink beer like a German; which does not prevent the *España*, a clerical newspaper of Madrid, from asserting that Victor Hugo does not exist, and that the real author of *Les Misérables* is called Satan. Here, dear sir, you have nearly all the details for which you ask me. Allow me to complete them by a cordial shake of the hand.

Translated from French by Elizabeth Wormeley Latimer

LOUISE MICHEL
Voyage to Exile

While I waited for deportation, I was kept in the Auberive prison. Once again I can see that prison, with its enormous cell blocks and its narrow white paths running under the pines. There is a gale blowing, and I can see the lines of silent women prisoners with their scarves folded at their necks and wearing white headdresses like peasants. In front of the pines burdened with snow during the long winter of 1872–73, the tired women prisoners passed slowly by, their wooden shoes ringing a sad cadence on the frozen earth.

My mother was still strong then, and I waited for my deportation to New Caledonia without seeing what I have seen since: the terrible and silent anguish under her calm appearance. She was staying at her sister's in Clermont, which was very near the Auberive prison, and I knew she was well. She brought me packages of cake and biscuits the way she used to when I was a student at Chaumont.

How many little gifts her old hands sent me, even in the last year she was alive. We revolutionaries bring so little happiness to our families, yet the more they suffer, the more we love them. The rare moments we have at home make us intensely happy, for we know that those moments are transient and our loved ones will miss them in the future.

According to the few pages remaining from my journal of the trip to New Caledonia, we left Auberive on Tuesday, 5th August 1873, between six and seven in the morning. The night before we left my mother came to say goodbye, and I noticed for the first time that her hair was turning white.

When I left for exile I wasn't bitter about deportation because it was better to be somewhere else and not see the collapse of our dreams. After what the Versailles government had done, I expected to find the savages in the South Pacific good, and perhaps I would find the New Caledonian sun better than the French one.

We were put on a train and while we were crossing through Langres on the way to Paris, five or six metalworkers with bare arms black up to their elbows came out of their workshop. One white-haired worker flourished his hammer and let out a yell that the noise of the railroad carriage's rolling wheels almost drowned out. "Long live the Commune!" he cried. Something like a promise to stay worthy of his salute filled my heart.

Translated from French by Elizabeth Gunter and Bullitt Lowry

ERNEST ALFRED VIZETELLY
Zola Leaves France

From the latter part of the month of July 1898, down to the end of the ensuing August, a frequent heading to newspaper telegrams and paragraphs was the query, "Where is Zola?". The wildest suppositions concerning the eminent novelist's whereabouts were indulged in and the most contradictory reports were circulated. It was on July 18 that Zola was tried by default at Versailles and sentenced to twelve months' imprisonment on the charge of having libelled, in his letter "J'accuse", the military tribunal which had acquitted Commandant Esterhazy. On the evening of the 19th his disappearance was signalled by various telegrams from Paris. Most of these asserted that he had gone on a tour to Norway, a course which the *Daily News* correspondent declared to be very sensible on Zola's part, given the tropical heat which then prevailed in the French metropolis.

On the 20th, however, the telegrams gave out that Zola had left Paris on the previous evening by the 8.35 express for Lucerne, being accompanied by his wife and her maid. Later, the same day, appeared a graphic account of how he had dined at a Paris restaurant and thence despatched a waiter to the Eastern Railway Station to procure tickets for himself and a friend. The very numbers of these tickets were given! Yet a further telegram asserted that he had been recognised by a fellow-passenger, had left the train before reaching the Swiss frontier, and had gaily continued his journey on a bicycle. But another newspaper correspondent treated this account as pure invention, and pledged his word that Zola had gone to Holland by way of Brussels.

On July 21 his destination was again alleged to be Norway;

but — so desperate were the efforts made to reconcile all the conflicting rumours — his route was said to lie through Switzerland, Luxembourg, and the Netherlands. His wife (so the papers reported) was with him, and they were bicycling up hill and down dale through the aforenamed countries. Two days later it was declared that he had actually been recognised at a café in Brussels whence he had fled in consequence of the threats of the customers, who were enraged "by the presence of such a traitor". Then he repaired to Antwerp, where he was also recognised, and where he promptly embarked on board a steamer bound for Christiania.

However, on July 25, the *Petit Journal* authoritatively asserted that all the reports hitherto published were erroneous. Zola, said the Paris print, was simply hiding in the suburbs of Paris, hoping to reach Le Havre by night and thence sail for Southampton. But fortunately the Prefecture of Police was acquainted with his plans, and at the first movement he might make he would be arrested.

That same morning our own *Daily Chronicle* announced Zola's presence at a London hotel, and on the following day the *Morning Leader* was in a position to state that the hotel in question was the Grosvenor. Both the *Chronicle* and *Leader* were right; but as I had received pressing instructions to contradict all rumours of Zola's arrival in London, I did so in this instance through the medium of the Press Association. I here frankly acknowledge that I thus deceived both the Press and the public. I acted in this way, however, for weighty reasons, which will hereafter appear.

At this point I would simply say that Zola's interests were, in my estimation, of far more consequence than the claims of public curiosity, however well-meant and even flattering its nature.

One effect of the Press Association's contradiction was to revive the Norway and Switzerland stories. Several papers, while adhering to the statement that Zola had been in London, added that he had since left England with his wife, and that Hamburg was their immediate destination. And thus the game went merrily on. Zola's arrival at Hamburg was duly reported. Then he sailed on the *Capella* for Bergen, where his advent was chronicled by Reuter. Next he was setting out for Trondheim, whence in a few days he would join his friend Bjørnstjerne Bjørnson, the novelist, at the latter's estate of Aulestad in the Gudbrandsdalen. Bjørnson, as it happened, was then at Munich, in Germany, but this circumstance did not weigh for a moment with the newspapers. The Norway story was so generally accepted that a report was spread to the effect that Zola had solicited an audience of the Emperor William, who was in Norway about that time, and that the Kaiser had peremptorily refused to see him, so great was the imperial desire to do nothing of a nature to give umbrage to France.

As I have already mentioned, the only true reports (so far as London was concerned) were those of two English newspapers, but even they were inaccurate in several matters of detail. For instance, the lady currently spoken of as Mme. Zola was my own wife, who, it so happens, is a Frenchwoman. At a later stage the *Daily Mail* hit the nail on the head by signalling Zola's presence at the Oatlands Park Hotel; but so many reports having already proved erroneous, the *Mail* was by no means certain of the accuracy of its information, and the dubitative form in which its statement was couched prevented the matter from going further.

At last a period of comparative quiet set in, and though gentlemen of the Press were still anxious to extract information from me, nothing further appeared in print as to Zola's whereabouts until the *Times* Paris correspondent, M. de Blowitz, contributed to his paper, early in the present year, a most detailed and amusing account of Zola's flight from France and his subsequent movements in exile. In this narrative one found Mme. Zola equipping her husband with a nightgown for his perilous journey abroad, and secreting bank notes in the lining of his garments. Then, carrying a slip of paper in his hand, the novelist had been passed on through London from policeman to policeman, until he took a train to a village in Warwickshire, where the little daughter of an innkeeper had recognised him from seeing his portrait in one of the illustrated newspapers.

There was something also about his acquaintance with the vicar of the locality and a variety of other particulars, all of which helped to make up as pretty a romance as the *Times* readers had been favoured with for many a day. But excellent as was M. de Blowitz's narrative, from the romantic standpoint his information was sadly inaccurate. Of his bona fides there can be no doubt, but some of Zola's friends are rather partial to a little harmless joking, and it is evident that a trap was laid for the shrewd correspondent of the *Times*, and that he, in an unguarded moment, fell into it.

On the incidents which immediately preceded Zola's departure from France I shall here be brief; these incidents are only known to me by statements I have had from M. and Mme. Zola themselves. But the rest is well within my personal knowledge, as one of the first things which Zola did on arriving in England was to communicate with me and in certain respects place himself in my hands.

This, then, is a plain unvarnished narrative — firstly, of the steps that I took in the matter, in conjunction with a friend, who is by profession a solicitor; and, secondly, of the principal incidents which marked Zola's views on some matters of interest, as imparted by him to me at various times. But, ultimately, Zola will himself pen his own private impressions, and on these I shall not trespass. It is because, according to his own statements to me, his book on his English impressions (should he write it) could not possibly appear for another twelve months, that I have put these notes together.

The real circumstances, then, of Zola's departure from France are these: on July 18, the day fixed for his second trial at Versailles, he left Paris in a livery-stable brougham hired for the occasion at a cost of fifty francs. His companion was his *fidus Achates*, M. Fernand Desmoulin, the painter, who had already acted as his bodyguard at the time of the great trial in Paris. Versailles was reached in due course, and the judicial proceedings began under circumstances which have been chronicled too often to need mention here. When Zola had retired from the court, allowing judgment to go against him by default, he was joined by Maître Labori, his counsel, and the pair of them returned to Paris in the vehicle which had brought Zola from the city in the morning. M. Desmoulin found a seat in another carriage.

The brougham conveying Messrs. Zola and Labori was driven to the residence of M. Georges Charpentier, the eminent publisher, in the Avenue du Bois de Boulogne, and there they were presently joined by M. Georges Clemenceau, Mme. Zola, and a few others. It was then that the necessity of leaving France was pressed upon Zola, who, though he found the proposal little to his liking, eventually signified his acquiescence.

The points urged in favour of his departure abroad were as follows: He must do his utmost to avoid personal service of the judgment given against him by default, as the Government was anxious to cast him into prison and thus stifle his voice. If such service were effected the law would only allow him a few days in which to apply for a new trial, and as he could not make default a second time, and could not hope at that stage for fresh and decisive evidence in his favour, or for a change of tactics on the part of the judges, this would mean the absolute and irrevocable loss of his case.

On the other hand, by avoiding personal service of the judgment he would retain the right to claim a new trial at any moment he might find convenient; and thus not only could he prevent his own case from being closed against him and becoming a *chose jugée*, but he would contribute powerfully towards keeping the whole Dreyfus affair open, pending revelations which even then were foreseen. And, naturally, England which so freely gives asylum to all political offenders, was chosen as his proper place of exile.

The amusing story of the nightgown tucked under his arm and the bank notes sewn up in his coat is, of course, pure invention. A few toilet articles were pressed upon him, and his wife emptied her own purse into his own. That was all. Then he set out for the Northern Railway Station, where he caught the express leaving for Calais at 9 P.M.

CARD NO. 512210
Bisbee

We are waiting, brother, waiting
Tho' the night be dark and long
And we know 'tis in the making
Wondrous day of vanished wrongs.

They have herded us like cattle
Torn us from our homes and wives.
Yes, we've heard their rifles rattle
And have feared for our lives.

We have seen the workers, thousands,
Marched like bandits, down the street
Corporation gunmen round them
Yes, we've heard their tramping feet.

It was in the morning early
Of that fatal July 12th
And the year nineteen seventeen
This took place of which I tell.

Servants of the damned bourgeois
With white bands upon their arms
Drove and dragged us out with curses,
Threats, to kill on every hand.

Question, protest all were useless
To those hounds of hell let loose.
Nothing but an armed resistance
Would avail with these brutes.

There they held us, long lines weary waiting
'Neath the blazing desert sun.
Some with eyes bloodshot and bleary
Wished for water, but had none.

Yes, some brave wives brought us water
Loving hands and hearts were theirs.
But the gunmen, cursing often,
Poured it out upon the sands.

Down the streets in squads of fifty
We were marched, and some were chained,
Down to where shining rails
Stretched across the sandy plains.

Then in haste with kicks and curses
We were herded into cars
And it seemed our lungs were bursting
With the odor of the Yards.

Floors were inches deep in refuse
Left there from the Western herds.
Good enough for miners. Damn them.
May they soon be food for birds.

No farewells were then allowed us
Wives and babes were left behind,
Tho I saw their arms around us
As I closed my eyes and wept.

After what seemed weeks of torture
We were at our journey's end.
Left to starve upon the border
Almost on Carranza's land.

Then they rant of law and order,
Love of God, and fellow man,
Rave of freedom o'er the border
Being sent from promised lands.

Comes the day, ah! we'll remember
Sure as death relentless, too,
Grim-lipped toilers, their accusers
Let them call on God, not on you.

EMMA GOLDMAN
from *Living My Life*

Saturday, December 20 was a hectic day, with vague indications that it might be our last. We had been assured by the Ellis Island authorities that we were not likely to be sent away before Christmas, certainly not for several days to come. Meanwhile we were photographed, finger-printed, and tabulated like convicted criminals. The day was filled with visits from numerous friends who came individually and in groups. Self-evidently, reporters also did not fail to honour us. Did we know when we were going, and where? And what were my plans about Russia? "I will organize a Society of Russian Friends of American Freedom," I told them. "The American Friends of Russia have done much to help liberate that country. It is now the turn of free Russia to come to the aid of America."

Harry Weinberger was still very hopeful and full of fight. He would soon get me back to America, he insisted, and I should keep myself ready for it. Bob Minor smiled incredulously. He was greatly moved by our approaching departure; we had fought together in many battles and he was fond of me. Sasha he literally idolized and he felt his deportation as a severe personal loss. The pain of separation from Fitzi was somewhat mitigated by her decision to join us in Soviet Russia at the first opportunity. Our visitors were about to leave when Weinberger was officially notified that we were to remain on the island for several more days. We were glad of it and we arranged with our friends to come again, perhaps for the last time, on Monday, no callers being allowed on the island on the Lord's day.

I returned to the pen I was sharing with my two girl comrades.

The State charge of criminal anarchy against Ethel had been withdrawn, but she was to be deported just the same. She had been brought to America as a child; her entire family were in the country, as well as the man she loved, Samuel Lipman, sentenced to twenty years at Leavenworth. She had no affiliations in Russia and was unfamiliar with its language. But she was cheerful, saying that she had good cause to be proud: she was barely eighteen, yet she had already succeeded in making the powerful United States Government afraid of her.

Dora Lipkin's mother and sisters lived in Chicago. They were working people too poor to afford a trip to New York, and the girl knew that she would have to leave without even bidding her loved ones good-bye. Like Ethel, she had been in the country for a long time, slaving in factories and adding to the country's wealth. Now she was being kicked out, but fortunately her lover was also among the men to be deported.

I had not met either of the girls before, but our two weeks on Ellis Island had established a strong bond between us. This evening my room-mates again kept watch while I was hurriedly answering important mail and penning my last farewell to our people. It was almost midnight when suddenly I caught the sound of approaching footsteps. "Look out, someone's coming!" Ethel whispered. I snatched up my papers and letters and hid them under my pillow. Then we threw ourselves on our beds, covered up, and pretended to be asleep.

The steps halted at our room. There came the rattling of keys; the door was unlocked and noisily thrown open. Two guards and a matron entered. "Get up now," they commanded, "get your things ready!" The girls grew nervous. Ethel was shaking as in fever and helplessly rummaging among her bags. The guards became impatient. "Hurry, there! Hurry!" they ordered roughly. I could not restrain my indignation. "Leave us so we can get dressed!" I demanded. They walked out, the door remaining ajar. I was anxious about my letters. I did not want them to fall into the hands of the authorities, nor did I care to destroy them. Maybe I should find someone to entrust them to, I thought. I stuck them into the bosom of my dress and wrapped myself in a large shawl.

In a long corridor, dimly lit and unheated, we found the men deportees assembled, little Morris Becker among them. He had been delivered to the island only that afternoon with a number of other Russian boys. One of them was on crutches; another, suffering from an ulcerated stomach, had been carried from his bed in the island hospital. Sasha was busy helping the sick men pack their parcels and bundles. They had been hurried out of their cells without being allowed even time to gather up all their things. Routed from sleep at midnight, they were driven bag and baggage into the corridor. Some were still half-asleep, unable to realize what was happening.

I felt tired and cold. No chairs or benches were about, and we stood shivering in the barn-like place. The suddenness of the attack took the men by surprise and they filled the corridor with a hubbub of exclamations and questions and excited expostulations. Some had been promised a review of their cases, others were waiting to be bailed out pending final decision. They had received no notice of the nearness of their deportation and they were overwhelmed by the midnight assault. They stood helplessly about, at a loss what to do. Sasha gathered them in groups and suggested that an attempt be made to reach their relatives in the city. The men grasped desperately at that last hope and appointed him their representative and spokesman. He succeeded in prevailing upon the island commissioner to permit the men to telegraph, at their own expense, to their friends in New York for money and necessaries.

Messenger boys hurried back and forth, collecting special-delivery letters and wires hastily scribbled. The chance of reaching their people cheered the forlorn men. The island officials encouraged them and gathered in their messages, themselves collecting pay for delivery and assuring them that there was plenty of time to receive replies.

Hardly had the last wire been sent when the corridor filled with State and Federal detectives, officers of the Immigration Bureau and Coast Guards. I recognized Caminetti, Commissioner General of Immigration, at their head. The uniformed men stationed themselves along the walls, and then came the command: "Line up!" A sudden hush fell upon the room. "March!" It echoed through the corridor.

Deep snow lay on the ground; the air was cut by a biting wind. A row of armed civilians and soldiers stood along the road to the bank. Dimly the outlines of a barge were visible through the morning mist. One by one the deportees marched, flanked on each side by the uniformed men, curses and threats accompanying the thud of their feet on the frozen ground. When the last man had crossed the gangplank, the girls and I were ordered to follow, officers in front and in back of us.

We were led to a cabin. A large fire roared in the iron stove, filling the air with heat and fumes. We felt suffocating. There was no air nor water. Then came a violent lurch; we were on our way.

I looked at my watch. It was 4:20 A.M. on the day of our Lord, December 21, 1919. On the deck above us I could hear the men tramping up and down in the wintry blast. I felt dizzy, visioning a transport of politicals doomed to Siberia, the étape of former Russian days. Russia of the past rose before me and I saw the revolutionary martyrs being driven into exile. But no, it was New York, it was America, the land of liberty! Through the port-hole I could see the great city receding into the distance, its sky-line of buildings traceable by their rearing heads. It was my beloved city, the metropolis of the New World. It was America, indeed, America repeating the terrible scenes of tsarist Russia! I glanced up — the Statue of Liberty!

TEFFI
The Gadarene Swine

There are not many of them, of these refugees from Sovietdom.
A small group of people with nothing in common; a small motley
herd huddled by the cliff's edge before the final leap. Creatures of
different breeds and with coats of different colours, entirely alien to
one another, with natures that have perhaps always been mutually
antagonistic, they have wandered off together and collectively refer
to themselves as "we". They have wandered off for no purpose, for
no reason. Why?

The legend of the country of the Gadarenes comes to mind.
Men possessed by demons came out from among the tombs, and
Christ healed them by driving the demons into a herd of swine,
and the swine plunged from a cliff and drowned.

Herds of a single animal are rare in the East. More often they
are mixed. And in the herd of Gadarene swine there were evidently
some meek, frightened sheep. Seeing the crazed swine hurtling
along, these sheep took to their heels too.

"Is that *our* lot?"

"Yes, they're running for it!"

And the meek sheep plunged down after the swine and they all
perished together.

Had dialogue been possible in the course of this mad dash, it
might have resembled what we've been hearing so often in recent
days:

"Why are we running?" ask the meek.

"Everyone's running."

"Where are we running to?"

"Wherever everyone else is running."

"What are we doing with *them*? They're not our kind of people. We shouldn't be here with them. Maybe we ought to have stayed where we were. Where the men possessed by demons were coming out from the tombs. What are we doing? We've lost our way, we don't know what we're..."

But the swine running alongside them know very well what they're doing. They egg the meek on, grunting "Culture! We're running towards culture! We've got money sewn into the soles of our shoes. We've got diamonds stuck up our noses. Culture! Culture! Yes, we must save our culture!"

They hurtle on. Still on the run, they speculate. They buy up, they buy back, they sell on. They peddle rumours. The fleshy disc at the end of a pig's snout may only look like a five-kopek coin, but the swine are selling them now for a hundred roubles.

"Culture! We're saving culture! For the sake of culture!"

"How very strange!" say the meek. "'Culture' is our kind of word. It's a word we use ourselves. But now it sounds all wrong. Who is it you're running away from?"

"The Bolsheviks."

"How very strange!" the meek say sadly. "Because we're running away from the Bolsheviks, too."

If the swine are fleeing the Bolsheviks, then it seems that the meek should have stayed behind.

But they're in headlong flight. There's no time to think anything through.

They are indeed all running away from the Bolsheviks. But the crazed swine are escaping from Bolshevik *truth*, from socialist *principles*, from equality and justice, while the meek and frightened are escaping from *untruth*, from Bolshevism's black reality, from terror, injustice and violence.

"What was there for me to do back there?" asks one of the

meek. "I'm a professor of international law. I could only have died of hunger."

Indeed, what is there for a professor of international law to do — a man whose professional concern is the inviolability of principles that no longer exist? What use is he now? All he can do is give off an air of international law. And now he's on the run. During the brief stops he hurries about, trying to find someone in need of his international law. Sometimes he even finds a bit of work and manages to give a few lectures. But then the crazed swine break loose and sweep him along behind them.

"We have to run. Everyone is running."

Out-of-work lawyers, journalists, artists, actors and public figures — they're all on the run.

"Maybe we should have stayed behind and fought?"

Fought? But how? Make wonderful speeches when there's no one to hear them? Write powerful articles that there's nowhere to publish?

"And who should we have fought against?"

Should an impassioned knight enter into combat with a windmill, then — and please remember this — the windmill will always win. Even though this certainly does not mean — and please remember this too — that the windmill is right.

They're running. They're in torment, full of doubt, and they're on the run.

Alongside them, grunting and snorting and not doubting anything, are the speculators, former gendarmes, former Black Hundreds and a variety of other former scoundrels. Former though they may be, these groups retain their particularities.

There are heroic natures who stride joyfully and passionately through blood and fire towards — *ta-rum-pum-pum!* — a new life!

And there are tender natures who are willing, with no less joy and no less passion, to sacrifice their lives for what is most wonderful and unique, but without the *ta-rum-pum-pum*. With a prayer rather than a drum roll.

Wild screams and bloodshed extinguish all light and colour from their souls. Their energy fades and their resources vanish. The rivulet of blood glimpsed in the morning at the gates of the commissariat, a rivulet creeping slowly across the pavement, cuts across the road of life for ever. It's impossible to step over it.

It's impossible to go any further. Impossible to do anything but turn and run.

And so these tender natures run.

The rivulet of blood has cut them off for ever, and they shall never return.

Then there are the more everyday people, those who are neither good nor bad but entirely average, the all-too-real people who make up the bulk of what we call humanity. The ones for whom science and art, comfort and culture, religion and laws were created. Neither heroes nor scoundrels — in a word, just plain, ordinary people.

To exist without the everyday, to hang in the air without any familiar footing — with no sure, firm earthly footing — is something only heroes and madmen can do.

A "normal person" needs the trappings of life, life's earthly flesh — that is, the everyday.

Where there's no religion, no law, no conventions, no settled routine (even if only the routine of a prison or a penal camp), an ordinary, everyday person cannot exist.

At first he'll try to adapt. Deprived of his breakfast roll, he'll eat bread; deprived of bread, he'll settle for husks full of grit; deprived of husks, he'll eat rotten herring — but he'll eat all of this with the same look on his face and the same attitude as if he were eating his usual breakfast roll.

But what if there's nothing to eat at all? He loses his way, his light fades, the colours of life turn pale for him.

Now and then there's a brief flicker from some tremulous beam of light.

"Apparently *they* take bribes too! Did you know? Have you heard?"

The happy news takes wing, travelling by word of mouth — a promise of life, like "Christ is Risen!"

Bribery! The everyday, the routine, a way of life we know as our own! Something earthly and solid!

But bribery alone does not allow you to settle down and thrive.

You must run. In pursuit of your daily bread in the biblical sense of the word: food, clothing, shelter, and labour that provides these things and law that protects them.

Children must acquire the knowledge needed for work, and people of mature years must apply this knowledge to the business of everyday life.

So it has always been, and it cannot of course be otherwise.

There are heady days in the history of nations — days that have to be lived through, but that one can't go on living in for ever.

"Enough carousing — time to get down to work."

Does this mean, then, that we have to do things in some new way? What time should we go to work? What time should we have lunch? Which school should we prepare the children for? We're ordinary people, the levers, belts, screws, wheels and drives of a vast machine, we're the core, the very thick of humanity — what do you want us to do?

"We want you to do all manner of foolish things. Instead of screws we'll have belts, we'll use belts to screw in nuts. And levers instead of wheels. And a wheel will do the job of a belt. Impossible? Outdated prejudice! At the sharp end of a bayonet, nothing is impossible. A theology professor can bake gingerbread and a porter give lectures on aesthetics. A surgeon can sweep the street and a laundress preside over the courtroom."

"We're afraid! We can't do it, we don't know how. A porter lecturing on aesthetics may believe in the value of what he is doing, but a professor baking gingerbread knows only too well that his gingerbread may be anything under the sun — but it certainly isn't gingerbread."

Take to your heels! Run!

Somewhere over there... in Kiev... in Yekaterinburg... in Odessa... some place where children are studying and people are working, it'll still be possible to live a little... For the time being.

And so on they run.

But they are few and they are becoming fewer still. They're growing weak, falling by the wayside. They're running after a way of life that is itself on the run.

And now that the motley herd has wandered onto the Gadarene cliff for its final leap, we can see how very small it is. It could be gathered up into some little ark and sent out to sea. But there the seven unclean pairs would devour the seven clean pairs and then die of overeating.[8]

And the souls of the clean would weep over the dead ark:

"It grieves us to have suffered the same fate as the unclean, to have died together with them on the ark."

---

8 A slightly inaccurate reference to a passage in Genesis, where God tells Noah, "Of every clean beast thou shalt take to thee by sevens, the male and the female: and of beasts that are not clean by two, the male and the female."

Yes, my dears. There's not much you can do about it. You'll all die together. Some from eating, some from being eaten. But "impartial history" will make no distinction. You will all be numbered together.

"And the entire herd plunged from the cliff and drowned."

Translated from Russian by Anne Marie Jackson

JOSÉ CARLOS MARIÁTEGUI
The Exile of Trotsky

Trotsky exiled from Soviet Russia: here is an event to which international revolutionary opinion cannot become easily accustomed. Revolutionary optimism never admitted the possibility that this revolution would end, like the French, condemning its heroes. But what in good sense should not have been expected is that the task of organizing the first great socialist state would be fulfilled with unanimous agreement, without debate or violent conflicts, by a party of more than a million impassioned militants. Trotskyist opinion has a useful role in Soviet politics. It represents, if one wishes to define it in two words, Marxist orthodoxy, confronting the overflowing and unruly current of Russian reality. It exemplifies the working-class, urban, industrial sense of the socialist revolution. The Russian revolution owes its international, ecumenical value, its character as a precursor of the rise of a new civilization, to the ideas that Trotsky and his comrades insist upon in their full strength and import. Without vigilant criticism, which is the best proof of the vitality of the Bolshevik Party, the Soviet government would probably run the risk of falling into a formalist, mechanical bureaucratism.

But, to this point, events have not proven Trotskyism correct from the point of view of its ability to replace Stalin in power with a greater objective capacity to realize the Marxist programme. The essential part of the Trotskyist opposition's platform is its critical part. But in the estimation of those elements who might plot against Soviet policies, neither Stalin nor Bukharin is very far from subscribing to most of the fundamental concepts of Trotsky and his adepts. The Trotskyist proposals and solutions, on the other hand, do not have the same solidity. In most of what relates to agrarian and industrial policies and the struggle against bureaucratism and the NEP spirit, Trotskyism tastes of a theoretical radicalism that has not been condensed into concrete and precise formulas. On this terrain, Stalin and the majority, along with having the responsibility for administration, have a more real sense of the possibilities.

The Russian revolution, which, like any great revolution, advances along a difficult path that it clears with its own impetus, has not yet known easy or idle days. It is the work of heroic and exceptional men, and for this very reason has only been possible through the greatest and most tremendous creative tension. The Bolshevik Party, therefore, neither is nor can be a peaceful and unanimous school. Lenin imposed his creative leadership until shortly before his death, but not even with this extraordinary leader's immense and unique authority were violent debates unusual inside the party. Lenin gained his authority with his own strength; he later maintained it through the superiority and perspicacity of his thought. His points of view always prevailed because they best corresponded to reality. Many times, though, they had to defeat the resistance of his own lieutenants of the Bolshevik old guard.

Lenin's death, which left vacant the post of creative leader with immense personal authority, would have been followed by a period of profound disequilibrium in any party less disciplined and organic than the Russian Communist Party. Trotsky stood out from all his comrades because of the brilliant distinctiveness of his personality. But he not only lacked a solid and long-standing connection with the Leninist team. His relationship with the majority of its members had been quite uncordial before the revolution. Trotsky, as is well known, had an almost individual position among Russian revolutionaries until 1917. He did not belong to the Bolshevik Party, whose leaders, even Lenin himself, polemicized bitterly with him more than once. Lenin intelligently and generously appreciated the value of collaborating with Trotsky, who himself — as the volume of his writings on the revolution's leader attests — unreservedly and unjealously respected an authority consecrated by the most inspiring and enthralling work of revolutionary consciousness. But if almost all the distance between Lenin and Trotsky could be erased, the identification between Trotsky and the party itself could not be equally complete. Trotsky could not count on the full confidence of the party, as much as his performance as people's commissar merited unanimous admiration. The party machinery was in the hands of members of the old Leninist guard, who always felt themselves a bit distant from and alien to Trotsky, who, for his part, was not able to fully join them in a single bloc. Moreover, Trotsky, it seems, does not possess the special talents of a politician as Lenin did to the greatest degree. He does not know how to gather men; he is not acquainted with the secrets of managing a party. His singular position — equidistant from Bolshevism and Menshevism — during the years between 1905 and 1917, besides disconnecting him from the revolutionary team that prepared and realized the revolution with Lenin, must have disaccustomed him to the concrete practice of a party leader.

As long as the mobilization of all revolutionary energies against the threats of reaction continued, Bolshevik unity was ensured by the pathos of war. But once the work of stabilization and normalization began, the discrepancies between individuals and tendencies had to manifest themselves. The lack of an exceptional personality like Trotsky would have reduced the opposition to more modest terms. In this case, it would not have come to a violent schism. But with Trotsky at the command post, the opposition quickly took an insurrectionary and combative tone to which the majority and the government could not be indifferent.

Trotsky, moreover, is a man of the cosmopolis. Zinoviev, at another moment during a Communist congress, accused him of ignoring and neglecting the peasant. He has, in any case, an international sense of the socialist revolution. His notable writings on the transitory stabilization of capitalism are among the most alert and sagacious criticisms of the era. But this very international sense of the revolution, which gives him such prestige on the world scene, momentarily robs him of his power in the practice of Russian politics. The Russian revolution is in a period of national organization. It is not a matter, at the moment, of establishing socialism internationally, but of realizing it in a nation that, while being a territory populated by 130 million inhabitants that overflows onto two continents, does not yet constitute a geographical and historical unit. It is logical that, in this stage, the Russian revolution is represented by men who more deeply sense its national character and problems. Stalin, a pure Slav, is one of these men. He belongs to a phalanx of revolutionaries who always remained rooted in the Russian soil, while Trotsky, Radek and Rakovsky belong to a phalanx that passed the larger part of their lives in exile. They were apprenticed as international revolutionaries in exile, an apprenticeship that has given the Russian revolution its universalist language and its ecumenical vision. For now, alone with its problems, Russia prefers more simply and purely Russian men.

Translated from Spanish by Michael Pearlman

LEON TROTSKY
Letter to the Workers of the USSR

Greetings to the Soviet workers, collective farmers, soldiers of the Red Army and sailors of the Red Navy! Greetings from distant Mexico where I found refuge after the Stalinist clique had exiled me to Turkey and after the bourgeoisie had hounded me from country to country! Dear Comrades! The lying Stalinist press has been maliciously deceiving you for a long time on all questions, including those which relate to myself and my political co-thinkers. You possess no workers' press; you read only the press of the bureaucracy, which lies systematically so as to keep you in darkness and thus render secure the rule of a privileged parasitic caste. Those who dare raise their voices against the universally hated bureaucracy are called "Trotskyists", agents of a foreign power; branded as spies — yesterday it was spies of Germany, today it is spies of England and France — and then sent to face the firing squad. Tens of thousands of revolutionary fighters have fallen before the muzzles of GPU Mausers in the USSR and in countries abroad, especially in Spain. All of them were depicted as agents of Fascism. Do not believe this abominable slander! Their crime consisted of defending workers and peasants against the brutality and rapacity of the bureaucracy. The entire Old Guard of Bolshevism, all the collaborators and assistants of Lenin, all the fighters of the October revolution, all the heroes of the Civil War, have been murdered by Stalin. In the annals of history Stalin's name will for ever be recorded with the infamous brand of Cain!

The October revolution was accomplished for the sake of the toilers and not for the sake of new parasites. But due to the lag of the world revolution, due to the fatigue and, to a large measure, the backwardness of the Russian workers and especially the Russian peasants, there raised itself over the Soviet Republic and against its peoples a new oppressive and parasitic caste, whose leader is Stalin. The former Bolshevik Party was turned into an apparatus of the caste. The world organization which the Communist International once was is today a pliant tool of the Moscow oligarchy. Soviets of Workers and Peasants have long perished. They have been replaced by degenerate Commissars, Secretaries and GPU agents. But, fortunately, among the surviving conquests of the October revolution are the nationalized industry and the collectivized Soviet economy. Upon this foundation Workers' Soviets can build a new and happier society. This foundation cannot be surrendered by us to the world bourgeoisie under any conditions. It is the duty of revolutionists to defend tooth and nail every position gained by the working class, whether it involves democratic rights, wage scales, or so colossal a conquest of mankind as the nationalization of the means of production and planned economy. Those who are incapable of defending conquests already gained can never fight for new cries. Against the imperialist foe we will defend the USSR with all our might. However, the conquests of the October revolution will serve the people only if they prove themselves capable of dealing with the Stalinist bureaucracy, as in their day they dealt with the Tsarist bureaucracy and the bourgeoisie.

If Soviet economic life had been conducted in the interests of the people; if the bureaucracy had not devoured and vainly wasted the major portion of the national income; if the bureaucracy had not trampled underfoot the vital interests of the population, then the USSR would have been a great magnetic pole of attraction for the toilers of the world and the inviolability of the Soviet Union would have been assured. But the infamous oppressive regime of Stalin has deprived the USSR of its attractive power. During the war with Finland, not only the majority of the Finnish peasants but also the majority of the Finnish workers, proved to be on the side of their bourgeoisie. This is hardly surprising since they know of the unprecedented oppression to which the Stalinist bureaucracy subjects the workers of near-by Leningrad and the whole of the USSR. The Stalinist bureaucracy, so bloodthirsty and ruthless at home and so cowardly before the imperialist enemies, has thus become the main source of war danger to the Soviet Union. The old Bolshevik Party and the Third International have disintegrated and decomposed. The honest and advanced revolutionists have organized abroad the Fourth International, which has sections already established in most of the countries of the world. I am a member of this new International. In participating in this work I remain under the very same banner that I served together with you or your fathers and your older brothers in 1917 and throughout the years of the Civil War, the very same banner under which, together with Lenin, we built the Soviet state and the Red Army.

The goal of the Fourth International is to extend the October revolution to the whole world and at the same time to regenerate the USSR by purging it of the parasitic bureaucracy. This can be achieved only in one way: By the workers, peasants, Red Army soldiers and Red Navy sailors, rising against the new caste of oppressors and parasites. To prepare this uprising, a new party is needed — a bold and honest revolutionary organization of the advanced workers. The Fourth International sets as its task the building of such a party in the USSR. Advance, workers! Be the first to rally to the banner of Marx and Lenin which is now the banner of the Fourth International! Learn how to create, in the conditions of Stalinist illegality, tightly fused, reliable revolution-ary circles! Establish contacts between these circles! Learn how to establish contacts through loyal and reliable people, especially the sailors, with your revolutionary co-thinkers in bourgeois lands! It is difficult, but it can be done. The present war will spread more and more, piling ruins on ruins, breeding more and more sorrow, despair and protest, driving the whole world towards new revolutionary explosions. The world revolution shall reinvigorate the Soviet working masses with new courage and resoluteness and shall undermine the bureaucratic props of Stalin's caste. It is necessary to prepare for this hour by stubborn systematic revolutionary work. The fate of our country, the future of our people, the destiny of our children and grandchildren are at stake.

Down With Cain Stalin and his Camarilla!
Down With the Rapacious Bureaucracy!
Long Live the Soviet Union, the Fortress of the Toilers!
Long Live the World Socialist Revolution!

Fraternally,
LEON TROTSKY
May, 1940

Translated from Russian by the Fourth International

VICTOR SERGE
from *Mexican Notebooks*

4th April 1942

Stefan Zweig committed suicide in Rio at the end of March. I was in Veracruz, waiting for the *Nyassa*, about whose fate grim rumours were circulating which I didn't take seriously (and yet it seemed inconceivable that Laurette was arriving). I read about it in a newspaper. Aged sixty; with his wife, some thirty years younger. Barbiturates. A magazine photo shows them lying in bed, asleep beside each other. On the bedside table, a glass, a bottle of mineral water, a box of matches; life's last trifling objects, practical, of no interest, of the kind we no longer see. His latest book has just been published: *Brazil, Land of the Future* [...] I have no doubt he is sincere. Not the same future, a land, a man, a couple. His suicide note says he can no longer live like this, amidst the collapse of a culture and a world, in reality a foreigner, as he must have felt in the Americas. Vaguely thought, more felt, Zweig was never a fighter, nothing but a great, refined intellectual, an artist — and ultimately feeble, feeble through being accustomed to comfort, through his idea of culture as something definitively acquired and of unique value, through being accustomed to literary success and the good life. I remember his home; it was the home of a hugely privileged patrician, on one of Salzburg's hills, in a most serene, romantic place, most beautiful to look at, one of the most civilized in the world [...] I understood a lot about the nature of the man in admiring his house; he felt he was read in the name of Art. At the time fairly good on the psychology of emotions in the novel, easy success, but of good quality all the same. It all lacked fundamental vigour, humanism that was only skin-deep and intellectually shallow, based on a superficial vision of the tragedy of today's world. Repression in the face of this tragedy; let me live with my noble thoughts, the psychologist and poet is entitled to this delightful house on the peaceful hillside, entitled to music, entitled to a privileged life, for his nobility enriches the world. That intelligentsia is being torn up and crushed by the hurricane, it will only be able to rediscover its purpose in life by understanding the hurricane and flinging itself into it heart and soul. True, for a social category, impossible for most of those who comprise it. His end seems logical and courageous. Nothing more natural than the dignified refusal to live in conditions that are unacceptable. Being uprooted, the void, age too with its declining faculties, the fear that one is not sufficiently alive to attain moments that are worth living for, the fear of physical deterioration. Above all the torpor of a mind that has lost its source of sustenance, the exchanges that stimulated it. Under the harsh Rio sun, it must have been particularly palpable: unbearable.

Translated from French by Ros Schwartz

MARINA TSVETAYEVA
Homesickness

Homesickness! Silly fallacy
laid bare so long ago.
It's all the same where I'm to be
entirely alone —

it's all the same across what stones
I lug my shopping basket,
towards some house as alien
as a hospital or barracks.

I do not care what faces see
me bristle like a captive lion,
or out of which society
I'm quickly forced into my own

fenced realm of silent feelings.
I'm like an iceless polar bear —
just where I fail to fit (won't try!)
and am belittled, I don't care.

My native tongue will not delude
me with its milky call.
I won't, I can't be understood
in any tongue at all

by passers-by (voracious eaters
of newspapers, milkers of rumour) —
they're of the twentieth century,
and me — no time is home to me!

Dumbfounded, like a log that fell
on an abandoned lane,
all is the same to me, all, all
the same, and what has been

most dear to me now matters least.
All signs, all memories and dates
have been erased:
a soul born — any place.

My homeland cared for me so little
that the most clever snoop
could search my soul for birthmarks — he'll
find nothing with his loupe!

Yes, every house is strange to me
and every temple — barren.
All, all the same. Yet, if I see,
alone along the verge — a rowan...

Translated from Russian by Boris Dralyuk

ANNA SEGHERS
from *Transit*

"The Germans are now the real masters here. And since you presumably are a member of that nation, you must know what German 'order' means, Nazi order, which they're now all boasting about here. It has nothing to do with World Order, the old one. It is a kind of control. The Germans are not going to miss the chance to thoroughly control and check all people leaving Europe. In the process they might find some troublemaker for whom they've been hunting for decades."

"All right. All right. But after you're checked out, after you have a visa what significance is the transit visa? Why does it expire? What is it actually? Why aren't people allowed to travel through countries on their way to their new homes in other countries?"

He said, "My son, it's all because each country is afraid that instead of just travelling through, we'll want to stay. A transit visa — that gives you permission to travel through a country with the stipulations that you don't plan to stay."

Suddenly he changed his approach. He addressed me in a different, very solemn, tone of voice that fathers use only when they're finally sending their sons out into the world. "Young man," he said, "you came here with scarcely any baggage, alone and without a destination. You don't even have a visa. You're not the least concerned that the Marseilles Prefect will not let you stay here if you don't have a visa. Now, let's assume that by some stroke of luck, or by your own efforts, something happens, though it rarely does, or maybe because when you least expect it, a friend reaches out a hand from the dark, that is, from across the ocean, or maybe through Providence itself, or maybe with the help of a committee, anyway, let's assume you get a visa. For one brief moment you're happy. But you soon realize that the problem isn't solved so easily. You have a destination — no big deal, everybody has that. But you can't just get to that country by sheer force of will, through the stratosphere. You have to travel on oceans, through the countries between. You need a transit visa. For that you need your wits. And time. You have no idea how much time it takes. For me time is of the essence. But when I look at you, I think time is even more precious for you. Time is youth itself. But you must not fly off in too many directions. You must think only of the transit visa. If I may say so, you have to forget your destination for a while, for at this moment only the countries in between are what matter, otherwise you won't be able to leave. What matters now is to make the consul see that you're serious, that you're not one of those fellows who want to stay in a place that is only a transit country. And there are ways to prove this. Any consul will ask for such proof. Let's assume you're lucky and have a berth on a ship and the trip as such is a certainty, which is really a miracle when you consider how many want to leave and how few available ships there are. If you're a Jew, which you're not, then you might be able to secure a berth on board a ship with the help of Jewish aid groups. If you're Aryan, then maybe Christian groups can help. If you're nothing, or godless, or a Red, then for God's sake, or with the help of your party, or others like you, you might be able to get a berth. But don't think, my son, that your transit visa will be assured, and even if it were! In the meantime, so much time has passed that the main goal, your primary one, has disappeared. Your visa has expired, and as vital as the transit visa is, it isn't worth anything without a visa, and so on and so forth. Now, son, imagine that you've managed to do it. Good, let's both dream that you've done it. You have them all — your visa, your transit visa, your exit visa. You're ready

237

to start your journey. You've said goodbye to your loved ones and tossed your life over your shoulder. You're thinking only of your goal, your destination. You finally want to board the ship. For example: yesterday, I was talking with a young man your age. He had everything. But then when he was ready to board his ship, the harbour authorities refused to give him the last stamp he needed."

"Why?"

"He had escaped from a camp when the Germans were coming." The old man said this in the weary tone of voice he had been using before. He seemed to sink into himself. Yet his posture was too erect — it was more that he sagged. "The fellow didn't have a certificate of release from the camp — so it was all for nothing."

Translated from German by Margot Bettauer Dembo

CESARE PAVESE
Lo Steddazzu

The lonely man wakes while the sea is still dark
and the stars are shuddering. A warmish breeze
rises from the shore, where the seabed lies,
to sweeten one's breath. This is the hour when nothing
can happen. Even the pipe between his teeth
hangs unlit. Nocturnal is the water's subdued swash.
The lonely man has already lit a bonfire of branches
and watches it redden the landscape. Even the sea
will soon resemble the fire and its blazing shine.

There's nothing more bitter than the dawn of a day
when nothing will happen. Nothing more bitter
than pointlessness. A greenish star hangs
exhausted in the sky, taken aback by the dawn.
It watches the still-dark sea and the blotch of fire
where the man keeps warm, if only to stay busy;
it watches and falls sleep-heavy between murky mountains
where a bed of snow awaits it. The slowness of this hour
is ruthless to those who no longer expect anything.

Is there a point to the sun rising from the sea
and for the long day to begin? Tomorrow,
the warmish dawn will return with its silky light,
it'll be like yesterday and nothing will happen.
The lonely man would like only to sleep.

When the last star goes dead in the sky,
the man carefully fills his pipe, and lights it.

Translated from Italian by André Naffis-Sahely

YANNIS RITSOS
A Break in Routine

They came to the door and read names from a list.
If you heard your name you had to get ready fast:
a busted suitcase, a bundle you might carry
over your shoulder, perhaps; forget the rest.
With each new departure, the place seemed to shrink.

Finally, those who were left agreed to bunk
in a single room, which no one thought odd.
They found an old alarm clock
and placed it just here, in the hearth,
a little household god,
and made a rota for who would wind it and set it
to ring at six-thirty, in time for their needle-bath.

Once, it went off at midnight, whereat they woke
and sluiced themselves under the moon, then sat
in a circle round the clock
to smoke the last of their cigarettes.

Translated from Greek by David Harsent

CARLOS BULOSAN
American History

"... this is what I say: I am suffering because
I am a radical, and indeed I am a radical;
I have suffered because I was an Italian, and indeed
I am an Italian. I have suffered more for my family
than for myself; but I am so convinced to be right
that you can only kill me once but if you could
execute me two other times, I would live again
to do what I have done already. I have finished.
Thank you..."

        Vanzetti, the dreamy fish-peddler,
hurt but not alone in the alien courtroom,
voicing the sentiments of millions in his voice;
to scorning men voicing the voice of nations
in one stream of sentiments in his gentle voice,
that justice and tolerance might live for every one.

"... but remember always, Dante, in the play
of happiness, don't use all for yourself only,
but down yourself just one step, at your side
and help the weak ones that cry for help: they are
your friends: they are the comrades that fight
for the conquest of the joy of freedom for all.
In this struggle of life you will find more love
and you will be loved..."

Sacco, the good shoemaker,
dreaming of the future with the poet that never was,
in spheres of tragic light, dreaming of the world
that never was, as each tragic moment passed
in streams of vivid light, to radiate a harmony
of thought and action that never came to pass.

Our agony is our triumph: Sacco and Vanzetti.

BARBARA TOPORSKA
The Chronicle

In memory of Stanisław Kodź (1898-1966)

Dr (of Law) A. Lonely
political émigré
died
on Sunday
of heart failure
at a Munich hotel.

There is snow in the street
this November in Munich
the walls swayed like veils
the ceiling came down
and dusk glazed the windows
with a silver-like silence
then night brushed it off
with the glare of the streetlights.

In the morning the phone rang
servants knocked at the door
locksmith
policeman
doctor —
death was sudden and lonely.

While Lonely — he sails
far away by his lonesome

on this ashen grey Sunday
with snow at the window
growing younger each moment
than all things on the course
of this Europe in autumn
this Munich in autumn.

*

Full stop. End of entry.
"Political commentary?"
cold
cigarette
smoke
in a lump of soil from the homeland.

Translated from Polish by Boris Dralyuk

SILVA KAPUTIKYAN
Perhaps

Perhaps you became so small, Armenia
so we could carry you in our hearts.
Perhaps you changed into charred parchment
so we would tremble lest you fall apart.
Perhaps your handful of soil was meant
as talisman, lesson, and exercise.
Your name became the symbol, perhaps,
for purification in a world of lies.

Translated from Armenian by Diana Der-Hovanessian

ALESSANDRO SPINA
The Fort at Régima

Captain Valentini received the order to join the regiment stationed at Régima to the south of the city. "You'll miss everything there," his predecessor had warned him, "not just danger or action, there isn't even a reason for keeping the place garrisoned. You never get any orders. You must look on the High Command the way one beholds a higher power. It's useless to ask for any signs or explanations. The High Command won't remember you until they need you to go somewhere, or want you to come back, that is if they even remember that you're still out there." The Captain was nevertheless glad to go. His departure for that fort presented itself as an opportunity to subtract himself from everything: General Occhipinti and the military parades, the Officers' Club, the speeches by the Secretary of the local Fascist party, the five German girls and their papier-mâché train at the Berenice Cinema and the evening walks alongside the main avenue... all would be swept away. Solitude, he reflected, is the epitome of subtracting oneself from life and it is blessed for this very reason. The fort was situated on a hill. The brief walk to the top was pleasant. The path was slightly uneven. Not a single tree in sight for over thirty miles. The fort, one part of which lay in complete abandon, had a medieval feel to it, a feature the original builders had probably wanted (first the Turks, then the Italian colonial government), and had decided to enhance it with useless battlements. However, time had worked its magic on those imitation battlements, and the inclemency of the elements had endowed the fort with a hard-edged, aristocratic sheen. More than Western medieval structures, it recalled the castles the knights had built in Greece during the

Fourth Crusade. The landscape was identical. The Captain's armoured car tottered along a path strewn with stones. Sometimes it ventured into open fields, where the ground was often more level than the path itself. "Had I come on horseback, the journey might have been more comfortable." As with the celebrated Knight of La Mancha, the Captain had many famous examples in mind: *Anseau de Cayeux, Thierry de Tenremonde, Orry de Lisle, Guido di Conflans, Macario de Sainte Menehould, Bègue de Fransures, Conon de Béthume, Milon le Brèbant, Païen d'Orléans, Peter of Bracieux, Baldovino di Beauvoir, Hugues de Beaumetz, Gautier d'Escornai, Dreux de Beaurain...* the Captain proved unable to stop thinking about the legacies of these knights. They had conquered Constantinople, made and unmade emperors, and had carved the vast empire into feuds; they had scrambled hither and thither throughout the lengths of the Empire vainly trying to sustain an order, which, lacking any roots in that country, was ultimately fated to die. All that remained of those knights was their fortresses, like gigantic carcasses of vanquished animals. Nothing connected those knights to anything that had come before them, and nothing survived their slaughter. The empire had simply swatted them away, like flies. As the Captain bounced around in his armoured car, it struck him that repeating the same sequence of events so many centuries later was both cruel and unbearable.

Translated from Italian by André Naffis-Sahely

MIGUEL MARTINEZ
Spanish Anarchists in Exile in Algeria

On 19th March 1939, my father was forced to flee Spain due to the victory of Franco's troops. With him went his partner and two children, which was unusual, for the vast majority of fugitives had been forced to set off alone as per instructions from their trade unions or, more rarely, for personal reasons. I was seven years old at the time. The war that ended in defeat for the anti-Francoists lingered as the backdrop to my childhood. All I can remember of it are a few striking eruptions. On the other hand, I spent the long period of exile that followed surrounded throughout my childhood and early youth by comrades who had themselves also been landed in Oran, then a French colonial port, from a trawler in March 1939. Our exile started once we were ashore. The French police were waiting for us on the dockside. We found ourselves being treated, not as fighters against fascist rule, but as common criminals. We were lashed and scattered through concentration camps, some of us never to return. The camps in Colomb-Béchar, Boghari and Djelfa were nothing better than punishment centres. My father spent six months in Boghari, at the end of which he was transferred to Carnot where his wife and two children had been waiting for him to be released from prison. Carnot was a family reunification camp which I have to admit could not be compared with the sinister prisons named earlier. My father eventually secured a certificate allowing him to take up a job at a hairdressers' in Orleansville and we were allowed to leave Carnot after an enforced stay of over a year. Fleeing the malaria raging on the Cheliff plains, we moved on to the capital, Algiers, where a number of other comrades had also sought refuge.

It was in Algiers that I grew up. I shared the life of my exiled elders, targeted for all manner of problems reserved for outsiders and driven by just one hope: of returning to Spain once Franco had been overthrown. Of itself, this obsession of theirs explains their stand-offishness as a cultural group; they kept out of the events that were to shape Algerian history. But there were ideological grounds too for this undeniable remoteness (on the part of the libertarians at any rate) from a land that they regarded, right up until the end, as simply a place of transit, and from its inhabitants. In fact, when the colonized rose in violent revolt against their colonizers in November 1954, a ferocious seven-year war ensued. During which terrorism and a trail of bereavement, hatred and thirst for vengeance would become standard practice. The libertarian "Spanish refugees" would take no part in the conflict, although right from the start they were sympathetic to the fact that the oppressed had finally rebelled against their colonial masters. But they could not see how their own struggle could be squared with a fight for national independence and the creation of an Algerian state. During rare contacts with the local leadership of the National Liberation Front (FLN), the comrades tried to persuade them that all their people would be doing would be exchanging one master for another, an Algerian exploiter for a French one. They also criticized the complacency with which the Movement played along with the Muslim religion. And they disapproved of the rebels' tactics of using terrorist outrages as a fighting method, something that was to lead to their murdering more than one of our comrades on the grounds that he was a "roumi", a European like all the rest. This reflected a sordidly racist, inhuman behaviour like the one that drove their colonialist opponents. In short, the Spanish libertarians could not see anything in that struggle around which to mobilize. In Spain, they had fought for an end to

250

capitalist society and to install a regime of exemplary justice for all the peoples of the earth.

Besides, had they, in spite of everything, thrown their weight somehow behind the uprising, they were still Spaniards, i.e. foreigners, utterly forbidden to interfere with French government domestic policy. Breaching that ban amounted to illegal interference and that would have jeopardized their special residency status which entitled them to go on living in Algeria, or in France. Finally, the last but undeniable factor preventing engagement with the insurgent movement was the aforementioned obsession they had with some day returning to Spain. After twenty years in exile, this still-vivid dream impelled them to devote all of their efforts to making a reality of that dream. All of which explains of course why no history of the Algerian war, so far as I am aware, ever mentions the presence of Spanish refugees or tackles their stance on events in Algeria. Does that not mean that they should be lumped together with the masses of "Algerian French"? That is hard to say, they being "refugee Spaniards". Nor can they be lumped with the *pieds noirs*. For the reasons set out, the libertarians never backed the cause of an Algerian Algeria, but it is equally true that they did actively oppose the criminal activity of the OAS, some at the risk of their lives, as in the case of comrade Suria who used to sell anarchist newspapers in the bars of Bab-el-Oued; he was murdered by OAS thugs and his remains dumped in a sack labelled "So perish all traitors". But then again, as far as the libertarians were concerned, opposing the OAS, which had secured support from Spain, boiled down to fighting Francoism rather than participating in the Algerian people's national liberation struggle. Even though it is a fact that on the whole they had always been openly hostile to the colonial population, which they held to be reactionary in political terms, their stance was a non-interventionist one. This fight was not their fight. They were neither for a French Algeria nor for an Algerian Algeria.

After the declaration of independence (and the Evian Treaty of 1962) the vast majority of the "Spanish refugees in Algeria" opted for exile in metropolitan France. In my own case, having taken French nationality and become a teacher, I stayed on in Algeria to help out. This enabled me to witness the birth of the Algerian state and to see confirmation of the analysis earlier offered by libertarian comrades. The fellagha populace of the Mitidja, workers from Belcourt or Bab-el-Oued still worshipped Allah and found themselves under new masters. The only change was that they and the masters were now citizens of a now Algerian Algeria.

Translated from French by Paul Sharkey

MARTHA NASIBÚ
from *Memories of an Ethiopian Princess*

It sometimes seemed that Fascist officials decided our fate, using us like pawns on a chessboard. After a long period of calm, two *carabinieri* knocked at our door and informed us that we had to leave Naples. They would come and take us away the next day. Evidently, our travails hadn't ended. At daybreak one day in May 1938, the eleven of us hastily boarded a ship that was going to the island of Rhodes, in the Aegean Sea. Mother entrusted our kind neighbours to inform the schools of our absence *sine die*.

When we got to the island we were sent to a villa with a sprawling garden. The kids were quick to notice a wonderful swing hooked to the highest branch of a soaring walnut tree. It was our consolation, and the fulcrum of our games. The first thing we did was divide parts of the tree between us. Fassil, the only one who could venture up to the topmost branches, took over that section. Those of us who were smaller acquired the more modest lower branches. Upon awakening each morning, we made our way to the gigantic tree and climbed exultant on our own branch and began daydreaming.

So many adventures took place on that venerable tree! We used the swing to see who could launch themselves the highest into the air and who, from that height, could jump the farthest onto the ground. There were so many thrills, and so much laughter that leavened our days! At any rate, nature, as the saying goes, is generous with those who live peacefully with her. The tree rewarded us for lavishing it with attention and distracting it from its loneliness by bearing fruit in abundance. We made huge feasts out of its exquisite walnuts. But Mother was the bulwark that put our hearts at ease. Her inner strength flowed from the faith she had in a divine plan, which was always the fount of her inspiration. Atzede continued believing that the impossible could become real with God's help.

Mother, who tirelessly advocated for the usefulness of our studies despite the constant movements that rudely interrupted them, enrolled us in new schools wherever we went. This time, however, in Rhodes, she didn't find religious schools willing to take us in, and so we had to remain at home. "God will provide, don't be afraid." She comforted us and never stopped hoping for better days, when we would finally be able to live normal lives. The military surveillance was very discreet in Rhodes. Wherever we went, we never saw them. "Look! They're hiding in the bushes!" Fassil shouted to get under our skin when we least expected it. Or, "Watch out for our shadows behind those plants!", and so on. It was torture. Always the prankster, he never hesitated to joke to make us laugh. But when Mother happened to hear him being a smart-aleck, she always cautioned him. "Careful, Fassil, these people don't play around!"

We could roam around Rhodes feeling something quite like freedom. I have a wonderful recollection of the island, bright and bursting with greenery, where the intense blue of the sea and the white houses mirroring one another created a suggestive contrast, and the streets were paved with natural-coloured mosaics — ochre, burnt sienna, evergreen, grey, black and white — that left magnificent arabesques on the pavement. The islanders were obliging and jocular. Guided by friends from the area, we could admire art and architecture and visit the *botteghe* of consummate goldsmiths who fashioned ornate, filigreed objects, mostly Maltese crosses, the symbol of the Knights Hospitaller. Our coerced stay, however, lasted only three months. On October 2nd, 1938 we were yet again put on a steamer that brought us back to Naples, where we stayed until July 1939.

It was as if the Fascists were trying to hide us from encroaching spirits. It's impossible to give a sensible explanation for such paranoid frenzy. We had become cumbersome merchandise and could no longer make sense of our movements. In Italy, however, word was going around that Mussolini no longer wanted "these Abyssinian negroes" in Italian territory. Whether or not that was true, on 19th July 1939 we were once more cast out to sea and making our way to Tripoli. The more I think of it, calendars no longer had any use in our nomadic lives. Only the shifts in climate told us that spring or winter had arrived. We changed schools, teachers, and friends with each move from one country to another, and this went on for who knows how long. We attended a school just in time to learn some geography, the formation of clouds and their names: cumulus, cirrus, cumulonimbus, cirrus stratus, etc... Or the history of Rome: Romulus and Remus, the she-wolf, Numa Pompilius and the other kings. Just when we smiled at one of our classmates, in the hope of finally finding a little friend, we were forced to embark towards a new destination.

Translated from Italian by Aaron Robertson

ELENA SHVARTS
Why, Let the Stricken Deer Go Weep

QUEEN: *If it be, why seems it so particular with thee?*
HAMLET: *'Seems', madam – nay, it is, I know not 'seems'.*

I.

In February 1942 the Leningrad Theatre Institute, or at least, what was left of it, was evacuated from besieged Leningrad to Pyatigorsk, together with the Philharmonic and Radlov's Theatre Company. They had barely settled or begun recovering a little from their starvation, when the Germans began a sudden and unexpected offensive in the Caucasus and reached Pyatigorsk with unimaginable speed. The soldiers and the town's administration all fled south to Tbilisi. Almost everyone in the Theatre Institute set off in their wake, the students walking, some hitching lifts on the last military lorries going in that direction. Initially my mother and her friend had the luck to be offered a ride, but then the soldiers began harassing them, and finally, angered by their aloofness, they threw them back out onto the road. Not everyone left. One Jewish girl wouldn't believe that the Germans were annihilating the Jews. "They are a cultured nation," she insisted. Another girl, a friend of the first, said nothing, and stayed on too. When the Germans arrived, a Russian family looked after the Jewish girl. One day she went to the market and met her old friend there. The friend was keen to find out where she was living, and when she returned home, a German firing squad was waiting for her. The family who had sheltered her had already been shot. In the few hours between the arrival of the Germans and the departure of the town's administration, Radlov and his theatre company had a meeting to decide whether to stay or to leave. Many of them decided to remain in the town, however Boris Smirnov, the handsome young lead, refused to stay and, together with his wife, who was still breastfeeding their child, fled by foot on the road through the Caucasus.

Radlov's Theatre subsequently toured its production of *Hamlet* all around Germany, with Nikolai Kriukov in the role of Prince Hamlet. There were rumours that Hitler had seen the production. It seems likely that for Radlov the hidden meaning of the performance was that it was about "life in thrall to a villain". But was it worth exchanging one villain for another? In the end Radlov's Theatre met a tragic fate. The French handed them over to the Soviet Union and the Radlovs themselves were arrested in the airport upon arrival, although the actors were spared for some unknown reason. But that is another story altogether. I am writing here about *Hamlet*, which was performed in a translation by Anna Radlova, the wife of Sergei Radlov and a famous poet in her own right who later died in a camp. Kriukov was also imprisoned, and after his release became a film actor — I remember him in the film *The Last Inch*. You could just about work out what sort of Hamlet he might have made: a rather cold, rational Hamlet. (How many faces Hamlet has — is there no end to the different ways of being Hamlet? Every generation sees him anew, every generation sees in him the true man of the age. He's sometimes played as an old man, or a freak, or then again "one of the boys" — and he's been played by women, and six people all at once, just like the many-headed Hydra...) My mother, Dina Shvarts, saw Radlov's *Hamlet* twenty-five times whilst she was still at school. She always said that Radlova's translation was the best of all of them, at least in theatrical terms. But what would you expect — after all, Radlova was translating it for her own theatre, her own director. Everything in it is easy to say, workable, theatrical, even if Pasternak's translation is more profound and poetically brilliant.

II.

After my mother died I began reading *Hamlet* feverishly, in all its different translations, picking it up in various different places — end, beginning, middle. I was drawn to it, as a sick animal is drawn to the herb that will cure it. For a long time I couldn't work out where this obsession came from, I merely drank it down, like the dark, bitter drug it was. Then I realised something apparently quite obvious about the tragedy, something which has until now gone unnoticed, and it is this: *Hamlet* is about being orphaned, about being completely orphaned. At the very beginning we learn about the murder of two fathers. Most of the characters (all of the main characters!) are the children of murdered parents: Hamlet, Ophelia, Laertes and Fortinbras. Hamlet Senior kills Fortinbras Junior, and Hamlet Junior kills his potential father-in-law. Shakespeare circles around the slaying of fathers with extraordinary relentlessness, as if compelled to do so. Perhaps the Shakespeare authorship problem might be solved by addressing this compulsion. The author of *Hamlet* was not of course Shakespeare, the son of a butcher, who came to theatre accidentally, watching over the horses left in the theatre courtyard, and not, of course a group of aristocrats, as Yury Liubimov recently proclaimed. Marlowe? Rutland? The feelings associated with the death of a parent are so strong in this play I think the author is someone who lost a father in about 1600…

And for all of them, apart from Fortinbras, the death of a parent leads to their own death. If the play is all about coming to terms with the death of a loved one, then no one manages it — Ophelia goes mad (and certainly not out of love for Hamlet), Laertes lets himself be killed, and Hamlet too, both apparently moved by the idea of revenge. But is it really revenge that guides them? "The time is out of joint" (is translated beautifully but approximately by Pasternak as "the thread that strings the days is torn"; Radlova's version cleaves much closer to the text — "the age is dislocated"). This is exactly the feeling you have when you lose a much-loved parent, the one who carried in themselves the conceiving of your own time. Since my mother died the days have dragged like years, or flown past like moments, and what happened yesterday is buried in the memory, in the sands and lost corners of shadowy death. This loss is inevitable for almost all of us, and this orphan of a play is about all of us. The meaning of this rather lightly worn piece of prose is that *Hamlet* is a play about orphans, a play about the orphans lost in the world, who have nothing to revenge themselves upon, except perhaps death itself. In no other play by Shakespeare is there such a circling of thought around a single axis — death: the mysteries of death, its meaning and meaninglessness, Yorick, poor Yorick and the gravediggers, and the leaping into the grave. And it moves all the characters like a puppeteer — there it is, not love, nor ambition, but pitiless, incomprehensible death.

Translated from Russian by Sasha Dugdale

ELIAS KHOURY
from *My Name Is Adam*

When I saw Claude Lanzmann's movie "Shoah", I was struck
dumb. It was in 1991, at the house of an American Jewish doctor
called Sam Horovitz who had decided to return to the Promised
Land and had taken up residence in Ramat Aviv. The guy was a
model of courtesy and good nature. He called me up to discuss an
article of mine about Umm Kulsoum's song *"Ahl al-Hawa"* that had
been published in *Kol Ha'ir*. Sam and his wife Kate were lovers of
Arabic music and regularly attended video-screenings of Egyptian
movies. He called me and we met more than once. He declared
his admiration for my articles, with their openness towards Arab
culture, and said he'd never met another Jew so open to the culture
of the region.

He asked me to explain oriental musical modes and the concept of the quarter-tone, and I was astonished by his love of Arabic
culture. He said he'd read *Diary of a Country Prosecutor* by the
Egyptian writer Tawfiq al-Hakim, translated into English by Aba
Eban (sometime Israeli minister of foreign affairs), and had fallen
under the spell of that writer, who had managed to present the
social issues of the poverty-stricken Egyptian countryside in the
form of a detective novel. He had daring ideas on the necessity of
Israel's integration into the Arab region and showed sympathy for
the cause of the Palestinian refugees living in wretched camps.
Once, after a long discussion over coffee, I told him I wanted to
ask him a question but was hesitant to do so and afraid of upsetting him.

I asked him why he had gone there. "You love Arabic culture but Israel is a project with a Western bent that despises the

culture of the country's original inhabitants, so why did you come here?"

He answered me that he'd come because of Claude Lanzmann and spoke at length about the genius of that great leftist man of culture, friend of Jean-Paul Sartre and Simone de Beauvoir. He said Lanzmann's movie "Shoah" had changed his life and was one of the reasons for his adoption of his Jewish identity and his decision to return to the Promised Land.

"Lanzmann was the portal to my identity. Umm Kulsoum, though, is the magic of the East that captivated my heart when I came here.

"Have you seen the movie?" he asked me.

"No. I've heard of it, but the hype here in Israel made me reluctant to go and see it. I don't like blockbusters."

"This time, you're wrong," he said, and he invited me to his house, where I spent six hours transfixed in front of the small screen witnessing savagery in its most extreme manifestations.

"I'm bowled over," I told Sam.

A movie unlike any other, stories unlike any others, and one tragedy giving birth to itself inside another.

Despite Lanzmann's Zionism, his peacock-like personality, and his later movie "Tsahal", in which he glorifies the Israeli army with a blind partiality informed by a loathsomely romantic attitude towards an armed force that hides its amorality under claims of morality, my admiration for "Shoah" has never gone away. I regard it as a humane work in which the content is greater than the form, and one that succeeds in telling what cannot be told.

Nevertheless, I feel perplexed when faced by fate's coincidences and try to find an explanation for them, which I cannot. The coincidence of my meeting with Murad is understandable and logical: falafel, hummus and nostalgia led the seventy-year-old to the Palm Tree restaurant. But what possessed Claude Lanzmann to bring a group of Holocaust survivors and men who'd worked in the *Sonderkommando* teams to the Ben Shemen colony, just outside Lydda, to tell of their suffering when burning victims, victims who were of their own people? We may be sure that Lanzmann was unaware of the existence of a Palestinian ghetto in Lydda. Even if echoes of the great expulsion of 1948 ever reached him, it's certain that, if he'd had to choose between it and the stories of the Nazi Holocaust that he decided to tell in his movie, he would have granted that marginal event no consideration. All that is understandable — or, let us say, something that I try to understand, having drunk that experience to its dregs, and adopted the identity; indeed, at one stage of my life I believed I was Jewish, the son of a survivor of the Warsaw Ghetto. However, my recall of scenes from that coincidental event fifteen years before my encounter with Murad al-Alami, who witnessed the transformation of the Palestinian youth of the ghetto into a new form of *Sonderkommando*, shook me to the core.

Why did Claude Lanzmann bring the Jewish men of the *Sonderkommando* to Lydda?

And would the Franco-Jewish writer and movie-maker have been able to imagine a possible encounter between those poor men and Murad and his comrades, who carried out the burning of the corpses of the people of Lydda in obedience to the orders of the men of Tsahal?

I have no idea, but what makes me angry is that no one confronted the French director with this truth, which was known to all the youth of the Lydda ghetto. Maybe the tragedy has to remain enveloped in silence, because any discussion of its details would disfigure the nobility of that silence.

Murad was right to be silent.

Murad's silence resembles that of Waddah al-Yaman. Now I understand why Murad severed all ties with me and why Waddah al-Yaman rejected my attempt to identify with his story.

It's the story of the sheep that was driven to slaughter and never opened its mouth.

That is the story of the children of the ghetto.

I don't want to draw a comparison between the Holocaust and the Nakba. I hate such comparisons and I believe the numbers game is vulgar and nauseating. I have nothing but contempt for Roger Garaudy and others who deny the Nazi Holocaust. Garaudy, who walked the tightrope of ideology from Marxism to Christianity to Islam and who ended up a mercenary at the doorsteps of the Arab oil sheikhdoms, committed the crime of playing with numbers, reducing that of the Jews who died at the hands of the Nazis from six million to three million. No, Monsieur Garaudy, in the Holocaust everybody died, for whoever kills one innocent person is like him who kills all humankind. As it says in the Mighty Book, *Whosoever slays a soul not to retaliate for a soul slain, nor for corruption done in the land, shall be as if he had slain humankind altogether.*

That said, what is the meaning of the chance encounter of these two incidents? Did they meet so that the banality of evil, the naïvety of humankind and the insanity of history could be laid bare?

Or does their encounter point to the apotheosis of the Jewish issue at the hands of the Zionist movement, which transformed the Jews from victims into executioners, destroyed the philosophy of existential Jewish exile and, indeed, turned that exile into a property of its Palestinian victims?

I swear I have no idea! But I do know that I am sorrowful

unto death, as Jesus the Nazarene said when he beheld the fate of humankind in a vision.

Translated from Arabic by Humphrey Davies

ASHUR ETWEBI

A Dog Hides Its Tail in the Darkness of Night

In my village, Etwebia, in the last drop of wine in the glass
I see the tree I planted in front of the guest room

I see its yellow flowers blossom in winter
where I used to sit with the red-chested bird
I drink my glass cold, the way I like it
and he takes peanuts from my hat the way he likes

Oh, my tree, my winter tree!
Oh, my Etwebia, captured by militias

I used to enjoy the pouring rain
I used to hear it falling through thirsty sand

Now, in a country ravaged by death, rain loses its sound
Drops tangle in blue, fall, fall, fall silent

A dog hides its tail in the darkness of night
The water rises high. The olive tree listens in

Translated from Arabic by Ashur Etwebi and James Byrne

MOHSEN EMADI

from *The Poem*

VII.

In my language
every time everybody suddenly falls silent,
a policeman is born.
In my language
on the back of each frightened bicycle,
three thousand dead words are sitting.
In my language,
in murmurs, they make confessions,
in whispers, they wear black,
in silence,
they get buried.
My language is silence.
Who will translate my silence?
How can I cross this border?

Translated from Persian by Lyn Coffin

COSMOPOLITANISM AND
ROOTLESSNESS

T HE CHILEAN POET AND diplomat Gabriela Mistral (1889–
1957) was the first Latin American to receive the Nobel
Prize in Literature (1945), aside from being only the fifth woman,
and second non-European after Rabindranath Tagore, and while
Mistral isn't as widely read today as when she was alive, her work
has consistently attracted passionate readers and gifted translators,
not least of whom Langston Hughes and Ursula K. Le Guin. One
of Mistral's most commented-on poems is "La extranjera" ("The
Foreign Woman"), which some critics claimed prophesied Mistral's
death far away from her native home.

As the translator Stephen Kessler has noted: "The murder of
Federico García Lorca (1898–1936) and the scattering of others
into exile or into the mountains to defend the Republic against
Francisco Franco's fascist invaders was a cultural cataclysm to

match the political and military catastrophe of the next three years — a catastrophe that turned into the protracted nightmare of a four-decades-long dictatorship. In 1938, when things were looking especially bleak in Spain, Luis Cernuda (1902–63) accepted an invitation to lecture in London and simply never returned. He taught there and in Glasgow, Scotland, until 1947, when he took a position at Mount Holyoke, a women's college in Massachusetts, where he wouldn't even have the invigorating experience of lusting after his students. Openly homosexual in his life and his writing, Cernuda chronicled his misery during these years of exile in the north even as he continued to create some of his best poems and to establish himself as one of his generation's most astute and respected critics."

Arguably one of the most famous of the Spanish Generation of '27 poets, Cernuda's "Impression of Exile", most likely written either in 1939 or 1940, finds the poet mingling with a crowd in the "salon of the old Temple, in London" and suddenly overhearing, "From someone's lips", "Heavy as a falling teardrop", the single word "Spain", which carries with it all the emotional burdens of the Republic's downfall and the permanent loss of his motherland, given that Cernuda would perish in exile twelve years before the death of Francisco Franco.

Another poet fated to die in exile before witnessing the demise of the dictatorship that exiled them in the first place was the Díli-born author Fernando Sylvan (1917–93), a Timorese poet who died in Portugal a mere six years before Indonesia ended its military occupation of East Timor (1975–99). Despite living in the womb of the colonial power that dominated his homeland for close to three centuries, Sylvan devoted his creative energies to the resurrection of an independent artistic consciousness among the Timorese, and as one of his translators, David Shook, has pointed out, the distance from his homeland did not diminish his appeal, given that his work was "clandestinely distributed through occupied East Timor in facsimile editions".

After marrying a woman of Vietnamese descent, which was then illegal in his native country, in 1975 the South African painter, poet and activist Breyten Breytenbach (1939–) snuck back to South Africa on behalf of Okhela, the anti-apartheid organization he had helped establish, in order to secure funds for pro-African National Congress activities and establish a network of contacts. Ironically, it was members of the ANC who eventually gave him up to the South African government, which, he later discovered, had been kept abreast of his every step from the outset of his clandestine return. Convicted in late 1975, Breytenbach served two years in solitary confinement in the maximum-security section of Pretoria's prison, incarcerated in a six-by-five cell. In his groundbreaking collection of essays, *Notes from the Middle World* (2009), part of Breytenbach's "Middle World Quartet", the South African poet and painter sketches out his definition of what he has called the Middle World, essentially an elusive transnational cultural space that lies beyond one's origins and even one's exile from one's origins. As Breytenbach writes: "To be of the Middle World is to have broken away from the parochial, to have left 'home' for good (or for worse) whilst carrying all of it with you and to have arrived on foreign shores (at the outset you thought of it as 'destination', but not for long) feeling at ease there without ever being 'at home'." Is this just exile, he asks?

> Maybe. But exile is a memory disease expressing itself in spastic social behaviour: people find it a mysterious ailment and pity you greatly [...] Exile could be a passage and you may well speak of "passage people". Yet, the

Middle World is finality beyond exile. For a while at least the reference pole will remain the land from which you had wrenched yourself free or from where you were expelled. Then, exile itself will become the habitat. And in due time, when there's nothing to go back to or you've lost interest, MOR[9] will take shape and you may start inhabiting the in-between. The terrain is rugged, the stage bathed in a dusty grey light. It is not an easy perch.

Writers like the Pakistani-born Aamer Hussein (1955–) appear to exist very comfortably in Breytenbach's Middle World, as is evidenced by "Nine Postcards from Sanlucar de Barrameda", the first story in Hussein's short-story collection *Insomnia* (2007), which was written in the wake of the 7/7 terrorist bombings in the UK in 2005, and which explores the rising tide of Islamophobia in Britain and elsewhere. It features a Venezuelan complaining of how "Muslims in Europe are a demographic problem", to which the narrator replies: "I guess I'm a Muslim in Europe too [...] And foreign wherever I go."

---

9   Breytenbach's acronym for 'Middle World.'

GABRIELA MISTRAL
The Foreign Woman

"She speaks with an accent of her savage seas,
with who knows what algae and who knows what sands;
she recites prayer to God without baggage or burden,
aged as if she were dying.
In the vegetable garden that made us foreign,
she has placed cactus and unfurled herbs.
She glows with the desert's heavy breath,
and she has loved with a passion that bleaches her,
that she never talks about and that if she told us
would be like mapping some other star.
She will live among us for eighty years,
but always as if she's just arrived,
speaking a language that gasps and moans,
understood just by little beasties.
And she's going to die in our midst,
some night she most suffers,
with only her fate for a pillow,
from a death both quiet and foreign."

Translated from Spanish by Alana Marie Levinson-LaBrosse and David Shook

NELLY SACHS
I'm searching for my Right to Roots

I'm searching for my Right to Roots
through this Geography of Countries at Night
where Arms opened to Love
hang crucified along the Lines of Latitude
fathomless in Expectation —

Translated from German by Martin Kratz

LUIS CERNUDA
Impression of Exile

It was last spring,
Nearly a year now,
In the salon of the old Temple, in London,
With its old furniture. The windows looked out,
Past old buildings, in the distance,
Between the lawns, on a grey zigzag of river.
Everything was grey and looked tired
Like the dull sheen of a sick pearl.

There were elderly gentlemen, old ladies
With dusty feathers in their hats;
A murmur of voices coming from the corners
Near tables with yellow tulips,
Family portraits and empty teapots.
The shadows falling
With a cat-like smell
Were stirring up sounds in kitchens.

A very quiet man was seated
Near me. I could see
The shadow of his long profile at times
Looking up absently from the rim of his cup,
With the same weariness
Of a corpse coming back
From the grave to some mundane gathering.

From someone's lips,
Over in a corner
Where clusters of old folks were talking,
Heavy as a falling teardrop,
Came one word: Spain.
An unspeakable fatigue
Circled my skull.
The lights came on. We left.

After descending long, dim flights of stairs
I found myself in the street,
And next to me, when I turned,
I saw that quiet man again,
Who said something I didn't quite get
In a foreign accent,
A child's accent in a voice grown old.

He followed me, walking
As if all alone beneath an invisible weight,
Hauling his own gravestone;
But then he stopped.
"Spain?" he said. "A name.
Spain is dead." The little street
Suddenly turned a corner.
I watched him vanish into the damp shadows.

Translated from Spanish by Stephen Kessler

FERNANDO SYLVAN
Invasion

They wanted to separate my heart from my island

But I had a green ribbon of palm leaf
On my head
And I crossed the riverbank where
My brothers the crocodiles lived
And because of the emblem of the green ribbon of palm
They didn't devour me
They remembered
That it was me
The prince
Who thousands of years ago saved
The first one of them all
From the fiery sand
And covered him in water

They wanted to separate my heart from my island

And men from far away searched for me
From Cupão to Lautém

And finally they saw me
Crossing the riverbank

And once I was on the other bank
they entered the waters

But no one separated my heart from my island . . .

They didn't have green ribbons of palm leaf
On their heads

Translated from Portuguese by David Shook

GISÈLE PRASSINOS
Nobody Is Going Anywhere

There is someone who is lost.
The world is so compact
the trees and the houses rise up for breath
in the blue there's high alert
the streets are dying muffled strangled.

We push on thinking we navigate
through flesh through sounds through encounters
but nobody is going anywhere.
The defeated core still chases after life.

Whoever is lost and who knows it
lets their arms dangle
they will sleep
eyes shuttered down upon
a bird no longer in the sky.

Translated from French by Jade Cuttle

ROQUE DALTON
Spite

Homeland you don't exist
you're just a bad outline of myself
words of the enemy I believed

Before I used to believe you were so small
you reached neither
north nor south
but now I know you don't exist
and it doesn't seem as though anybody needs you
I haven't heard any mothers speak of you

That makes me happy
because it proves I made up a country
although I might end up in an institution for it

Then I am a little god at your coast

(I mean: if I am an expatriate
you are an ex-country)

Translated from Spanish by Luis Gonzalez Serrano

BREYTEN BREYTENBACH
from *Notes from the Middle World*

To be of the Middle World is to have broken away from the parochial, to have left "home" for good (or for worse) whilst carrying
all of it with you and to have arrived on foreign shores (at the
outset you thought of it as "destination", but not for long) feeling
at ease there without ever being "at home". Sensing too, that one
has now fatally lost the place you may have wanted to run back
to. Have you also lost face, or is the "original face" now unveiled?
Exile? Maybe. But exile is a memory disease expressing itself in
spastic social behaviour: people find it a mysterious ailment and
pity you greatly. (J.M.G. Le Clézio has this evocative definition of
exile as "he or she who has left the island"; the exile, one assumes,
leaves the I-land of self to become water lapping at the continent
of we-ness, of belonging.)

Exile could be a passage and you may well speak of "passage
people". Yet, the Middle World is finality beyond exile. For a while
at least the reference pole will remain the land from which you
had wrenched yourself free or from where you were expelled.
Then, exile itself will become the habitat. And in due time, when
there's nothing to go back to or you've lost interest, MOR will take
shape and you may start inhabiting the in-between. The terrain
is rugged, the stage bathed in a dusty grey light. It is not an easy
perch. Wieseltier, in another of his barbed aphorisms, says: "In the
modern world, the cruellest thing you can do to people is to make
them ashamed of their complexity."

One location of the Middle World is where the turfs of the out-
cast, the outsider and the outlaw overlap. It could be a dominion
of outers. Is it all shame, therefore? Not on your life! Listen to this

poem written in the year 1080 by a Chinese world-traveller, Su Tung-p'o, a functionary who had carnal knowledge of prison and banishment:

> A hundred years, free to go, and it's almost spring;
> for the years left, pleasure will be my chief concern.
> Out the gate, I do a dance, wind blows my face;
> our galloping horses race along as magpies cheer.
> I face the wine cup and it's all a dream,
> pick up a poem brush, already inspired.
> Why try to fix the blame for troubles past?
> Years now I've stolen posts I never should have had.

(The translator, Burton Watson, adds that line 3, "I do a dance", may as well be interpreted as "I stop to piss".)

Now let me draw the line a little more clearly by proposing a very partial and partisan list of people I consider to be (or have been) of the Middle World; these well-known names make the night of the nameless ones even darker, of course.

I won't touch upon religion or science — the Dalai Lama is there by definition, and Einstein was surely an uncitizen of MOR — "*I am truly a 'lone traveller' and have never belonged to my country, my home, my friends, or even my immediate family, with my whole heart; in the face of all these ties, I have never lost a sense of distance and a need for solitude*"; nor music (Mozart was one and so was John Cage with his glass silences), or business (I suspect that Maxwell, the news mogul who became a whale, was also an uncitizen, and Soros may well be there as philosopher-pirate); nor politics (Mandela, for ever driven into self-presentation by prison, burnt clean of attachments, may just be of the Middle World, Trotsky who wore round glasses and a little pointed beard in order to remember his singular self touched the black walls of this night-land, and so ultimately did Gandhi, impaled on the flash-knife of not "belonging" sufficiently).

You will take me to task for my choices, which depend more on feeling than verifiable assessment, but my sketchy picture includes: Kundera — for a while before he became French; Nureyev; Vidiadhar Surajprasad Naipaul — adrift whilst denying it; Rushdie — neither East nor West but enjoying the party immensely; Bruce Chatwin, exploring the nomadic roads all leading to death; Homi Bhabha — *"we now locate the question of culture in the realm of the beyond"*; Ieoh Ming Pei, the international architect, and so was Gaudí; Juan Goytisolo; "Saint" John of the Cross and his girlfriend, Teresa of Ávila; Yeats and Pound and Auden, but not Eliot; Erich von Stroheim, but somehow neither Dietrich nor Chaplin; Edward Said — very intermittently so; Bei Dao, the Chinese exile poet, is in the process of getting his uncitizen papers; Brecht, from the time after he returned to East Germany; Adorno, who relished it, particularly in his late style; Borges — very nearly, tapping his white cane against the gates; Freud — unwittingly, which is not so strange because he fancied himself a scientist when he was in fact but an interesting writer — and probably also Jung; Samuel Beckett, who visualized the workrooms of Middle Worldliness on stage; Pessoa, populating his head with alienated explorers of the self, that slippery slope to damnation; Vladimir Nabokov, although he tried his best to dissimulate it; Joseph Conrad of the dark heart; J.M.G. Le Clézio; Henri Michaux — *"hell is the rhythm of the other"*; Rimbaud — both as poet and trader; Victor Segalen; the toothless Artaud and the mutilated Van Gogh, and Cioran, who considered it a shame to have been born, and Max Ernst and Man Ray and Mayakovsky with the hole in the head, and the mild revolutionary Aimé Césaire and Lautréamont (Isidore Ducasse), and Django Reinhardt, and Primo Levi fatally drawn to the downward spiral of the dark stairwell, and Jimi Hendrix and Tristan Tzara; Leonardo da Vinci, painting backwards to the unknowable I as if to light; Faulkner going down into the thickets of language; Henry Miller, in painful lust, and his buddy, Larry Durrell; Han Shan the Cold Mountain poet and Gary Snyder his disciple; the al-Andalus explorers and historians; Elias Canetti; Mahmoud Darwish — *"Where should we go after the last frontiers? Where should the birds fly after the last sky?"*; Frantz Fanon and Franz Kafka; Brodsky and Walcott, angrily; Bessy Head and Amos Tutuola in their worlds of spirits; Cervantes of the Missing Hand and Goya with the Screaming Mind; Morandi and Giacometti; Carlos Fuentes but not Octavio Paz and certainly not Vargas Llosa; Frida Kahlo but not Diego Rivera; the Zapatistas of Chiapas but not the Shining Path guerrillas; Pasolini but not Fellini; Ryszard Kapuściński; Robert Walser — *"how fortunate I am not to be able to see in myself anything worth respecting and watching"*; Albert Camus; Alexandra David-Neel; William Burroughs, maybe Jack Kerouac, but, I imagine, somehow not Allen Ginsberg; the Chinese wandering monks/artists/poets/exiles; Gauguin, maybe Degas, probably Bacon with the raw meat of his thinking, and Matisse, but neither Picasso nor Cézanne nor Velázquez; Billie Holiday, but not Ella Fitzgerald; Hannah Arendt — *"I am more than ever of the opinion that a decent human existence is possible today only on the fringes of society, where one then runs the risk of starving or being stoned to death. In these circumstances a sense of humour is of great help."* And so many more down the ages...

Was Nietzsche of the detribalized tribe? Or was he more German than mad? And of his acolytes I'd include only Foucault, who had the baldness and the loud taste in attire so typically uncitizen, and perhaps Deleuze, for he did sport extraordinarily long fingernails — although he gradually glad-mouthed himself back to the closed-in compulsiveness of self-indulgent French rhetoric before throwing his body like a stinking dog carcass out the window; the others (Barthes, Derrida, Kristeva) remain too rooted in a Jacobin arrogance where doubt is a cover for self-accretion, they suffer from the blindness of brilliance and besides, the text of itself (and for itself) being skein stretching over rotting body, cannot be the Middle World.

Is one always of the Middle World? It may happen, as in the case of Beckett who walked in order to fall down, and Paul Celan who never escaped, not even when he became a bloated dead goose bobbing on the oily blackness of the Seine. But one may also grow out of it. One is not normally born there, and your children cannot inherit uncitizenship.

How does one draw the map of MOR? Wherever its uncitizens are, there the Middle World is. I don't have a complete topography because cities and countries may change their colouring on the map and the forces of conformism are voracious. Once more, I'll not argue the nuances. It should be pointed out that Middle Worlders paradoxically have a sharpened awareness of place (*topoï*, *locus*) — as with nomads, the environment may be constantly changing and one does not possess it, but it is always a potentially dangerous framework with which you must interact — and therefore they will know cloud and well and star and fire better than sedentary citizens do.

Alexandria was Middle World territory (by the way, the Middle World has nothing to do with modernity) and so was Beirut once upon a time; Sarajevo belonged before the pigs slaughtered it to "purity"; Hong Kong was an outpost (the poet P.K. Leung wrote, in an admirable volume called *City at the End of Time*: "*Ironically, Hong Kong as a colony provides an alternative space for Chinese people and culture to exist, a hybrid for one to reflect upon the problems of a 'pure' and 'original' state"*); Paris used to be a section of MOR when it still had a proletariat, many of whom were of foreign origin, living within the walls (by the way, the Middle World has nothing to do with riches or urban sophistication); Cuba may be of the Middle World despite its best efforts at being communist; Berlin, still, although it is now becoming "normalized" as the pan-Germanic capital; Jerusalem, even though its present rulers try to stamp it with the seal of fanatic exclusivity; South Africa went through the birth pains, it was close to understanding a cardinal Middle World law — that you can only survive and move forward by continuing to invent yourself — but then it became a majority-led and majority-smothered democracy instead; New York, except when it is too close to America; I have heard tales of tolerance and centre-insouciance from a town once known as Mogador, now Essaouira; Tangier, where I celebrated my twenty-first birthday (bird-day) wrapped in a burnoose, was a refuge despite the closed warren of its Casbah; Timbuktu — how could I forget that sand-whispering place, and the other holy sites of books that could only be reached on the swaying backs of camels — Chinguetti, Ouadane, Ti-chit and Oualâta; Gorée, Sal, Lamu, Zanzibar, Haiti and the other Caribbean islands — most islands tend to be natural outcrops of MOR; Palestine most certainly — "exodus" can be a high road to the Middle World, and what is now termed the Territories (a euphemism for ghettos and Bantustans, subject to Apartheid) will breed a new generation of uncitizens.

MIMI KHALVATI
The Soul Travels on Horseback

and the road is beset with obstacles and thorns.
But let it take its time for I have hours and hours to wait

here, snowbound in Lisbon, glad of this sunlit café
outside Departures, for an evening flight to Heathrow.

Being my soul's steed, I should like to know its name
and breed — a Marwari of India, Barb of North Africa,

the Akhal-Teke of Western Asia or a Turkoman,
now extinct? Is it the burnt chestnut colour of the ant,

grey as a Bedouin wind, the four winds that made it?
O Drinker of the Wind, I travel by air, sea, land

and wherever I am, there you are behind my back
pounding the cloud streets, trailing banners of cirrus

or as Platero once did, from fear or chill, hoofing a stream,
breaking the moon into a swarm of clear, crystal roses.

No, no matter your thirst, ride swiftly, mare, stallion,
mother, father, for without you I feel for ever homesick.

MICHAEL SCHMIDT
The Freeze

We can't sleep tonight. The ice has formed —
from thin skin at evening
to deep stone. With midnight
the boat's aground in it.
Planks shriek against the hardening.

Below deck a film of frost pales everything.
Our breath makes beads of ice. We pace
between the hatch and bunks.
The world would end by ice
tonight, for sure, if we lay down.

Come outside: the wind has sculpted
sails to marble drapery;
on the line our laundry freezes to
a rigor mortis of our bodies' clothes.
Night will hardly darken all this glass —

the stars are treble on its rippled plane.
Birds stiffen on the surface,
bellies up, like fish.
We started from a tropic on whose shore
the lizards' tongues were flames of malachite

in leaves that trailed on to the tide,
and crimson fish were couriers there
to caverns where eels uncoiled their sting.

Night plankton burned our wake —
for years we have been heading north.

When lips are tucked away for good
and rigid as ice-starched shirt and trousers
we pass the climax of our slow miasma,
and the river hardens in the arteries
till the heart with the hull surrenders

to stillness and is broken like a stone,
when our histories are minuted, adjourned,
our faces upturned to a Sabbath star,
this will be the scene if we can see,
the fish arrested with the drifting tyres,

the dry snow driven into dunes of ash.
It was not like this in the other place —
there all was fire and water,
nothing stilled the waves
that might be furious though they never died

to the intolerable vacancy
we pace to keep the blood awake. Come down.
We'll light the burner, thaw our fingers out.
We are the ashes that will cover us,
our inch of life, our mile, our field of breathing.

AAMER HUSSEIN

from *Nine Postcards from Sanlucar de Barrameda*

6.

Later, on the beach. Pavese called the sea a field. Tonight it is, a silver field.

The sky reddens, darkens, scatters stars.

"We're at the mouth of the Guadalquivir," my neighbour says. "The Arabs called it something like wad-el-kabir."

"Andalusian hospitality, too, is Arab," someone says.

But this is not the sea. The yellow strand is not a beach. I'll stick to my terms.

Sea or river, the line of water remains a silver field.

7.

We eat water-creatures: anchovies and anemones, cockles, langoustines and bream. My neighbour speaks to me of ragged love and separation. My mind and tongue unlock their Spanish. We are, at fifty, childless. My companion, eleven years younger, has a son.

"You should have a child, the two of you," my neighbour says.

"Ah, I tell her, but we're not lovers."

"We're best friends," my companion adds.

"Do you still feel Pakistani?" The Venezuelan to my left asks me.

"I do, when I feel anything at all."

The Venezuelan drones on.

"Muslims in Europe are a demographic problem. In Andalusia,

I hear, they want to reclaim ancient sacred places. They should be loyal to their country of adoption. Wouldn't you say?"

"I guess I'm a Muslim in Europe too," I say. "And foreign everywhere I go."

With one desultory gesture I dismiss an uncongenial conversation.

"I'm tired of romance," I overhear my companion saying.

"But without love life's an uphill climb," my sister muses.

Now, as I drink manzanilla, I see you in my glass. Perhaps I haven't thought of you as yet, left you behind with other things in London. Finger dipped in ink of manzanilla, I bring you into being from your place of absence, think of writing you into this narrative. (Like me, I remember, you can't swim.) Why do we see yesterday as shadow, tell me, call memory a haunting? Echoed crooked smiles, linked fingers, can thrill, become a sudden presence. Should I write: sometimes I think of you and wonder if you really happened, on occasion wish you were here to taste the green figs and the summer wine — or remind you of an evening's words that spiralled from life's work into euphoria, an empty bottle's cork I kept at dawn, some other things you left behind?

FRED D'AGUIAR
At the Grave of the Unknown African

This poem, dedicated to the Guyanese poet Martin Carter, was inspired by a visit to Henbury Parish Church, near Bristol, where the gravestone of an eighteenth-century servant includes couplets in praise of his unflagging devotion but fails to give his name.

I.
Two round, cocoa faces, carved on whitewashed headstone,
protect your grave against hellfire and brimstone.

Those cherubs with puffed cheeks, as if chewing gum,
signal how you got here and where you came from.

More than two and a half centuries after your death,
the barefaced fact that you're unnamed feels like defeat.

I got here via White Ladies' Road and Black Boy's Hill,
clues lost in these lopsided stones that Henbury's vandal

helps to the ground and Henbury's conservationist
tries to rectify, cleaning the vandal's pissy love-nest.

African slave without a name, I'd call this home
by now. Would you? Your unknown soldier's tomb

stands for shipload after shipload that docked,
unloaded, watered, scrubbed, exercised and restocked

thousands more souls for sale in Bristol's port.
Cab-drivers speak of it all with yesterday's hurt.

The good conservationist calls it her 300-year war;
those raids, deals, deceits and capture (a sore still raw).

St Paul's, Toxteth, Brixton, Tiger Bay and Handsworth:
petrol bombs flower in the middle of roads, a sudden growth

at the feet of police lines longer than any cricket pitch.
African slave, your namelessness is the wick and petrol mix.

Each generation catches the one fever love can't appease,
nor molotov cocktails, nor when they embrace in a peace

far from that three-named, two-bit vandal and conservationist
binning beer cans, condoms and headstones in big puzzle-pieces.

II.
Stop there black Englishman before you tell a bigger lie.
You mean me well by what you say but I can't stand idly by.

The vandal who keeps coming and does what he calls fucks
on the cool gravestones also pillages and wrecks.

If he knew not so much my name but what happened to Africans,
he'd maybe put in an hour or two collecting his Heinekens;

like the good old conservationist, who's earned her column
inch, who you knock, who I love without knowing her name.

The dead can't write, nor can we sing (nor can most living).
Our ears (if you can call them ears) make no good listening.

Say what happened to me and countless like me, all anon.
Say it urgently. Mean times may bring back the water cannon.

I died young, but to age as a slave would have been worse.
What can you call me? Mohammed. Homer. Hannibal. Jesus.

Would it be too much to have them all? What are couples up to
when one reclines on the stones and is ridden by the other?

Will our talk excite the vandal? He woz ere, like you are now,
armed with a knife. I could see trouble on his creased brow,

love trouble, not for some girl but for this village.
I share his love and would have let him spoil my image,

if it wasn't for his blade in the shadow of the church wall
taking me back to my capture and long sail to Bristol,

then my sale on Black Boy's Hill and disease ending my days:
I sent a rumble up to his sole; he scooted, shocked and dazed.

Here the sentence is the wait and the weight is the sentence.
I've had enough of a parish where the congregation can't sing.

Take me where the hymns sound like a fountain-washed canary, *and the beer-swilling, condom-wielding vandal of Henbury*

reclines on the stones and the conservationist mounts him,
and in my crumbly ears there's only the sound of them sinning.

FARHAD PIRBAL
Waste

I was born in Hewlêr, I got to know Lenin in Baghdad, I began feeling my statelessness in Tehran, my Kurdishness in Damascus, I opened my eyes in Spáňov, I got my passport in Aalborg, in Copenhagen, I faced thoughts of suicide, in Stockholm, for the first time, I slept with a European woman, in Paris, I got my first foreign diploma, in Kraków, my ears were purified by the music of Chopin, in Santiago, with love, in Düsseldorf, with hatred...

Now I want, like the Austrian-Jewish businessmen of World War II, to go work for a while in Canada and then marry a Brazilian woman, then come back to Europe and publish a book in London, finally I will go to Amsterdam to kill myself: my corpse, like a rotting sack of potatoes, tossed into a dumpster, known to no one.

Translated from Kurdish by Alana Marie Levinson-LaBrosse

IMAN MERSAL
The Idea of Houses

I sold my earrings at the gold store to buy a silver ring in the market. I swapped that for old ink and a black notebook. This was before I forgot my pages on the seat of a train that was supposed to take me home. Whenever I arrived in a city, I felt my home was in a different one.

Olga says, without my having told her any of this, "Your home is never really home until you sell it. Then you discover all the things you could do with the garden and the big rooms — as if seeing it through the eyes of a broker. You've stored your nightmares in the attic and now you have to pack them in a suitcase or two at best." Olga goes silent then smiles suddenly, like a queen among her subjects, there in the kitchen between her coffee machine and a window with a view of flowers.

Olga's husband wasn't there to witness this regal episode. Maybe this is why he still thinks the house will be a loyal friend when he goes blind — a house whose foundations will hold him steady and whose stairs, out of mercy, will protect him from falls in the dark.

I'm looking for a key that always gets lost at the bottom of my handbag, where neither Olga nor her husband can see me, drilling myself in reality until I give up on the idea of houses.

Every time you go back home with the dirt of the world under your nails, you stuff everything you were able to carry with you into its closets. But you refuse to define home as the future of junk — a place where dead things were once confused with hope. Let home be that place where you never notice the bad lighting, let it be a wall whose cracks keep growing until one day you take them for doors.

Translated from Arabic by Robyn Creswell

SHOLEH WOLPÉ

The World Grows Blackthorn Walls

Tall, stiff and spiny.
Try to make it to the other side
and risk savage thorns.

We who left home in our teens,
children who crossed boundaries and were torn
by its thousand serrated tongues,

                who have we become?

We who bear scars that bloom and bloom
beneath healed skins,

              where are we going?

I ask myself
is home my ghost?

Does it wear my underwear
folded neatly in the antique chest
of drawers I bought twenty years ago?
Or nest inside my blouse that hangs
from a metal hanger I've been meaning to discard?
Is it lost between the lines of books
shelved alphabetically in a language
I was not born to? Or here on the lip
of this chipped cup left behind
by a lover long gone?

Why do they call us *alien,*
as if we come from other planets?

I carry seeds in my mouth, plant
turmeric, cardamom, and tiny
aromatic cucumbers in this garden,
water them with rain I wring
from my grandmother's songs.
They will grow, I know, against
these blackthorn walls. They are magic.
They can push through anything,

                                    uncut.

I left home at thirteen.
I hadn't lived enough to know how
not to love.
Home was the Caspian Sea, the busy bazaars,
the aroma of kebab and rice, Friday
lunches, picnics by mountain streams.
                    I never meant to stay away.

But they said come back
and you will die.

Exile is a suitcase full of meanings. I fill up
a hundred notebooks with scribbles.
And when I am done I throw them into fire
and begin to write again; this time
tattooing the words on my forehead.
This time, writing only not to forget.

Complacency is communicable
like the common cold.
I swim upstream to lay my purple eggs.

Spirits urge and spirits go,
but I write postcards only to the future.
What is a transplanted tree
but a *time being*
who has adapted to adoption?

They say draw sustenance from this land,
but look how my fruits hang in spirals
and smell of old notebooks and lace.

Perhaps it's only in exile that spirits arrive.
They weep and wail at the door of the temple
where I sit at the edge of an abyss.
But even this is an illusion.

KAVEH BASSIRI
99 Names of Exile

Adam & Eve	Exotic	Outcast
Afflicted	Expatriated	Outlaw
Afraid	Expelled	Outsider
Alien	Extraterrestrial	Overseas
Banished	Foreign	Pariah
Beggar	Forsaken	Queer
Castaway	Fugitive	Refugee
Colonist	Guilty	Resident Alien
Condemned	Heretic	Runaway
Crippled	Homeless	Scapegoat
Dangerous	Homesick	Squatter
Dark	Impure	Stateless
Deportee	Infectious	Stranger
Deserter	Inhuman	Street Arab
Detested	Insurgent	Terrorist
Different	Invisible	Traitor
Dirty	Ishmael	Trespasser
Disgraced	Jew	Unclean
Disinherited	Kashmiri	Uncorrectable
Dismissed	Lost	Undesirable
Disowned	Malefactor	Undomesticated
Displaced	Marooned	Unfit
Dispossessed	Mysterious	Unfortunate
Dyke	Nigger	Unidentified
Emigrant	Non-citizen	Uninvited
Ethnic	Non-conformist	Unknown
Evil	Other	Unnamed

300

Unrecognized	Unwanted	Wanderer
Unskilled	Unwilling	Witch
Unspeakable	Unworthy	Wrong
Unthinkable	Victim	X
Untouchable	Villain	Yellow
Unusual	Virus	Zero

FADY JOUDAH
He came, the humanitarian man

He came, the humanitarian man, and
In the solitude of giving, he befriended
A stray dog as mirror.

Every day after the long arduous hours
Of the humane, he would come home
To be consoled: the dog

Waiting inside the door,
Wagging and panting, in a rave.
He named him

Nothing foreign to the population
So as not to offend anyone.
He trained him

To sit on the cheap sofa
One finds in places of conscious exile.
And the dog got to know the front seat of the car,

His tongue licking the air, hair
Blowing, children cheering barefoot.
Then it was time

To make the dog part of his family
Of dogs back home, but the cruel
Government of the wretched refused:

There was no identity card.
And no mirror inside the mirror
Could console the dog, slumped by the door

In hunger strike until it died.
He came, the humanitarian man,
He came and loved, then he went.

JEE LEONG KOH
To a Young Poet

Quit the country soon as you can
before you're set on a career path or marrying
the home ownership scheme.
Pay no heed to the village elders.
They are secretly ashamed that they did not leave.

Quit the country but do not
shake the dust off your feet against it.
Leave instead with a secret smile
for all that leaving has to teach you.

Learn what it is to be welcomed
for the coin in your purse, for strong hips
in pushing a cart uphill, a firm voice in a good cause.
When the welcome wears off, as it will,
learn to leave again, this time by the sea.

Be always on your way, and on arrival
sleep with anyone who asks. You never know
what gift they may have for you in the morning.
You will discover, suddenly or over the course of a winter night,
what gift you have for them.
Always kiss goodbye on the lips.

There will be seasons of great loneliness.
You cannot outrun it, so sit and survey
the thunderless desert.

In every town, pick up the local accent
and blend it into yours, already impure,
as a secret ingredient is fused into the top note of a perfume.
Hearing you, the taberna will wonder where you are from.
Drink deep of their wonderment. Do not betray it.

JENNY XIE
Rootless

Between Hanoi and Sapa there are clean slabs of rice fields
and no two brick houses in a row.

I mean, no *three* —
See, counting's hard in half-sleep, and the rain pulls a sheet

over the sugar palms and their untroubled leaves.
Hours ago, I crossed a motorbike with a hog strapped to its seat,

the size of a date pit from a distance.
Can this solitude be rootless, unhooked from the ground?

No matter. The mind resides both inside and out.
It can think itself and think itself into existence.

I sponge off the eyes, no worse for wear.
My frugal mouth spends the only foreign words it owns.

At present, on this sleeper train, there's nowhere to arrive.
Me? I'm just here in my traveler's clothes, trying on each passing town for size

EDITOR'S AFTERWORD

Exile begins with loss, when one is torn from one's roots and prevented from returning, either temporarily or permanently. For some this can represent new beginnings, while for others it is an insurmountable calamity, or, as Edward Said called it, the "unhealable rift". Regardless, once one finds oneself, as Joseph Conrad once put it, in some "obscure corner of the earth", one must either busy oneself with returning home, like Ulysses did, or grow reconciled with one's lot, like the Pakistani writer Aamer Hussein, who finds comfort in "feeling foreign" wherever he goes. To speak of exile, however, is inevitably to speak of human history, and my aim with this anthology, quite simply, was to produce a miniature history of humanity as seen through the prism of exile. As such, *The Heart of a Stranger* is to be read as a series of meditations which, while acknowledging the narratives of time and nation, is otherwise focused on showcasing a wide spectrum of exilic experiences through verse, fiction, letters and memoirs.

Over the course of the past three years, I have sought to assemble a modest picture of what it means to be an exile and the emotions that it engenders, while simultaneously attempting to portray the myriad situations that might lead one to becoming an exile in the first place. Thus, while the initial sections, "Origins and Myths" and "Dark Ages and Renaissances", follow a conventionally linear approach to history, taking the reader from Egypt to Israel, Greece, Rome, China, Muslim Sicily, the Byzantine Empire and Renaissance Italy, the authors selected to represent these cultures and epochs do not necessarily belong to the time in question, as is made evident by my selection of Naguib Mahfouz's adaptation of the ancient Egyptian myth of Sinuhe as the opening contribution. The following four sections of this anthology, "Expulsions, Explorations and Migrations", "Dynasties, Mercenaries and Nations", "Revolutions, Counter-Revolutions and Persecutions" and "Cosmopolitanism and Rootlessness", have instead been arranged chronologically by the date of their authors' births, while taking a more sharply thematic direction than the preceding two sections.

While the mechanisms of how exile occurs can be relatively simple and straightforward — brutality and unlawful extirpation being the primary tools in most cases — what happens *after* one is deracinated is often left to fate and the causality of context. Therefore, I have sought to portray as vast an array of "exilic" situations as possible. Although the Ovidian conception of exile has taught us to see the "Exile" as a whiny, withered husk forever longing for the branch it was unhappily torn from, I wanted this anthology to showcase an alternative genealogy of misfits, rebels, heretics, contrarians, activists and revolutionaries, particularly in the later sections of the book. Exile, this anthology argues, can be defiant, like Emma Goldman aboard the USS *Buford*, or Leon Trotsky's stirring "Letter to the Workers of the USSR", written months before Stalin's pickaxe found him in Mexico City; it can be horrifying, as the Polish legionnaires learnt while fighting to oppress a people they knew nothing about in Haiti; it can be depressing, like Giacomo Leopardi's poem on Italy's sorry state following the tumults of the Napoleonic Wars; it can speak of heroism, like the sacrifices made by poets such as Yannis Ritsos and Abdellatif Laâbi, all of whom spent long years in prison for their peaceful activism, or for their "crimes of opinion"; some exiles even end in triumph, the way the revolutionaries of 1905 returned to rule in 1917 — a political sea-change crystallized in the image of Lenin arriving at Finland Station.

All too often, however, exile ends in tragedy, as it does for Ribka Sibhatu's Eritrean refugees aboard their ramshackle boats while attempting to cross the Mediterranean to begin new lives in Fortress Europe. On the other hand, fleeing one's home may gain one a kingdom, as is shown by the excerpt from John Barbour's (c.1320–95) *The Bruce of Bannockburn*, which details the rise to power of Robert the Bruce, King of Scots (1274–1329). Indeed, while history has taught us to look upon exile as a judgement passed by inscrutable higher powers or power-drunk despots, it is abundantly clear that exile can also be a choice. As Robert W. Service tells us in "The Spell of the Yukon", "I wanted the gold, and I sought it", which appears as popular a reason to leave home as any. Encouraging one to go into self-imposed exile can also be sound advice, as Jee Leong Koh does in "To a Young Poet": "Quit the country soon as you can" he counsels, adding "Pay no heed to the village elders. / They are secretly ashamed that they did not leave." After all, what does "home" truly mean if it does not truly accept who you are? While this anthology does not seek to define exile, what should hopefully be clear by the time one has read this book cover to cover is that there never has been — and never will be — a definitive definition for this famously elusive condition.

Entirely unsurprisingly, I am indebted to the translators featured in these pages for their warmth, generosity and enthusiasm for this project. The overabundance of material uncovered during my research was probably as daunting as the condition of exile itself, and I must therefore beg the reader's forgiveness for the sins of omission I will undoubtedly have committed. In the end, I was forced to discard more than three times the number of poems and stories than what eventually made the cut. I agonized over certain decisions, while others proved far easier. The reader will see nothing here by favorites of mine such as Abdelrahman Munif, Bertolt Brecht, Pablo Neruda, W.H. Auden, James Baldwin and Gore Vidal, none of whose works I could afford to feature in these pages. As there was no attempt on my part to put together a "canonic" portrait of the literature of exile, this was no great restriction. In fact, this allowed me to make the anthology more pronouncedly political. Rather than focus on clichéd accounts of happy lives in sunny climes — Paul Gauguin in Tahiti or Robert Louis Stevenson in Samoa spring to mind — I wanted the reader to experience Madame de Staël's thoughts on Napoleon's tyranny, or to picture the Communard Louise Michel on her way to the penal colony in New Caledonia, or to see the parallel to our present times in Mary Antin's campaigns for immigrant rights during a particularly xenophobic moment in American history.

In addition, I feel it necessary to add here that the fetishization of privileged cliques who took to "exile" like some take to resort holidays has never held any interest for me; ergo my decision to overlook the Lost Generation of the 1920s — Gertrude Stein, Ezra Pound, Djuna Barnes and Ernest Hemingway — since they've all been amply dissected over the course of the past century. There is something sickeningly self-satisfied about the self-imposed exiles of James Joyce in Trieste, the Beats in Morocco or Joseph Brodsky in Venice. If you're going to stare into a mirror, you might as well do that at home, especially if you are fortunate enough to have one. As an exile myself, I have little love for well-heeled "literary expatriates" who write the same books elsewhere that they could have written in their home towns, and as such tend to think of most of them as "parasites in paradise", to borrow from Ngũgĩ wa Thiong'o's description of European settlers in Kenya.

What readers will find here, instead, especially in the more contemporary sections of the anthology, are non-Western poets who deserve far more attention in the English-speaking world than they have thus far received: examples here include the Iraqi-Assyrian poet Sargon Boulus, the Chinese Uyghur poet Ahmatjan Osman, the East Timorese poet Fernando Sylvan and the Egyptian poet Iman Mersal, to name only a few. In conclusion, owing to its historical scope, I must stress that this anthology does not seek to give an accurate portrayal of what exilic literature looks like today and this is a task I am sure will be taken on by younger poets in not too distant a time. I imagine such an endeavor would spill into several volumes — many thousands of pages at least — and I certainly hope someone will undertake that task in the near future. After all, we have been banishing one another for ethnic, religious, sexual and political reasons for longer than we can remember, and unfortunately, as the first two decades of the twenty-first century have shown us, since we do not appear to have tired of these practices, the topic remains as ripe for investigation as ever.

André Naffis-Sahely
Los Angeles, November 2018

ACKNOWLEDGEMENTS

The introductory prose in this volume was published in serial form by *PN Review* in their January–February, March–April and May–June issues in 2019. I would also like to extend my gratitude to the editors of the magazines in which some of these translations first appeared: *Ambit, Asymptote, Jewish Quarterly, Journal of World Literature, Modern Poetry in Translation* and *New Left Review*. The editor and publishers are grateful for permission to reproduce the following copyright material. Any errors in the list below are entirely unintentional.

Naguib Mahfouz, "The Return of Sinuhe", from *Voices from the Other World: Ancient Egyptian Tales* (American University in Cairo Press, 2006). Translated by Raymond Stock. Reprinted by permission of the translator and publisher.

Anonymous, Exodus 23:9, from *Holy Bible: King James Version* (Collins, 2011). Reprinted by permission of the publisher.

Anonymous, Psalm 137, The Book of Psalms, from *Holy Bible, New International Version* (Biblica, 1978). Reprinted by permission of the publisher.

"Now at their native realms the Greeks arrived", from Book I of *The Odyssey of Homer*, translated by Alexander Pope.

Sappho, "Fragment 98B", from *If Not, Winter: Fragments of Sappho* (Vintage, 2003). Translated by Anne Carson. Reprinted by permission of the translator and publisher.

Xenophanes, "Fragment 22", translated by André Naffis-Sahely. All rights reserved. Copyright © 2019.

Seneca the Younger, "Letter LXXXII", from *Moral Letters to Lucilius / Epistulae morales ad Lucilium* (Loeb Classical Library, 1917). Translated by Richard Mott Gummere.

Plutarch, "The Life of Cleomenes", from *The Parallel Lives* (Loeb Classical Library, 1921). Translated by Bernadotte Perrin.

The Desert Fathers, "Abba Longinus", from *The Desert Fathers: Sayings of the Early Christian Monks* (Penguin Classics, 2003). Translated by Benedicta Ward. Reprinted by permission of the translator and publisher.

Abd al-Rahman I, "The Palm Tree", from *Gardens, Landscape, and Vision in the Palaces of Islamic Spain* (Penn State University Press, 2003). Translated by D. Fairchild Ruggles. Reprinted by permission of the translator and publisher.

Du Fu, "Dreaming of Li Bai", from *The Anchor Book of Chinese Poetry* (Anchor, 2005). Translated by Tony Barnstone and Chou Ping. Reprinted by permission of the translators and publisher.

Bai Juyi, "Song of the Lute", from *The Anchor Book of Chinese Poetry* (Anchor, 2005). Translated by Tony Barnstone and Chou Ping. Reprinted by permission of the translators and publisher.

Christopher of Mytilene, "On the ex- emperor Michael Kalaphates, when he was arrested and blinded for having banished the Empress Zoe from imperial rule", from *The Poems of Christopher of Mytilene and John Mauropous* (Dumbarton Oaks Medieval Library, 2018). Translated by Floris Bernard and Christopher Livanos. Reprinted by permission of the translators and publisher.

Ibn Hamdis, "Oh sea, you conceal my paradise", from Giuseppe Quatriglio, *A Thousand Years in Sicily: From the Arabs to the Bourbons* (Legas Publishing, 1999). Translated by Giuseppe Quatriglio and Justin Vitiello. Reprinted by permission of the publisher.

Moses ibn Ezra, "I am weary of roaming about the world", from Salo Wittmayer Baron, *A Social and Religious History of the Jews: High Middle Ages, 500–1200* (Columbia University Press, 1957). Translated by Salo Wittmayer Baron. Reprinted by permission of the publisher.

Anna Komnene, from *The Alexiad of the Princess Anna Comnena: Being the History of the Reign of Her Father, Alexius I, Emperor of the Romans, 1081–1118 A.D.* (Routledge, Kegan, Paul, 1928). Translated by Elizabeth A. S. Dawes.

Attar, "Parable of a Pauper in Love with a King", from *The Conference of the Birds* (W.W. Norton & Company, 2017). Translated by Sholeh Wolpé. Reprinted by permission of the translator.

Dante, "Cacciaguida's Prophecy", from Canto XVII of *Paradiso, The Divine Comedy* (Forum Italicum, 2000). Translated by James Finn Cotter. Reprinted by permission of the translator.

John Barbour, from *The Bruce of Bannockburn* (E. Mackay, 1914). Translated by Michael MacMillan.

Michael Marullus, "De exilio suo". Translation by Amy S. Lewis. All rights reserved. Copyright © 2019.

William Shakespeare, from *Coriolanus* (Arden Shakespeare, 1976).

Andrias MacMarcuis, "The Flight of the Earls", from David H. Greene, *An Anthology of Irish Literature* (NYU Press, 1985). Translated by Robin Flower.

Henry Wadsworth Longfellow, from *Evangeline: A Tale of Acadie*, in Charles W. Eliot, *The English Poetry III: From Tennyson to Whitman* (P.F. Collier & Son, 1914).

Olaudah Equiano, "The Middle Passage", from *The Interesting Narrative of the Life of Olaudah Equiano, or Gustavus Vassa, the African, written by Himself* (London, 1789).

Mirza Sheikh I'tesamuddin, from *The Wonders of Vilayet: Being the Memoir, Originally in Persian, of a Visit to France and Britain in 1765* (Peepal Tree Press, 2002). Translated by Kaiser Haq. Reprinted by permission of the translator and publisher.

Phillis Wheatley, "A Farewell to America", from *Poems on Various Subjects, Religious and Moral* (A. Bell, 1773).

Francis Baily, from *Journal of a tour in unsettled parts of North America in 1796 & 1797* (Baily Bros, 1856).

Mary Shelley, from *Voltaire, Rousseau, Condorcet, Mirabeau, Madame Roland, Madame De Staël* (Lea and Blanchard, 1840).

Emma Lazarus, "The New Colossus", from Hamilton Fish Armstrong, *The Book of New York Verse* (G.P. Putnam's Sons, 1917).

Robert W. Service, "The Spell of the Yukon", in *The Spell of the Yukon and Other Verses* (Barse & Hopkins Publishers, 1907).

Solomon Tshekisho Plaatje, from *Native Life in South Africa, Before and Since the European War and the Boer Rebellion* (Tsala Ea Batho, 1920).

Mary Antin, from *They Who Knock at Our Gates* (Houghton Mifflin, 1914).

A.C. Jacobs, "Immigration", from *Nameless Country: Selected Poems* (Carcanet Press, 2018). Edited by Merle Bachman and Anthony Rudolf. Reprinted by permission of the publisher.

Ngũgĩ wa Thiong'o, "A Colonial Affair!", from *Detained: A Writer's Prison Diary* (Heinemann, 1981). Reprinted by permission of the publisher.

Sargon Boulus, "Du Fu in Exile". Translated by Sinan Antoon. Reprinted by permission of the translator. All rights reserved. Copyright © 2019.

Luis Cernuda, "Impression of Exile", in *Forbidden Pleasures: New Selected Poems, 1924–1949* (Black Widow Press, 2015). Translated by Stephen Kessler.

Fernando Sylvan, "Invasion", in *7 Poemas de Timor* (Lisbon, 1965). Translated by David Shook. Reprinted by permission of the translator. All rights reserved. Copyright © 2019.

Gisèle Prassinos, "Nobody Is Going Anywhere", in *La vie, la voix* (Flammarion, 1971). Translated by Jade Cuttle. Reprinted by permission of the translator. All rights reserved. Copyright © 2019.

Roque Dalton, "Spite", in *Cordite Poetry Review*, 2013. Translated by Luis Gonzalez Serrano. Reprinted by permission of the translator. All rights reserved. Copyright © 2019.

Breyten Breytenbach, from *Notes from the Middle World* (Haymarket Books, 2009). Reprinted by permission of the author and the publisher.

Mimi Khalvati, "The Soul Travels on Horseback", in *The Weather Wheel* (Carcanet, 2014). Reprinted by permission of the author and the publisher.

Michael Schmidt, "The Freeze", in *Poetry Nation 5*, 1975. Reprinted by permission of the author.

Aamer Hussein, from "Nine Postcards from Sanlucar de Barrameda", in *Insomnia* (Telegram Books, 2007). Reprinted by permission of the author and the publisher.

Pushkin Press

Pushkin Press was founded in 1997, and publishes novels, essays, memoirs, children's books—everything from timeless classics to the urgent and contemporary.

Our books represent exciting, high-quality writing from around the world: we publish some of the twentieth century's most widely acclaimed, brilliant authors such as Stefan Zweig, Marcel Aymé, Teffi, Antal Szerb, Gaito Gazdanov and Yasushi Inoue, as well as compelling and award-winning contemporary writers, including Andrés Neuman, Edith Pearlman, Eka Kurniawan, Ayelet Gundar-Goshen and Chigozie Obioma.

Pushkin Press publishes the world's best stories, to be read and read again. To discover more, visit www.pushkinpress.com.

THE SPECTRE OF ALEXANDER WOLF
GAITO GAZDANOV
'A mesmerising work of literature' Antony Beevor

SUMMER BEFORE THE DARK
VOLKER WEIDERMANN
'For such a slim book to convey with such poignancy the extinction of a generation of "Great Europeans" is a triumph' *Sunday Telegraph*

MESSAGES FROM A LOST WORLD
STEFAN ZWEIG
'At a time of monetary crisis and political disorder... Zweig's celebration of the brotherhood of peoples reminds us that there is another way' *The Nation*

THE EVENINGS
GERARD REVE
'Not only a masterpiece but a cornerstone manqué of modern European literature' Tim Parks, *Guardian*

BINOCULAR VISION

EDITH PEARLMAN

'A genius of the short story' Mark Lawson, *Guardian*

IN THE BEGINNING WAS THE SEA

TOMÁS GONZÁLEZ

'Smoothly intriguing narrative, with its touches of sinister, Patricia Highsmith-like menace' *Irish Times*

BEWARE OF PITY

STEFAN ZWEIG

'Zweig's fictional masterpiece' *Guardian*

THE ENCOUNTER

PETRU POPESCU

'A book that suggests new ways of looking at the world and our place within it' *Sunday Telegraph*

WAKE UP, SIR!

JONATHAN AMES

'The novel is extremely funny but it is also sad and poignant, and almost incredibly clever' *Guardian*

THE WORLD OF YESTERDAY

STEFAN ZWEIG

'*The World of Yesterday* is one of the greatest memoirs of the twentieth century, as perfect in its evocation of the world Zweig loved, as it is in its portrayal of how that world was destroyed' David Hare

WAKING LIONS

AYELET GUNDAR-GOSHEN

'A literary thriller that is used as a vehicle to explore big moral issues. I loved everything about it' *Daily Mail*

FOR A LITTLE WHILE

RICK BASS

'Bass is, hands down, a master of the short form, creating in a few pages a natural world of mythic proportions' *New York Times Book Review*

JOURNEY BY MOONLIGHT
ANTAL SZERB

'Just divine… makes you imagine the author has had private access to your own soul' Nicholas Lezard, *Guardian*

BEFORE THE FEAST
SAŠA STANIŠIĆ

'Exceptional… cleverly done, and so mesmerising from the off… thought-provoking and energetic' *Big Issue*

A SIMPLE STORY
LEILA GUERRIERO

'An epic of noble proportions… [Guerriero] is a mistress of the telling phrase or the revealing detail' *Spectator*

FORTUNES OF FRANCE
ROBERT MERLE

1 *The Brethren*
2 *City of Wisdom and Blood*
3 *Heretic Dawn*

'Swashbuckling historical fiction' *Guardian*

TRAVELLER OF THE CENTURY
ANDRÉS NEUMAN

'A beautiful, accomplished novel: as ambitious as it is generous, as moving as it is smart' Juan Gabriel Vásquez, *Guardian*

A WORLD GONE MAD
ASTRID LINDGREN

'A remarkable portrait of domestic life in a country maintaining a fragile peace while war raged all around' *New Statesman*

MIRROR, SHOULDER, SIGNAL
DORTHE NORS

'Dorthe Nors is fantastic!' Junot Díaz

RED LOVE: THE STORY OF AN EAST GERMAN FAMILY
MAXIM LEO

'Beautiful and supremely touching… an unbearably poignant description of a world that no longer exists' *Sunday Telegraph*